NAMELESS THINGS

Survive the terror lurking beneath your feet...

ERNEST JENSEN

Text copyright © 2024 by Louise Jensen

All rights reserved. For information regarding reproduction in total or in part, contact Rising Action Publishing Co. at http://www.risingactionpublishingco.com

Cover Illustration © Nat Mack
Distributed by Simon & Schuster
Proofread by Sally O'Keef

ISBN: 978-1-998076-96-3
Ebook: 978-1-998076-97-0

FIC015000   FICTION / Horror

#NamelessThings

Follow Rising Action on our socials!
Twitter: @RAPubCollective
Instagram: @risingactionpublishingco
Tiktok: @risingactionpublishingco

For Duffbowl, always.

NAMELESS THINGS

Chapter 1

The rain pounded against my face as I squinted to catch a glimpse of Wade's dripping silhouette. There was no sign of him among the drenched spruce and scrub oak. My feet squelched inside my boots, rain pelted endlessly, and I was miserable. Even more miserable than when we'd started, or perhaps miserable in a different way.

It shouldn't be allowed to rain when you head out for a week's hiking to take your mind off things. Sadly, no one had informed the weather of my mood. I'd checked the forecast before we set off, and it'd been clear skies, but now it was nothing but grey overcast. The steep rock walls of the park formed a massive unbroken ring around us, effectively blocking cell phone signals, so we couldn't even check the upcoming forecast and had to hope it'd clear.

"*Miiiiike!*" Wade bellowed at me from up the trail. "Come on, old man."

Damned cheek for someone only a few months younger than me, and excuse me, but I was old. Mid-thirties wasn't old and there was still time for things to work out; I still had time. As I scrubbed at my face, trying to stifle my thoughts, Wade disappeared again.

I lumbered up the incline, boots slipping on wet rock, heavy drops from the leaf canopy above smacking me on the head.

He was waiting at the lookout, and I was huffing by the time I got there. Even in the wet, the view made me gasp. The Devil's Cup State

Park was an ancient volcanic caldera over fifty miles across in a great basin shape, hence the name.

From where we stood, we could see across the now-distant stone rim, cliffs rising above tumbled rocky foothills within a sea of blue-green treetops. Everything was blurry under the wet, grey blanket of lowering clouds.

"Hey, Slothapotamus, you want a break?" Wade peered at me from under his hood.

He'd tightened the strings around his face, so he looked like an Ewok. I shook my head. Trying to make it less obvious I was out of puff, I stared across the valley. We couldn't see the lake from the lookout, but we'd caught occasional glimpses as we hiked the south fork trail, the surface ashen to match the sky.

"Where's the pass from here?" I asked.

The way we'd come in was across the giant basin we'd slogged through, the only place accessible on foot. There were a couple of other points that could be scaled, but neither Wade nor I were climbers.

"Somewhere over there." Wade pointed in the misty rain.

We were hoping to get a few of the best trails in, none of the particularly difficult ones, just a nice hike. Not much chance of that in this weather.

"How're you holding up?" Wade asked, his face serious for once.

I glanced at him, unsure if this was a dig at my general lack of fitness or if he was enquiring about my mental state. Neither were topics I cared to discuss.

"I'm fine," I said.

My recent breakup was still red raw. It'd been difficult all round, with a lot of 'he said-he said,' and fighting over who got custody of the furniture, friends, and favorite sports bar. I'd been a sitting duck when

Wade's girlfriend cancelled on this trip last minute and he'd called to see if I wanted to fill in.

He caught me at a low ebb, when I'd reached the unfortunate stage of breakup angst when you began pondering the big questions in life: Was I going to die alone? How the hell did I rent a new apartment without a dishwasher? That kind of thing. So, foolishly, the idea of a hike had appealed. Now, the cold, wet, muddy reality of it was not so appealing.

Wade grinned at me now. "You sure you don't want to take a break?"

"No, I'm good," I said, which was a lie in more ways than one.

I'd made a firm commitment not to think about Ben on the trip or everything that had gone wrong. Which naturally meant I spent all my spare time thinking about it. Also, I underestimated exactly how much I'd miss my phone.

"Let's get going," I said, hitching the straps of my pack and making it move. "You've held us up long enough."

He snorted at me and turned back onto the trail. Wade was big into hiking; me, not so much. I mean, I liked it, but I didn't know all the woodsy stuff like he did. It'd taken me all of five minutes on the first day to work out I didn't like hiking when it was miserable and rainy.

I'd also conclusively shelved my long-held misbelief of walking the Appalachian Trail one day. I tried to tell myself it was nice to be out, though, away from work and the interminable paperwork, office politics, and trying to put on a happy face every day.

From the lookout, we headed back into the gloom under the trees. The odd cottonwood and maple showed among the oak and fir now, our footsteps hollow on built-up leaf mold. The rain never stopped, so it was surprising when the sky brightened from a dull grey to a sickly white ten or fifteen minutes later. We'd come out through patchy trees into a small clearing, and I thought at first it was the effect of that, of coming into the open again, that made it seem to be getting lighter. With the low, overcast sky, it was obvious the sun wasn't coming out.

We both paused, looking up. Around us, everything was still, and there was no sound aside from the patter of rain and the steady drip from the trees. Then, faintly there was a sizzling noise. A little twinge twisted in my stomach. Everything lightened. Odd shadows appeared on the ground. Across the snippet of the sky above us blazed a streak of white fire, a great ball of light with a tail shrouded by a dank cloud. I froze, head tipped back.

"What the hell...?" was as far as I got.

"It must—" Wade's high-pitched words were cut off by an almighty boom as what it was hit the ground. Or maybe it wasn't because a second later, there was another deafening bang. Through the trees came a shockwave like a hurricane wind. My face was blasted with dirt and leaves. A giant hand knocked me off my feet, buffeting me aside with casual brutality. I hit the ground, hard, the shock jarring through my joints, stunning me.

Then the ground shook; I could feel it through my ass, where I'd fallen. I had trouble catching my breath. The smell of damp and rotten leaves clotted my nostrils. A distant rumble lasted for a few seconds, and then everything went quiet again. I wiped my eyes with a shaking hand. Wade and I looked at each other from where we were sprawled. I could feel my heartbeat in my ears.

"Wow," he said. "I think it was a meteor."

For some reason I hadn't expected you'd be able to see a meteor in the day. I guess I'd always pictured shooting stars. A warm tide rushed into my chest. We were okay—whatever it was had missed us, passed us by, and everything was okay.

"Man, did it hit in the park?" Wade was wide-eyed, which made him look manic. I inspected him; the idiot was excited.

"Holy shit, dude," I said, which earned me a frown. I was still feeling that welcome reprieve, and also, occasionally, I like to 'forget' some things that had stuck with Wade from his days as a teacher. Before he came to his senses, Wade taught high school English, and his schtick on swearing was it was 'lazy.' There are better words apparently. Whatever—after he'd dragged me out into the endlessly soggy wilderness, I was entitled to some laziness.

"Seriously?" I threw a twig in his direction. "If that's not worth bad language, I don't know what the fuck is."

He shook his head, recognizing this as blatant provocation, and crawled forward onto his knees.

Righting myself while wearing a full, heavy pack, I discovered it took strategy, patience, and balance, all things I appeared to be having difficulty with. I scrabbled around, twigs and pebbles grinding under my palms and knees. Eventually, I accepted a hand up from Wade, struggling to my feet like an overladen camel.

"Thanks." He'd slipped out of his pack before standing up. "Well fuck," I said, mainly to annoy him.

We stood and tried to see through the screen of trees toward where the thing had hit. Even in the grey overcast, a great plume was visible, though whether of smoke or dust, I couldn't tell. I stared at it, my forehead wrinkling. Was that normal?

"Do you reckon it's near the pass?" Wade said.

"Pretty close if not," I said.

We looked at each other again.

"I guess we should go see?" I offered.

It'd take us more than a day to get back to the park entrance, and I had to admit, I didn't think it had hit the pass. I mean, talk about a bullseye if it had. What I was thinking was, if we went back to the pass, we could climb over the pass. And then down the mile or so to the Forest

Service parking lot where Wade's trusty Mazda waited to take us back to civilization. Or at least somewhere warm and dry—if it had beer and pizza, it would be a bonus.

To my pleasant surprise, Wade agreed we should start heading back. If he hadn't said anything about cutting our waterlogged outing short, I was sure I could persuade him once we got there. Besides, who didn't want to see where a meteor hit?

We set off again, slogging back down the trail we'd come out of. Everything was still and silent, and I presumed any wildlife had been well and truly scared into hiding.

"Do you think there'll be a crater?" I asked.

I kept looking at the rising column of smoke, which was visible through the canopy now. At this distance, it was a thin finger rising to the sky, but it must be massive where it hit. If it wasn't so wet, I'd have thought a wildfire had started.

"Maybe. Maybe not. I think mostly they break up before hitting the ground."

"Felt like it hit something."

"Could've been just shockwave."

"No way."

"Yes way."

It was obvious Wade and I have been friends since elementary.

It took us most of the day to return to Harper's Meadow, a designated campground. Not exactly sure why, given there was nothing there besides a wide empty plateau among the trees, with no shelter or outhouse like in some of the parks. The rain had stopped briefly but everything was still sodden, and the low misty cloud made it clear rain would recommence as soon as we tried to set up our tent.

Our arrival was heralded by a stuffed toy of a dog barreling down the trail at us at full yap. I had no idea what the barking was about, given it bounced around us in apparent delight. Don't get me wrong, I like dogs. It was cute, like a mop of red-orange hair with a little foxy face and ears, a Pomeranian-Spitz cross we found out later. It was a shocking patch of color in a landscape dampened to tones of grey and greyer.

We came out from the trees onto the campground and found a large tent set up on one side, the type you could stand up in, unlike Wade's compact A-frame. I flicked a glance around the space, checking for people but saw no one. A fire was burning in the middle of a ring of stones, the smoke rising straight up in the damp motionless air. Larger rocks were spaced around at intervals to serve as seating; one thing the park had in abundance was rock.

The dog joyously announced our arrival by running around and yapping some more. A woman came out of the tent to stand under its porch-like annex. She had short, dyed blonde hair, a snub nose, and eyes that disappeared when she squinted at us.

"Barney, get back here," she called in a voice that clearly said, 'I know the dog's not going to listen, but it's polite to seem like I'm trying.'

I remembered that voice from my last dog; I still missed him.

"Hi." We did the awkward wave thing. The woman smiled but gave us the once over to make sure we weren't crazed hillbillies toting banjos, I assumed. How could you tell when everyone's filthy and unshaven? I wasn't sure. General lack of stringed instruments, maybe?

I smiled so she could see I had all my teeth, then briefly considered introducing Wade as 'Cletus.' I was not sure he could pull it off, to be honest. I think we were both nondescript, as men go. Even in his mid-thirties, Wade still managed to look like a gangly adolescent with his round chin and close-cropped, curly hair; although he harbored the misconception, he looked like John Boyega. I was a little shorter than he was, and occasionally, people noticed a resemblance to Kit Harington, which I obviously encouraged, although it might be the wild hair.

"Mom, Mom!" a young boy, maybe eight or nine years old, belted out of the trail, which continued on the other side of the clearing, and fell abruptly silent when he noticed Cletus and me.

The kid continued to approach at a more sedate pace, looking us over as he did so. He was a snub-nosed copy of mom but with brown instead of streaked blonde hair. The dog tore over and cavorted around him like he'd been gone for a year. Dad appeared from the trail behind them, and we met the Taylor family: Dan, Mel, and their son, Josh.

Dan, we discovered, was a talker. He slightly resembled Jimmy Kimmel and sported an expensive trekking jacket. I'd looked at the same one online before deciding it was too rich for my blood. We stood around awkwardly for a few minutes as he explained he was camping, rather than hiking, because of his wife and kid.

"You know you're not supposed to have dogs in the park?" Wade said as he bent to pet the animal.

Mel turned to her husband. "See, I told you they weren't allowed."

Dan blew a raspberry, clearly unbothered. "He's fine. He's only little."

"Did you see the meteor?" the kid, Josh, asked us.

"Meteorite, kiddo," Dan said. "It's a meteor in the sky and a meteorite when it hits the ground."

Well, that was something I didn't know.

The boy considered, face scrunched in thought. "I have a Spiderman watch," he said at last. "It's new." He extended his arm to display this treasure to us.

Kids were not my thing.

"I'm hungry." Josh turned his attention back to his dad.

We set up on the opposite side of the clearing, as far from the Taylors as possible. There were a few hours of daylight left, but we weren't in such a great rush to get back to the pass. It was always better to set up camp when you could see too. Naturally, the rain started up. We came up short on one tent peg, and I knelt beside my pack, checking through again.

"Looks like you're going a bit thin on top there," Wade said. "Maybe you should get Emma to give you a cut. Shave off, you know." Wade's girlfriend was a hairdresser. "She could hide the bald spot for you."

I shook my head at him as he tried this one every time we hung out. "Fat chance. You'll have a full crop circle before I lose a hair."

Dan Taylor came up then and kept us company as we finished setting up the tent. His crop circle had been disguised by strategic forward brushing, I noticed, and I glanced at Wade to check he'd clocked it.

Dan appeared keen; we should know he'd done some serious hiking pre-marriage and family. Given his gift of the gab, he was a realtor, a revelation that completely failed to surprise me. The raindrops eased to a light mist almost as soon as we were done, but I left Wade to it and retreated to the tent. I hadn't the mental fortitude for the state of Boise real estate.

Inside, I rolled out my sleeping bag. It smelled musty, and I wrinkled my nose as I flopped on it. The Taylors seemed nice enough, even if I put Mel down as one of those women with kids instead of a personality.

That was why it was so surprising when she stumbled back into the clearing later, flapping her arms around and screeching like a banshee.

Chapter 2

We rushed over to check if she was okay. Technically, there could be bears, bobcats, mountain lions, and the like in the park, although sightings were rare. My face tightened as I scanned the edges of the campground, peering into the deepening shadows. I noticed Wade checking as well. He shook his head.

Mel kept rubbing at the back of her hand like she couldn't stop. "In the hole, oh God, it was there, there was an animal. Then the thing went into my hand. Oh God, oh God, oh God." She was incoherent, panting words.

"Mel, you're frightening Josh." Dan leaned in and did the hissing thing parents did as if their offspring were selectively deaf. "Here let me see." He reached out, took her hand gently, and looked at it. "There's nothing there; you've just rubbed it red." He showed her the place she'd been worrying about. "See?"

"I know what happened." She wrenched her hand back and chafed at it again.

"Where's the trowel?" Dan asked her.

Mel looked blankly at him, her mouth hanging open. "What? Have you even been listening?" She gestured back towards where she'd come from, a red flush running into her cheeks.

"Calm down," Dan said.

Hoo boy, even I knew that was not the thing to say to your agitated wife. Mel's face went red from forehead to chin. She was shaking slightly.

Dan's hands went to his hips. "Alright, I'll go and have a look." He heaved a sigh. "Come on, Joshy, let's go see."

"No!" Mel looked back. "Don't take him down there."

This was ignored by Dan and the kid, who headed off down the trail.

"Dan, I said don't take him. Josh, get back here!" Mel stood, hands on hips, but as they disappeared, she reluctantly followed. "Be careful down there. Do you hear me?"

Wade and I followed, too, as there wasn't a whole lot else happening, and a bit of entertainment wouldn't go astray. We tailed behind Mel as she led us off the path through scrub oak and chokeberry to a little clearing in a stand of blue spruce. Darkness from under the trees reached across it like fingers.

Dots of dug-over spots showed the family had been using it as a latrine area. Between them, raindrops clung to tufts of long grass. By the time we arrived, Dan was hunkered down beside a small hole, the trowel in his hand.

"There's nothing here, just some worms." He poked about with the little shovel.

Around us, nothing moved. Beyond the open space, the woods stretched silently into gloom.

"I'm telling you, there was something there. It was an animal. I saw it. It moved fast, like a fish." Mel's voice wavered.

Dan stared up at her. "An animal in the ground that moved like a fish?" He huffed a sigh and twisted his mouth at us. Mel didn't notice as she was trying to get Josh to come away from the hole.

"There's nothing here now." Dan bent forward, putting a knee to the damp ground, and reaching in with his hand. He tossed the loose wet mud about a bit, uncovering more of the wriggling worms. It was peculiarly quiet, the air still, as if muffled.

"Don't touch them." Mel's voice went up several octaves. She clutched an arm around her son and pulled him away. The boy looked like he was suffering near-terminal embarrassment. "It went in my hand," she hissed at Dan, again, as if Josh couldn't hear. She waved the offending body part at her husband as if to prove it.

I was sorry for her. The woman looked close to tears, her eyes bloodshot. I shuffled my feet a little in the long grass. Was she having some kind of breakdown? It felt embarrassing for me and Wade to be there to see it, like we should give her some privacy.

Josh took the opportunity of his mom's waving hand to make a spirited bid for freedom, only to be restrained more tightly.

"Dan, come away from there," Mel ordered him.

Dan responded with a snort. "Don't be ridiculous." He dug about a little more with the trowel. "I don't know what you thought you saw, but there's nothing here but some wrigglers." Dan reached in and scooped a trowel full of dirt and worms. "Come and see, Josh, they won't hurt you." He tipped the scoop onto his hand and brushed away the grit. I got a waft of an odd smell I couldn't place, though it was slightly astringent.

"No." Mel Taylor kept a tight hold of the boy and held him back.

"Look, they're only worms. Here, Joshy, give me your hand." Dan reached his hand out for the kid to see, nudging a few squirming specimens across his palm in a grotesque offering.

Mel made an odd choking noise and pulled the boy further away.

"Look, there's nothing to be scared of. Mommy's just being a bit silly." Dan poked at the worms.

Josh looked at the things undulating on his father's palm like they were steaming turds.

Dan stood and extended his hand to us so we could have a look. He wore an ostentatious, gold pinkie ring featuring an eagle with wings extravagantly spread. Wade and I leaned in and peered at the worms cupped in his palm. They were smaller than regular earthworms, fine and thread-like. Dan was right: nothing to make a fuss about. In fact, I wasn't sure which was worse, the tasteless ring or the worms.

As I watched, though, the things writhed unpleasantly, an obscene cross between maggots and spaghetti, and my palms itched looking at them. On Dan's hand, one of the worms rose up, almost like it was sniffing, and my nostrils crinkled faintly in response. Then, so fast it was nearly too quick to see, it arched up like an inchworm, whipped down, and disappeared into the skin of Dan's palm.

"Aaaah." Dan smacked his hands together wildly. "Ah, crap."

We all jerked back in shock. A hint of fright clawed through me.

"The damn thing bit me," Dan said. He brushed his hands together hard, his face tense. When he pulled his palms apart to look, there was a smear of blood. "Huh," he said. "I squished it, anyway." He wiped his hands roughly down his front.

Here was the thing, I didn't think that was what happened. I couldn't help backing up a few paces from Dan. He hadn't squashed the worm, or at least not the one I'd seen. I swallowed hard. The worm had stretched itself, needle fine, and disappeared like a hypodermic needle into his hand.

I met Wade's gaze, and we both took a few more steps back in the growing dark.

"Well, nothing to see," Dan announced like a cop to onlookers. He kicked the dirt back into the hole, flicked the trowel back and forth a couple of times, and then set off back up the hill like nothing had happened.

The rest of us followed the path, Wade and me, then Mel Taylor with the kid tucked under an arm like a mother hen. Wade looked back at her before muttering, "She doesn't look too good."

I glanced past him at the woman. She appeared hot and flustered, and I got the impression Josh might have been partially holding her up. She raised her head, and I was shocked at how bloodshot her eyes were. With unease, I wondered if she was actually on drugs.

"Do you need a hand?" I asked her.

"No, I'm fine, really. I just need to lie down." She clutched her son, and the two of them staggered up the path together.

When we trickled back into camp, two strangers, a man and a woman, were sprawled beside the fire. I put them in their early twenties. They were filthy in a 'forty days and forty nights in the wilderness' way that took me about a day to achieve. A few feet away, two enormous packs leaned back-to-back to keep them off the muddy ground. I glanced back, expecting the Taylor's dog to go ballistic, but there was no sign of him. I wondered if the animal had stayed down in the clearing, then couldn't remember if he'd even followed us there.

The pair by the fire jumped up as we approached, smiling but with slightly wary faces. They relaxed upon seeing Mel Taylor and the boy come up the path after Dan, Wade, and me.

The male half of the couple was tall and rangy with one of those 'I only drink craft beer' beards. The female part was attractive with a grimy Zendaya in Dune vibe, only curvier.

"Hey, did you guys see the meteor?" I couldn't place his accent. "I'm Pete, and this is Claire."

The young woman did the half-wave thing. "G'day."

Wade smiled broadly, hands on his hips. "Heck. Is there anywhere you can go and not find Aussie backpackers have been there?" The way Wade said 'Aussie' sounded more like 'ass-y.'

"Yeah, nah, mate," the answer came back from the beard, along with a lopsided grin. "Not even your mum."

I glanced at Wade to see how he'd take this, but he only grinned back, even if the grin was mostly for the female half of the couple.

"Dan Taylor." Coming around the firepit, Dan almost tripped over his tongue. "I almost went to Australia once. Sydney."

Josh Taylor followed his father to the two newcomers. "What's Sydney, Dad?"

Dan frowned at the kid but answered, "It's the capital of Australia, buddy. Australia's in the—"

"No, it's bloody not." Pete didn't look angry, more exasperated.

I checked to see if this would earn the newcomer the 'swear-bear' scowl from Mel or Wade, but Mel wasn't there. That was odd, as I expected she'd at least say 'hi' before disappearing. Dan was frowning at Pete, and I wondered if he would start arguing.

"Canberra, isn't it?" I said before Dan could open his gob and insert his foot.

"Yeah." Pete was still giving Dan the hairy eyeball as if waiting for him to disagree.

"No worries; it happens," Clare told Dan. "I always thought New York was the capital of America until we got here." Her lips quirked up.

I couldn't help a snort. Dan's mouth had an odd, outraged shape, and an unattractive flush ran up his neck.

"Dad." Josh tugged at Dan's jacket. "Mom's not feeling good; she wants you."

"For heaven's sake." Dan frowned again. "Yeah, alright." He rolled his eyes slightly at us before heading off towards their tent. "You can tell she's not outdoorsy." His glance back at Claire showed he appreciated her outdoorsiness, particularly in the chest area.

Taylor's dog reappeared. Uncharacteristically, he was completely disinterested in the newcomers and didn't even bother to bark at them. Pete tried clicking his fingers at the dog, but Barney ignored him. He was focused on the undergrowth around the campsite, digging and snuffling and making occasional whining and yipping sounds.

The shadows lengthened into dusk and the next hour or so passed as usual when you meet complete strangers in the wilderness. We sat around, telling each other where we were from and what we did for a living.

"I'm in city admin," I explained. "So, nothing too exciting there."

"I work construction," Wade put in, and I noticed he flexed his shoulders a little as he said it.

"Yeah." I grinned at him. "How is your dad's building company these days? Are you still looking after the office?"

He glared at me. "I don't just work in the office; I do construction. It's a change from teaching anyway."

"Wade used to be a teacher," I told Pete and Claire. "Five years of high school English made him want to hit something with a hammer."

Wade and I were the only locals, being from Billings. Dan and 'the wife and kid,' we already knew, were from Boise. The Australian couple were from a place called Queanbeyan, but when I tried to say it back, I butchered it. Pete worked in IT security, Claire was a graphic designer, and they seemed nice enough for kids their age. The meteor was a prime topic, and where we were when it happened.

"Did you guys see where it hit?" Claire looked across at me and Wade.

Wade frowned, schoolteacher-style. "We don't know if it hit anything; it might have broken up before impact."

I scoffed—where did the great plume of smoke come from then—but Pete jumped in before I could say anything.

"Oh, it hit something alright." I could hear the amusement in his voice. "It set off a rock fall too."

"Really?" Wade looked skeptical.

I sat up straight. "Whereabouts?"

"Yeah, we saw it," Claire said. "After the second bang, we could see right across, and part of the cliff collapsed." She made accompanying hand gestures.

"Where?" I asked again.

"Over on the pass side, but I don't know if it was near the pass. We were up on the lake trail and got a pretty good view."

Pete nodded in agreement. "Thought we'd better come and have a look."

"Yeah, us too," I said. Although I'd suggested the same to Wade, I hadn't actually been serious about the pass being blocked. The idea we might genuinely be trapped in here was disconcerting. "We should be alright, though," I said. "I mean, even if the pass is blocked, some kind of search and rescue will come get us eventually?"

No one appeared overly concerned. Wade and I had enough supplies for three more days, longer if we rationed them. Perhaps this would give us a good tale to tell, maybe even involve some mountain-man heroics that could later be worked into chat-up lines. Stupidly, I wasn't particularly worried.

The discussion naturally moved on to what trails we had been planning to do or had done, what equipment we had, and why it was better than what they had. The usual hiker-talk. After a while, Dan and Josh Taylor re-joined us at the fire. Their dog barely noticed them, being entirely focused on scratching at the outskirts of the clearing, occasionally barking at nothing.

"Mel's having a rest," Dan said, plonking himself unsubtly beside the Australian girl.

"Is she okay?" Claire asked, wiggling slightly away as if to give Dan more room.

"Yeah," Dan said. "Nothing to worry about; she's always getting herself worked up over nothing."

Sitting beside him, his son piped up, "Like the time you let me watch those *Deadpool* movies, Dad?"

Dan looked non-committal.

"I'm hungry," Josh added.

"Okay, bud," Dan said. "Why don't you go collect more sticks for the fire? Mom'll fix something when she's feeling better."

I couldn't help but notice Dan was rubbing at his palm.

"And tell Barney to shut up."

I caught a glimpse of movement in the dark. The little ball of fluff was in the undergrowth, digging furiously and then barking.

We turned in early, and the first scream woke us around one-thirty in the morning. It always took me a while to sleep on hard ground, so it felt like I'd barely drifted off. Nonetheless, I woke as if a fire alarm had gone off, dazed but instantaneously alert, trying to make sense of what was happening.

Chapter 3

I scrambled around in the dark to find our light, thinking it was possibly a bear or mountain lion attack. Wade was awake, struggling with his sleeping bag, and there was frantic movement from the Australians on the other side of the clearing. By the time I stumbled out with my flashlight, the couple were both up, flicking their beams around the camp. There was nothing large, hairy, or fanged, at least.

With the clouds covering the sky, there was no moon or stars, only a blank, black night. The shrieking was coming from the Taylors' tent, and it kept coming—awful, tortured, throat-tearing noises. As far as I could tell in the dancing flashlight, their shelter was all zipped up with no bear-sized holes ripped in it.

Pete reached it first and bellowed to compete with the screams. "What's going on?" He tripped on something under the annex flap and stumbled. The tent sides shook and there was furious movement inside.

"Open it, open it." Claire was leaning over Pete's shoulder, blocking my view.

"I'm trying ... shine your—" Pete was fumbling in the dark, pulling frantically at the flap, trying to find the opening.

There were brief breaks in the screaming, empty gaps filled with great sucking, gasping breaths before the ear-splitting racket started up again. This time there was whimpering and Dan Taylor's high, urgent voice. "Stop, stop, Mel—"

Another desperate howl drowned it all out, but Pete finally got the tent flap open. He and Claire shone their beams in, and I craned over their shoulders. The staccato pulse of their flashlights gave everything a surreal, stop-motion look. The tent was big compared to ours. Dan was on one side on his knees beside his wife, trying to hold her shoulders down. She was screaming and howling, her arms flapping wildly. I caught a flash of her eyes, a terrified glint of white.

Claire flicked her flashlight around the tent, and Josh's strained face stared back, luminous, like a deer caught in headlights. He was frozen, sitting bolt upright in his sleeping bag.

"What the hell's going on?" There was a gasping break in the shrieking as Pete threw himself down beside the Taylors, shining his light on Mel.

"I don't know, I don't know—" Dan almost sobbed. "I was asleep, I don't know what—"

Mel screamed again, a wall of howling that blocked everything. My ears hurt. She thrashed where she lay, arms flailing, legs kicking. I wondered, irrelevantly, if she'd wear herself out at some stage. Claire moved over to Josh, and I pushed in over Pete's shoulder.

"What's wrong?" I stupidly asked, as if Pete might have somehow worked it out.

Wade peered in behind me. I could not have been more useless.

"What's her name again?" Pete was patting lightly at the woman's face, as if trying to administer a hysteric-stopping slap but not wanting to hurt her. "Mel? Can you hear me? Mel, Mel?"

She went still and took another of those awful, deep, sucking breaths. We all leaned back marginally as if to give her air. Dan and Pete let go of her now-still arms.

Behind us, Claire was trying to comfort the kid. "... only a nightmare, nothing to—"

With a mad, violent burst, Mel Taylor hauled herself upright, sending both Dan and Pete sprawling, and I leaped backward. Pete fell into Claire, knocking her and the kid sideways.

The way the woman had burst from the ground wasn't right. Almost like her legs had pulled the rest of her up. Human bodies didn't move like that. A sick taste tingled across my tongue.

I stumbled a few steps back out of the tent and bumped into Wade before trying to tell myself I was being stupid and seeing things in the dark. The night around us was endless and primeval. We were far from civilization, far from help.

Then, Mel was out of the tent. She took two steps and began to fall. Wade and I jumped forward to catch her or soften her landing. All three of us sprawled to the ground, but we managed to take most of the impact. In my arms and lying partly across my legs, Mel was hot, burning, fever hot. I could feel the heat through the T-shirt and boxers I'd worn to sleep in.

Then, her head flung back abruptly, and she screamed again like a piercing siren. It stabbed my ears. Beneath my hands, wild tremors ran through her stiffened body. Rain pattered on us, but I barely noticed. Dan and Pete had scrambled out of the Taylor's tent, and we eased Mel to the ground as she went quiet but began to thrash again.

Flashlight beams lanced and flickered. Pete, Wade, and I looked at each other, but it was Wade who asked what we were all thinking, "What do we do?"

Dan was hopeless, rubbing his face and chanting, "Oh God, oh God, oh God, oh God—"

I glanced around, though heaven knew for what; did I expect an ambulance might suddenly have appeared?

I rolled my neck. "Let's get her into our tent," I said, looking at Wade for agreement. "Away from the kid."

We were the farthest from where the Taylors were camped, Pete and Claire having set up in between us. It was farther to carry her but farther from the little boy. The night pressed in around us, and a sharp, cold feeling rose in my chest.

Wade ran to arrange our sleeping bags into a bed. When Mel stopped thrashing to inhale, we picked her up as gently as we could and shuffled her into our tent. She flailed again before we got her settled, and we ended by heaving her onto the makeshift bed.

"I'll go check on Josh," Dan said, promptly disappearing.

My shoulders slumped as I looked at Mel. I had no idea what was going on, and I couldn't do anything to help. The sound, the sheer primal, animal pain she seemed to be in, was unearthly. I didn't know a human being could make noises like that. I kept expecting Dan to return, but he didn't.

By around three, Mel was quiet at last. No more screaming, no more gut-wrenching howls, just short, shallow, panting gasps. Rain tapped against the tent. Every now and again, odd twitches ran through her limbs. Somehow, I didn't think she was getting better. I tried to stay awake, and I guessed Wade and Pete, did too, but we didn't say a lot.

Dawn was a promise when Pete thumped me awake. "Mate, I think she's dead."

I didn't need the dim glow left by our lantern's batteries to know he was right. I reached a hand to touch Mel's forehead. She was cold. There were no more panting breaths; there were no breaths at all.

I was stunned. I was cold and sad. Mostly, I was tired. "Shit. We'd better get Dan."

I hauled myself to my feet as Pete reached to nudge Wade awake. The rain had stopped. There was a faint luminous whiteness to the sky. In the Taylor's tent, I found Claire asleep beside the kid. Dan was on the other side of the space, in his sleeping bag, flat on his back, snoring. Blood rushed to my head, and I had to fight the urge to kick him. I might have used my foot to nudge him awake, and I might not have been gentle. I didn't know, I was really tired.

When I got Dan out of the tent, Pete had disappeared, and Wade was poking the remains of the campfire awake. He looked up at us, then away. I guessed that meant I was breaking the news. I hadn't told Dan when I woke him, wanting to be as quiet as possible so not to disturb his son. I didn't know how to say it, so I took him to our tent and held the flap open.

I rubbed at my chin and said, straight out, "I'm sorry, but Mel's dead. She … died."

Dan peered in and turned back to gape at me. "Don't be stupid."

"I'm sorry." I didn't know what else to say.

Dan ducked into the tent. "She's not dead." He grabbed her shoulder, shaking her. "Wake up, Mel."

"She's got no pulse," I said. In the dim, dull light, Mel was grey.

"You must be doing it wrong, then. Look, she's still moving." He fumbled for her wrist.

What he said was true. Every now and again, a tiny tremor ran through her body.

"I don't know what to tell you," I said. "Bodies can twitch a bit after death, I think." My best guess, or what I hoped. I didn't even know what I feared.

"*She's not dead*!" Dan shouted it now, and there was a rustle of movement behind us from the Taylor's setup. Dan abruptly scrambled out of our tent. "I have to look after my son."

He stomped back across the clearing. I stood there, watching him go, gobsmacked. He was going to leave her here?

Rain dripped from the trees in a relentless patter that scraped across my nerves. I was so tired I was dizzy and disoriented. I didn't know what to do. I didn't even know what I expected Dan to do.

Over by the fire, Wade was slumped over, probably asleep, and there was still no sign of Pete. At last, I grabbed my pack from where Wade had hefted it out of the tent to make space for Mel. I pulled out my filthy clothes and struggled into them, leaned the pack against a rock, and then flopped against it. Everything was wet, but I didn't care; there was no way I was going back into our tent.

I woke from confused dreams of screams and red pain. Light was filtering through the denim-blue clouds. Pete and Claire sat silently by the fire and Wade was stretched full length now, his arm a pillow for his head.

My eyes were gritty, and I still felt queasy from not having enough sleep. I couldn't help but glance over to our tent, where the front flap was still open. A brief flurry of wings caught my attention on the other side of the clearing, and I twitched as a crow landed. It scratched a little at the ground, then pecked at something.

My eyelids drooped, yearning for darkness, but my bladder said no. Pete and Claire turned to look as I hauled myself to my feet but said nothing. I said nothing in reply; what was there to say?

I scrounged up my boots and, without bothering to tie the laces, staggered off to where the trees choked the daylight. Ducking behind a gnarled oak, I fumbled with my zipper and liquid gushed. I averted my gaze, focusing instead on a glossy-feathered crow. Its beak stabbed rhythmically at the soil, delving for unseen treasures. My noisy presence wasn't enough to scare it away. Beyond it, the woods dissolved into misty fog, shadows twisted into unidentifiable shapes. Apart from me and the bird, everything was still and unusually quiet in the pale morning light.

Something hefty hit the wet earth behind me as I was tucking the tackle away. I glanced back to where the sound came from, where the bird had been. The crow was gone, likely scared off by the sound. I paused, zipper at half-mast, and waited to see if I'd hear it again. Nothing. Just a tangled thicket of dripping leaves. Every rustle sent a jolt through my body, memories of last night's chaos flashing unbidden. My stomach growled, a stark reminder of missed meals. Grime caked my skin, and my eyelids felt like sandpaper. The promise of a warm bed tugged at me, urging escape from this waking nightmare.

By the time I got back to camp, Wade was awake, and Dan had joined the group around the fire. I hauled my pack over to dig out a protein bar and Wade handed me an enamel mug with coffee. The camping version of coffee: instant granules mixed with creamer powder and packed in a ziplock bag. Foul, but caffeinated.

"Thanks." I sat. It was too hot to drink, so I swirled the liquid around to cool it, and there was another of those odd, plopping noises off to the left of camp. "What the hell is that?"

"Dunno." Pete looked up. "Heard it a couple of times."

Dan stood abruptly, taking me by surprise. He strode over to our tent, with Mel's body still inside, and stooped to enter. The rest of us sat and looked at each other.

"Is Josh, okay?" I asked Claire, remembering her curled up beside him in the night.

"Yeah, he's asleep," she said, quietly. "He didn't get much kip last night." She looked down at her hands before flicking a glance over to our tent. "Best leave him as long as possible, I s'pose."

A couple of minutes later, Dan climbed out of the tent. He was white as bone.

"She's dead," he announced as if it'd be a revelation to us. "What the hell happened?"

I put down my mug of too-hot coffee and made my way over to him. His eyes, vacant and unfocused, stared through me. A subtle tremor ran through his frame, his hands quivering like leaves in a gentle breeze.

"Keep it down, buddy," I said as kindly as I could. As if I hadn't told him this exact news last night. "We don't want to wake your son."

"Fuck." Dan ignored me, hands clutched to either side of his head.

I peered in through the tent opening. In the full light of morning, it was obvious Mel was dead. The worst thing, though, was the odd little movements her body made, tiny twitches, every now and again. They were almost imperceptible. I tried not to look but every time it happened, my eyes snapped back. I tried to convince myself I wasn't seeing what I was seeing; it'd been a long, horrible night after all, with barely any sleep.

My feet dragged through damp leaves as I retreated to the fire's warmth. My skin crawled, urging me to put distance between myself and the lifeless form that was once Mel Taylor. Towering pines loomed overhead, their branches interlocking like gnarled fingers. Through their needle-laden canopy, a sliver of ashen sky peeked through, as cold and lifeless as the body behind me.

Dan eventually wandered back and collapsed beside us. "What am I going to do?"

We eyeballed each other. None of us knew what to do. To be fair this was pretty uncharted territory.

Wade had the first sensible suggestion. "We'll hike out and send help back for you." He glanced over at me. "If we go light, we can probably do it in a day, day and half?"

"What?" Dan stared at him like he was insane. "I'm not staying here."

My head felt full of glue, but I thought this over. "You want to leave her here?"

"You and," Dan flipped a finger toward Wade, "can stay with her and we'll go." He gave Claire and Pete a quick look, seeking agreement.

Wade and I shared questioning glances. Not sure why the Aussies got chosen to go and we didn't. I didn't say what I was thinking—I didn't want to stay here. Wade's eyes darted between the body and the tree line, his jaw clenched tight. His fingers twitched towards his backpack straps, mirroring my own restless hands. We exchanged a brief glance, a silent agreement passing between us.

"Where's Mom?"

We all whipped around to find Josh behind us. He stood on one bare, grubby foot, rubbing at the bottom of his Spiderman pajamas with the other.

Chapter 4

Dan drew in a long wavering lungful of air. "She had to go to the hospital."

We all turned to stare at him. He looked back at us and grimaced slightly. Josh frowned as if weighing his words. His gaze slid around the campground, and I was thankful Mel's body was inside our tent. It wasn't actively raining, but the air was damp. There was a soaking wetness that got into everything. The kid's toes curled into the loose leaf mold.

The boy turned back to Dan. "I have to go to the bathroom."

"Okay, Joshy." Dan looked around before obviously remembering. "Find somewhere to go. Don't dig a hole ... just go somewhere." He waved towards the dripping trees.

"I don't want to go by myself." Josh stood regarding Dan with the laser-like focus kids could get. "Why didn't Mom say goodbye to me?"

From beside me, Wade rose and ambled over to our tent. He casually flipped down the open flap and stood before it, blocking any view through the opening.

"Well, uh ... it was late, and she didn't want to wake you." Dan was a pretty shit liar, but luckily, his son didn't seem to notice.

"I have to go to the bathroom," the kid said again.

"Ah, okay." Dan looked over at Claire. She stared back at him, stony-faced.

I'd come across fathers like Dan Taylor before. Their kids were pretty much pets to them. They were happy to romp around with them when it was fun and games, but any of the actual work? That got handed off to someone else. The kind of guys who called looking after their own kids 'babysitting.'

So, this was why Wade and I had been delegated to stay here and babysit a dead body: so Dan could have Claire look after his kid. I turned to where she sat beside Pete and thought she might have different ideas.

There was an awkward pause as Josh jigged up and down, unaware of the silent communication. "Dad, I have to pee," he said at last.

Dan reluctantly got up, and the pair headed off.

"Wanker," Claire said when they were out of earshot.

We watched as father and son disappeared up the trail opposite to where Mel had led us yesterday. Tendrils of fog curled through the brush where their figures disappeared. I should have felt sorry for Dan. He'd lost his wife, but his whole attitude pissed me off. It was like he was annoyed at Mel for dying, like she'd inconvenienced him, let him down.

But what did I know? He was probably in shock. Then I remembered sitting beside Mel as agony wracked her body, as she screamed hour after excruciating hour without Dan, and I wanted to punch him in the nose.

When they were gone, Claire leaned towards us a little. "What was wrong with her?" she asked. "Did she get bitten by a snake?"

I shook my head. "No, I don't think so. She was fine when we turned up yesterday, maybe an hour or so before you got here." I glanced at Wade. "She was okay till after the whole digging business. Then she didn't look too good."

Wade coughed a little. "I saw a worm in her throat."

Pete, Claire, and I gawped at him like he'd lost his marbles.

"What are you talking about?" Claire asked. She looked exhausted, and dark rings accented her grimy-eyed expression.

"Last night. When she was ... when Mel was screaming, I saw a worm in her throat."

The unspoken skepticism was palpable.

"It was white. I saw it squirming." Wade was close to tears.

"That's crazy," I said. "It was a horrible night, and none of us got much sleep."

Instead of reassuring him, he glared at me.

It made me think too. It made me think about the worm, the day before, diving into Dan Taylor's palm and disappearing so swiftly into his flesh, like someone sucking in a tail end of spaghetti. I put a hand to my lips. It made me think about Mel saying the same thing had happened to her, about her rubbing at the back of her hand, about her horrific, tortured screams. Then I dismissed the idea.

"I know what I saw." Wade's face contorted, his upper lip curling while his brow furrowed deeply. His nostrils flared with each sharp breath, and his eyes narrowed to slits, darting between all of us and the ground.

I considered some more. "She couldn't scream like that if she had something in her throat. Think about it." I scratched the back of my head. "Maybe it was a vein or part of her throat or something?"

I had zero knowledge of anatomy, but saying it caused a little frond of relief to uncurl in me. What I suggested was undoubtedly true, as no one could make noises like she had with something in their throat. And where would the worm even have come from, her lungs? There was no possible way she screamed her life out with something in her lungs.

Wade looked doubtful. "It was right at the end, right around when she stopped...making noises."

The little squirm of dread curled back into my thoughts.

We sat static by the fire, and no one was able to muster the energy for anything. Not to say anything, not to do anything. I certainly couldn't.

I finished my revolting coffee along with the remains of my protein bar and hoped they'd help me give a fuck. I was tired, dead tired. The woods were quiet, grim and empty around us.

A rustle of leaves and snapping twigs broke the stillness. Dan's deep voice carried through the trees, followed by his son's higher pitch. Their approaching footsteps roused us from our stupor, heads turning in unison towards the sound. They were back sooner than I'd expected, but maybe I zoned out there for a while. I rubbed at my face and blinked repeatedly, staring at the ground. In the worn parts around the fire pit, knuckles of stone broke through the surface like long dead finger bones.

Dan sent the kid into the tent to get dressed while he retrieved their food bag from where it was tied, suspended from a tree branch. Watching him, it occurred to me I'd forgotten a couple of protein bars in my pack overnight. It was a good thing we hadn't been visited by hungry bears.

"Barneeeeeeey." Josh stuck his head out of the Taylor's tent and called for the dog.

I turned to Wade. "We should see what we can get out of our tent."

What I meant was, 'We need to check if we can salvage our sleeping bags,' but I didn't want to say it out loud. Wade looked back at me; he'd worked it out.

"Maybe we should see if we can move her somewhere else? So we can have the tent back?" he said.

It felt gruesome and callous, but I had to admit it made more sense. We could wrap the body in the ground sheet and move it. Then we could use the tent again, if not our sleeping bags. I flashed on the suspended food sacks, and my thoughts skittered away from what might happen if she was found by animals. Yeah, maybe we should take her away from camp.

"*Barney.*" Josh had wandered out of the tent now, half-dressed, holding a shoe. "Dad, where's Barney?"

"I don't know," Dan said, trying to stuff random things in a pack. "Get dressed."

"But Dad, I can't find Barney." The boy stood and stared at his father. "Did he go with Mom?"

"What? No." Dan's eyes slid past his son, unfocused and distant. His brow furrowed slightly, jaw working silently as if chewing on an unspoken thought. A nearby twig snapped under his son's foot, but Dan didn't flinch, his mind clearly elsewhere. "God, maybe, I don't know. Go and get dressed."

Josh shot an assessing glance at his father like he wasn't buying his dad's bullshit. The kid's mouth bunched a little and his bottom lip stuck out, but he went back into the tent.

Wade poked me.

"Okay, okay." I got to my feet and stood, rubbing my face again.

Dealing with Mel Taylor's corpse was the last thing I wanted, but those sleeping bags weren't getting any cleaner under her. My brain kept serving up unwelcome trivia about what happened to bodies postmortem. It made my skin crawl, but the faster we moved her, the better. We could wrap her in the ground sheet, and after the others had gone, we could shift her. Then we could move the tent and put it back up somewhere else. I didn't want to sleep right there where she'd died.

Wade indicated he needed to attend to a quick call of nature, so I made myself duck into the tent. I knelt beside Mel, and it hit me again. She wasn't just napping or passed out. She was stone cold. Done. My gut did a backflip, and I had to take a couple of deep inhalations to keep from hurling. Forcing my hands to move, I fumbled with the sleeping bags, trying to focus on the fabric and zippers instead of ... *well, you know*. Mine was fully under her, but Wade's was only partially beneath her, twisted around.

Something rippled under Mel's skin, like a shiver but ... wrong. Shit. My throat went dry, and I found myself leaning in without meaning to. I tried to shake it off, but then her eyelid freaking twitched. My heart did a nosedive into my gut, and I nearly fell on my ass as I leant back. Had we been wrong? Could she still be alive? The tent wall beside me billowed with a slight breeze, and light, stained blue from the canvas, danced across her face. Was that what I'd seen? I was frozen in place with a great ball of ice in my chest. From the corner of her eye came a teardrop, small, white, and round.

It wriggled.

From under her skin, another worm squirmed its way out into the air. It spooled out beneath her eye and waved its head about.

My stomach lurched. Before I could move, vomit splashed across Mel's front. Shit.

I scrambled back, colliding with the tent wall. The whole thing swayed. That reek of sour coffee hit me, and my gut heaved again. Hands shaking, I clawed at the tent flap. Stupid zipper jammed. I yanked harder, desperate for air.

My mouth burnt with acid, and I panted, my jaw hanging open.

"What are you doing?" Wade pulled back the tent flap and stuck his head in. My shoulder slammed into him. I stumbled out, legs wobbling as the ground rushed up to meet me. On my hands and knees, my body convulsed, heaving up whatever was left in my stomach.

"Hey, careful," Wade said, catching his footing. "What's wrong?"

Wade's lip curled, his eyes hard. Judgment was written all over his face. He hadn't seen what I'd just seen.

My finger trembled as I jabbed it at the tent. Words? *Forget it*. My lips were locked up tighter than a drum. But he needed to get his ass in there, needed to see it himself. No way he'd believe me if I told him. Hell, I barely believed it myself.

Wade frowned at me, then ducked into the tent.

"What's the problem? What am I supposed to— *uaaagh*."

Wade staggered out of the tent and bent over, hands on thighs, gaping. He didn't vomit, but he choked and spat, strings of saliva trailing.

We'd attracted attention by then, as Pete and Claire looked up from packing the last of their things. They travelled light with swags instead of a tent and had joked last night about swags being 'cultural,' whatever the hell that meant.

The pair came over, and Pete offered me a hand up from the ground where I was still sprawled.

"What's going on?"

I was shaking slightly. My lips parted, but I couldn't say anything. I turned to Wade, and he was upright again but stricken, sieving air through clenched teeth.

Dan, seeing us gathered, dropped his half-filled pack, and wandered over. I vaguely clocked Josh, drifting in and out of their tent, and hoped he'd stay there.

When we didn't say anything, Claire frowned and ducked to look in the tent. Pete followed to try and see over her shoulder.

"Oh God." Claire stood so abruptly she barreled into Pete, knocked him aside, and kept backing up till she was a good ten feet from the tent. Pete watched her, then bent to look as well.

"Oh Jesus." He stumbled a few steps back as well. "What the actual fuck?"

We were all wild eyed by then. We looked at each other, then to Dan.

"What's wrong?" he said. "Why are you all …"

No one could say anything. What could we say? Frowning at us, Dan went in.

Dan took one look and went ghostly white. He stumbled backwards, doubled over, and lost it. His retching broke the eerie silence. Splat after splat hit the ground.

Great. Fresh eyes, same reaction. Whatever was in that tent was as bad as I thought.

Horrible curiosity compelled me to go over and look again. God knew why. Both her eyes were now a squirming mass of worms. A couple dripped from her nostrils, and one started to squirm out from between her lips.

My belly contracted, but I had nothing left to expel. I stood upright and wiped at my mouth. There was the strange, acrid smell again. Another of those tremors ran through her body, but now I knew what it was.

Chapter 5

The movements were the sheer heft of the things inside her body, squirming as they consumed. I wrapped my arms around myself and backed away.

I remembered those tremors happening last night, when Mel had still been alive. I remembered the desperation in her bloodshot eyes as she screamed. Despite having nothing left to vomit, I upchucked acid and saliva, the taste sharp and foul.

In unspoken accord, we moved away from the tent, over to where Claire was standing, looking like she was considering the upchuck option herself. We stood in a semi-circle facing the tent, like we wanted to make sure nothing could sneak out of it.

"What the hell was that?" I asked.

Pete sounded near the end of his tether. "Are you crazy? It was worms. Fucking worms."

Thank you, Captain Obvious. I rubbed my sleeve across my forehead. "Christ. I know. I mean, it's ... do worms ... when someone dies ... is that normal?" I could hear the stupidity of this, even as I said it.

"No, it's not fucking normal."

Thanks again, Captain Obvo.

I became aware Dan was muttering over and over as he rubbed and scratched at his palm. I'd probably seem a bit dim, but it was only then

I fully realized the worms oozing out of Mel Taylor's face were identical to the ones from yesterday.

Now, I was both queasy and disoriented. My urge was to get as far away from both Mel's body and that damn patch of spruce as I could, right away.

"Oh God, oh God, oh God ..." Dan was hunched over, squatted into a ball, his hand extended, elbow resting on knee, as if to get it as far from himself as possible. His palm was red raw from where he'd been scratching and clawing at it and his hand was shaking.

"Oh God, it's going to happen to me." Dan looked up at us, face blank. "One of them went in my hand." His voice was high and squeaky, and he thrust his palm towards us. We'd all stepped back from him. "Oh God, oh God, why did she make me go down there? I can't, I can't—"

Across the clearing, Josh came out of the tent. "Dad, I can't find Barney."

The boy stomped towards our group only to stop, open-mouthed, when he saw his father's face.

"Dad, are you okay?" His brows were drawn together, and his voice was quavery, as if he knew something was badly wrong but wanted desperately to believe everything was alright. "Did something happen to Barney?"

Dan looked at the boy blankly for a second. "God. Shut up. I can't think." He clutched both hands to his head now, his concern over his palm seemingly forgotten.

"Oh, hey now." Wade stepped back towards Dan and shot me a look. It took my dazed brain an embarrassingly long time to realize the look meant 'get the kid out of here, you dimwit.'

Wade squatted beside Dan and patted him on the back. My palm crawled at the sight, and I wanted to grab Wade and pull him away from there. I turned and extended my arms in the universal herding gesture to the boy, as Wade was comforting his father.

"It's okay, if you were going to ... get sick, it would've happened by now. But you're okay. You were both ... bitten around the same time, yeah? Well, only maybe ten minutes later? See, and you're okay, you're okay. Maybe you weren't even bitten, we don't really know." Wade's voice was low and rapid.

I wondered if he believed what he was saying, whether he honestly hadn't seen the worm disappear into Dan's hand yesterday or if he was merely trying to calm the guy down.

"Let's go look for the dog," I said to the kid, for want of anything better to do.

Josh embraced this idea fervently. "Yes!" He raced off across the clearing to the trailhead.

Beneath the trees, the ground was black with moisture and squelched underfoot. I glanced back at Wade, wanting to tell him to be careful, but no suitable words presented themselves.

Josh bellowed at me from among the sodden brush, "Come ooooooooon already."

I glanced about as I followed the kid. Oddly, there were no birds, as normally you'd flush a few walking along the trail. Maybe the kid yelling 'Barney' every five seconds frightened them off early, but even so, it was ... unusual. Between Josh's shouts, there was only the dripping of wet trees. The hair on the back of my neck prickled.

I pushed back the hood of my jacket so I could see better, as the sides of it made me feel like I had blinkers on. There was nothing to see, though, and I didn't even hear any more of those odd, wet, thudding sounds, even though I kept listening for them.

With unerring precision, a drop of water fell into the back of my collar, sending a shiver down my spine. Everything was still, blank. We didn't find the dog, and eventually, I said we should head back. The woods were eerily quiet, and frankly, I didn't want to be there. Beneath the canopy, the tangles of creeper and rank brush had a bleak, lonely feel.

When we got back to camp twenty minutes later, Josh was sulky, wanting to keep looking for Barney. I tried to think when I'd noticed the dog last. It was before we'd all turned in. I'd not seen him in the night when Mel was ... well, when Mel died.

Had the animal been scared off by her screams? Run away into the woods and gotten lost? If so, he could be anywhere by now. Then I remembered his antics yesterday evening, digging, scratching, snuffling around. Had he followed us down to the spruce stand with the worms? I honestly couldn't remember.

When Josh and I came into the clearing, things had progressed. I couldn't believe how relieved I was to be back with adults. The Taylor's tent had been taken down, and Pete and Claire were packing the components. Their movements were quick and jerky, and both looked up and around often. Dan was sitting by the fire and seemed calmer, although his face was red and puffy, with tear trails running down his cheeks into his stubble. Wade had fixed him a mug of coffee, and he was holding it with trembling hands.

"Sorry," I told Dan. "We couldn't find the dog."

"What?" He looked at me blankly. "Oh yeah. Whatever."

I tried not to look in Josh's direction.

"Do you want more coffee, or should I pack this up?" Wade asked.

I desperately wanted more coffee. I tried not to think about where my earlier cup had ended up.

"I'm hungry," Josh said.

Pete tore his gaze from the scrub around the campsite and looked over to where Josh stood, hands on hips. Claire kept stuffing the kit, her eyes flicking up and about.

"Here, we kept these out for you." Pete came and handed over what looked like a couple of granola bars.

Josh's attention was rapidly distracted from his dad. Wade handed me an enamel mug of our coffee-like substance.

"I have to show you something," he said, his face turned away from Dan.

He grabbed a stick from beside the fire and led me over to a bit of bare, damp ground. Without a word, he used the stick to dig at the soil. It was soft after all the wet weather, and he easily gouged out a clod. Under it, and entwined in it, were a mass of worms. Squirming, wriggling, greyish white death. I involuntarily jerked back, took a couple of steps away from the hole, and spilled my coffee. Wade looked at me, then pointed to where I was now standing.

"They're everywhere," he said.

I eyeballed the ground, stunned, then the clearing around us. I was trying to process what I was standing on. Inside my boots, the soles of my feet tingled.

Back at the campfire, Josh was munching a granola bar. Between chewing, he was trying to engage his father in conversation. Wade and I gravitated to where the Australian couple were finishing up with the Taylor's gear and the four of us formed a little huddle.

"Did he show you the worms?" Claire asked quietly.

I nodded. I couldn't yet articulate the extent of my repulsion.

"Seriously, what the hell is this place?" Pete asked. He had a sheen of moisture on his forehead. "That woman was eaten by those bloody things, and they're everywhere. No one told us about this."

Both Wade and I stared at him like he'd grown another head.

"This is not normal, for fuck's sake," I said at last. "It's not like we go out camping and get eaten by worms all the time." I tried to calm what sounded like the start of hysteria. "I've never heard of anything like this."

I was trying to think. The caldera formed a massive stone basin. Anything in the soil would be entirely cut off from the outside. Had the worms here somehow mutated, turned into something new?

"What if they came from the meteorite?" Claire said.

"Maybe the worms here have, like, evolved?" I tried to explain my confused ideas. "Like those birds in the Galapagos?"

The silence was heavy. My mind drifted back to when we first got here. Those first couple of days, digging little holes in the dirt to do our business. Same as the Taylors. But back then? No worms. Zip. Nada.

And Wade? He hadn't said squat about seeing any creepy crawlies either. Something wasn't adding up.

"Could it have been something in the meteor?" Wade said.

I spun towards him, lightheaded. The meteor. Shit. It clicked into place like a sick jigsaw puzzle.

Crazy? Hell yeah. Impossible? Probably. But it fit. It all fucking fit.

The hair on the back of my neck stood up. That look on his face—he wasn't just spit balling—he believed it. And damn it, part of me did too.

"Maybe," I said, at the same time Pete raised his eyebrows at Wade's idea.

I glanced up to find Claire was scowling at us. I didn't know what the hell that was about, so I ignored it and thought some more.

"Wait, wait, wait." Pete raised his hands, palms out. "Are you honestly suggesting *worms* have come out of a meteor? Listen to yourself, that's insane."

My tired brain veered round to follow him. It was insane. What had I been thinking?

Claire looked thoughtful. "I don't think *my idea* is impossible, actually. Don't they reckon life might have started from a meteor?"

Pete's chin jutted. "How would that even work? The things burn up in the atmosphere."

"Maybe it's like tree seeds that need a bushfire to release them?" Claire said.

Pete frowned but was clearly considering it.

"But." I reflected. "If the worms are from the meteor, how did they get all the way over here? It only hit yesterday morning, and it was way over there." I gestured toward where the column of rising smoke was still visible. It occurred to me I didn't even know if that was normal either, whether meteor strike sites normally smoked.

"I dunno, maybe more than one of them hit?" Wade suggested.

Claire's lips quirked. "We only saw one."

"Or maybe the worms breed really fast?" Wade said it like he was making a joke.

I didn't know. Everything felt so bizarre that anything seemed possible. "Whatever the hell's going on, we have to let someone know as soon as we can," I said. "This whole place'll have to be like, I don't know, sprayed with DDT or something. I mean, what if whatever it is spreads outside the basin?"

Wade frowned. "I don't think it could. It'd be contained by the caldera. If the worms are only in the dirt, they won't be able to get out, right?" We all looked at him. "Unless they can climb up rock, they can't get out by the pass."

My mind refused to consider the possibility that worms could climb rocks. I felt that itch up under my feet again, inside my boots. Then, something else occurred to me.

"What if a bird picks one up and drops it outside?"

The full horror of the situation hit me, as I'd assumed it did the others. All I wanted was to book it. Get the hell out of Dodge. Find somewhere with four walls, a locked door, and cell service. Let the cops deal with this mess.

This was bigger than us. Way bigger.

"We gotta move. Now." My voice came out raspy, but urgent. "Park rangers, cops, fucking Army—whoever."

I was already scanning for the quickest way out. If those things spread beyond the park ... Jesus. Didn't even want to think about it.

We looked at each other, and no one said anything. There was nothing more to say; we had to go. Whatever the hell was going on, whatever it was, wherever it'd come from, we had to get out of here.

Chapter 6

We hustled Dan and his complaining son onto the trail, a thin down-trodden sliver that snaked between tree trunks and rock. The kid was outright mutinous, and I thought he wasn't going to follow.

"But we can't leave without Barney." His face was a thundercloud as he tagged along reluctantly. "We have to find him." He'd first refused to put his pack on and trailed it along the wet, muddy ground. "Daaaaaad."

But Dan Taylor was completely oblivious. He'd stalked ahead of us, setting a cracking pace I doubted his son would be able to manage for long.

His father's total lack of response appeared to confuse Josh eventually, and he quit whining, shut up, and looked worried. At last, he slipped his arms through the straps of his pack and stomped along.

Wade, who was bringing up the rear, tried to reassure him. "It'll be okay. Dogs can follow a scent. He'll be able to smell our trail and catch us up. And dogs can run a lot faster than we can walk."

Josh thought about this. "Yeah," he said, doubtfully. "I dunno. Barney's pretty stupid."

The kid had a point.

We walked fast for about an hour, then Josh flagged. His pack had some food and water, warm clothes, and a sleeping bag, so it wasn't heavy, but he wasn't empty-handed either. Wade, at the back, called out to suggest a quick break, and ahead of us, Pete had to jog to catch up with Dan and let him know. We dumped our packs and sat on them, as nobody wanted to risk sitting on the ground.

Around the trail, the woods were quiet, no birdsong, no calls. I was overheated and tired and there were more bugs than usual. Pete wandered off the side of the path, I assumed, for a pee. On his way back, he picked up a stick and scratched at the ground a little. I raised my eyebrows in question, and he nodded, his face set in stern lines.

After a few more minutes, Dan stood up and hauled on his pack. "Come on, we have to go."

Josh groaned.

"Joshy, on your feet, let's go."

I was annoyed with Dan but then thought, how would I feel if it was my kid out there? Yeah, I'd be all for hightailing it as fast as I could too.

"Yeah, come on, buddy," I said, standing and stretching. "We'll have a decent break at lunchtime, I promise; we just need to keep going now." I did shoot Dan a look though, as I hoisted my pack. It was much lighter without the tent, even though we'd redistributed some of the weight from Wade's pack.

"If you need, I can put anything heavy you've got in my pack?" I offered Josh. Maybe that would speed things up.

He shook his head and squinted at me like I'd threatened to steal his worldly possessions.

"You can't have my food," he said.

"Okay, bud." I smiled at his narrow-eyed look.

We set off, and I was glad to be moving again. I scanned the sides of the trail as we went, checking between the trees. I couldn't shake that crawling feeling I was missing something, but there was nothing, just mossy tree trunks marching away into the mist.

Josh became my shadow. I didn't know if it was because Dan was oblivious to his kid or if it was my in-depth knowledge of Spiderman, but he stuck by my side. I listened to the kid's piping voice on and off. Whenever the trail was wide enough for two abreast, he'd be there beside me, skipping to keep up.

"—And Nonna told Mom she'd look after Ralphie, but she wasn't gonna clean out his cage, no how. But it's okay because we won't be gone long, and do you think my mom's okay?"

Oh hell. I glanced down at the little upturned face. His hair needed brushing and was standing out from his head here and there. He stopped and looked up at me steadily. The miniature hands clutching the straps of his pack were grimy but balled so tight the knuckles were white.

He hadn't totally trusted his father's assurances his mom was fine. I had a hard knot inside because I knew he'd believe me. If I said his mom was okay, he'd believe me. His bottom lip quivered ever so slightly.

Annoyingly, Dan had been right about this too. I'd thought of him as a weasel not to tell the kid about Mel, but now I knew I'd been wrong. It was better to keep the news from the boy until we could get out. He needed to be able to walk and walk hard. Then his eyes filled with moisture, and I knew I'd hesitated too long.

"Here's the thing. Your mom's in the hospital, so she's not exactly okay, you see?" I could tell from his face this version was marginally more believable than his dad's. "After the doctors and nurses look after her, she'll be okay, but she might be there a while."

He nodded slowly, considering this.

"Then," I said with sudden inspiration. "When she comes home, she's going to need a lot of help. You'll have to help keep things tidy and ... and keep your room clean, okay?"

Josh's face cleared. It appeared this had enough ring of unpleasant childhood obligation to be plausible.

"You can do that for her, can't you?"

He nodded emphatically and smiled, the tangled hairball bouncing at the back of his head. He headed up the trail, and I followed, feeling about as low as a worm.

Dammit, don't think about worms.

We decided to stop for lunch a little before midday. It was early, but Josh was clearly exhausted, and the rest of us were tired and freaked out—at least I certainly was. There'd been a brief shower earlier, and the trees around us dripped endlessly in the silence.

We came across a little clearing with cut logs set up as seats, and this seemed a better choice than perching on our packs, so our little cavalcade stopped. We had to call Dan back again. The logs were wet and a bit slimy but felt okay. Josh dumped his pack at the first log but trailed over to where we were sitting.

I dug out the ubiquitous protein bars, surprised to find I was hungry. Then I remembered when I'd last eaten and where that bar had ended up. My appetite waned then, but I thought I should eat, so I dutifully unwrapped, bit, and chewed. It tasted like caramel cardboard, but I was suddenly hungry again.

The closed canopy of aspen and conifer around us crowded over the seating area, the bark of an occasional birch showing like luminous bone in the wet.

Dan dug a handful of granola bars out of his pack, tore one open, and ate it, leaving the rest cradled in his lap.

"You want to chuck some of those over here?" Claire said to him, pointing to his waiting son as Pete rummaged for their food.

Dan looked up. "No, he's got food in his pack." Upon reaching the clearing, he waved a hand to where the kid had dumped his load. It was almost the first thing Dan had said since we left camp this morning.

Claire frowned at Dan, and I had a spurt of annoyance with him myself. Then I thought it probably made sense to lighten the kid's pack first, not that granola bars weighed a whole hell of a lot. Josh groaned at having to get up again but huffed over to where he'd abandoned his pack. Instead of bringing his lunch back to sit with his dad, the kid stayed there, plonked down on a log away from all of us.

"How much longer d'you reckon till we get to the pass?" Pete asked. He and Claire had circled around on the high rim trail so hadn't hiked this route on their way in.

"By midday tomorrow, maybe?" Wade answered.

Dan had been looking dazed, but now his brows snapped together. "Tomorrow? No, we have to get there today. We can do it if we push on."

The rest of us clocked dubious expressions. It was only lunchtime, and Josh was already feeling the pace we'd set. Even if we didn't have the kid with us, I doubted we could've made the pass in a day. Had Dan forgotten how far it was?

"We need to get out of here today," Dan said forcefully, as if his tone would make it possible.

Across from us, Josh looked up from his pack. "But what about Barney?" he called. "If we leave today, he won't catch us up."

Dan gazed vacantly at the boy. "Um." He appeared to pull himself together with some effort. "He might be at the pass already, kiddo. Remember when he ran away at the park, and we looked and looked, and when we got home, he was there on the front porch?"

We all eyeballed Dan, and I wondered if he really thought Josh was stupid enough to believe this. The look the boy gave his father said the same thing. I wondered, guiltily, whether he'd really believed me about his mom. Was the fuss about the dog really about his mom? Did he know she was still back there? What was left of her?

None of us said anything for a while as we munched. I stared absently into the twisted tide of vegetation beneath the trees before narrowing my eyes. Had something moved in the tangle of dead twigs and branches? Maybe not.

I finished my bar and took a swig of water as I considered eating another. The day around us was dull and overcast. At least it wasn't raining, but among the trees, it was dim and muted, and everything was damp. I was clammy inside my jacket.

I kept trying not to think about Mel Taylor's face, the last time I'd seen it, but the more I tried to stuff it down, the more that snapshot popped back up. For some reason, the single, lone worm squirming out from between her blue lips was the most disturbing. I found myself rubbing my mouth.

People finished eating and made their way, one by one, into the undergrowth. More to distract myself than from actual need, I joined them and answered the call of nature. I went downhill, a little further from where Wade had gone a few minutes earlier, and found some lichen-covered stone to water—anything to avoid disturbing the ground.

On the way back, I put my hand out absently and grabbed at a sapling to haul myself up a steep rock. I was shocked when I tugged the tree over towards me instead of pulling myself up. It came out of the ground with a ripping sound and tilted over, its crown catching against other branches.

"Holy shit." I danced sideways, stumbling on the uneven ground and trying not to put my hands on anything for balance. I had a sharp flash of panic at the thought of falling and putting my palms on bare soil.

It hadn't been too small of a tree, but it'd come out of the ground like pulling a weed. I gave it a wide berth as I climbed uphill a couple of steps. The exposed root plate of the sapling was a mass of white, squirming awfulness. The unusual chemical smell I'd come to associate with the worms knifed into my nostrils, and my insides tried to climb out of my body.

There was a flash of something else in the hollow left by the roots among the shadows. Something black against the dark, muddy brown and scattered, wriggling flecks was gone too quickly for me to identify. I gulped, trying to tamp down unease, and took a few more steps up the hill. I looked at the other trees looming around me, then reached out a hand and pushed at one.

Not a small, overgrown sapling this time, but a decent looking trunk, the notched bark almost black in the wet. It moved. It didn't tip over, but I distinctly felt it give a little. If I'd pushed it hard, it would have gone over. Turning back, I looked down at the gooey bulk of the sapling's root ball, the upturned mass mushy and porous. I stood stock still as a horrible suspicion occurred to me. The whole slope, the whole area around me, was so full of worms that the actual ground was destabilized.

I stared at the other trees on the slope and felt oddly giddy for a brief second. It was too big to take in. I reached out again, poked at a spruce trunk, and watched as it listed drunkenly. Hands jittery, I moved back from it and stamped a foot.

Beneath my boot was still the firm, rotted-down hollowness you got in the woods. The top layer of the slope felt normal, so whatever was going on must be further down, deep where the taproots of the trees ran. We were a long way from where the meteor had hit. Was the entire basin undermined? Or were ... my head reared back ... were the worms following us underground? Swarming?

I thought about pushing another tree to check—you know, in case the world had righted itself while I was having my own personal break-down—but my hands were shaking too much. Despite knowing the worms were beneath us, until now, my surroundings had remained normal. Yes, there was a problem, but I'd still been in the everyday world.

Now a curious disorientation hit me, that the park wasn't safe. The actual environment wasn't safe. The *world* wasn't safe. The knowledge of the sheer bulk of worms below us made me gag. I picked my way back up and into the clearing as carefully as I could.

"What were you doing down there?" Wade asked, looking over as I emerged from among the trees. "We could hear you crashing around like bigfoot."

To my surprise, I found myself making a noise at him like an angry Marge Simpson. I was still suffering from that strange, unsteady realization.

"The trees aren't safe," I said, sitting myself down shakily. "I knocked one over."

Chapter 7

Everyone looked at me like I was out of my mind, which was hardly surprising.

I brushed my palms down my front. "I think the worms have destabilized the roots. The ground's soft or something. Deep down." This sounded crazy even as I said it.

"That's impossible," Wade said.

I looked at him, more tired than I'd ever been in my life.

"You try," I told him. "Go on, push one." I waved at the towering firs around us.

Wade raised his eyebrows at me, then flicked a glance around the group as if to apologize for the poor, deluded city boy he'd brought into the wilderness. He got up, though, and took a step towards the closest tree.

"Not there, dingus. There'll be worms and shit." I waved down the trail. "Go down a bit, away from us."

I'm sure he rolled his eyes but headed further down the path. He reached a tree and turned back towards us, his hand out to the trunk. He posed dramatically, looking at us with an expression that clearly said, 'Watch me humor the idiot.'

Wade leaned against the trunk. It juddered and dropped down the slope upright, almost like it had gone down a step on an escalator.

"Oh, heck." He jigged away from it exactly like I'd done with my tree.

How about that, our very own dance, the Douglas Fir Polka. Yeah, lack of sleep was still hitting me.

Pete, Claire, and Dan were on their feet now.

Pete moved cautiously down the trail to where Wade was. He reached out a hand.

"Don't, you idiot—" Claire shouted at him a second before he pushed at a trunk.

"Holy shit." Pete staggered back from the tree.

This one actually fell. Slowly, almost gracefully, with a great ripping as its roots turned up out of the ground. Wade and Pete hauled ass back up the trail, their rapid footfalls hollow on the path. The tree Wade had pushed went over a heartbeat later.

"Tim-berrrr," I said. I couldn't help it.

The fir crashed through its neighbors and caused a cascade, as several other trees below it went over as well. We stood frozen, watching in awestruck horror, listening to the roar as trees crashed down through the hillside. At last, it stopped.

"Bloody hell," Claire whispered into the silence, her face drained.

A snootful of that chemical waft came up the hill, and I could taste it in the back of my throat. Dan was frozen and tense, Pete had a hand in front of his mouth and Wade was panting in short, shallow gasps. I guessed everyone was mentally catching up, because our surroundings were basically inimical to life. That the world around us was fucked. It was disorienting, and they wouldn't be feeling good.

"Told you so," I said.

We stood there looking at each other for a while. No birds had been roused by the trees collapsing. Although, by this time, I'd probably have been surprised to hear any. There were no sounds, just that rank smell.

"What the hell are we going to do?" Pete asked. "Does the trail go up through trees the whole way?"

I tried to remember. "Pretty much, I think."

"Doesn't matter, we've still got to get out of here," Dan said.

"Yes, but we've got to be more careful," Wade said, his forehead wrinkled and tense. "Way more careful."

We looked at the trees above us on the slope. Firs and spruce mostly, big, looming. A light breeze ruffled their upper branches. What was going to happen when it got windy?

A gunshot hammered the air, a flat hard *blat*.

It wasn't close, but there were echoes from the distant stone cliffs. We looked around, but it was impossible to tell where it'd come from. Until then, I'd honestly not thought about anyone else in the park; my rickety world had shrunk to our little group.

"Jesus, is someone shooting at worms?" I asked.

"Maybe they're trying to get attention?" Claire said.

I met her look. I could imagine what kind of trouble some other hiker might be in, and from the faces around me, the others could too. We waited, but the sound wasn't repeated.

"Should we go try to find them?" Wade ventured, but even he sounded dubious.

"We don't have time," Dan said. "And it's not safe. We've gotta get out of here."

Claire worried at her thumbnail. "He's right. We don't even know where it came from, so we could spend hours wandering and not find anyone."

I had to admit this was a relief. Besides, even if we could reach whoever it was, we could do nothing for them, and I didn't want to come across another Mel Taylor. I didn't want to listen to someone else scream their life out as they were eaten alive, to have to sit beside them, this time knowing what was going on inside of them. And wondering whether I'd be next. We just needed to get the hell out of here as fast as we could.

"We should get on then," I said. "We should probably—"

"Where's Josh?" Dan asked.

I turned to look around the clearing, but the boy wasn't there. Not in the open area, not among the trees. Everyone began to peer into the brush.

"Where's Josh?" Dan demanded this time as if one of us had hidden the kid.

We moved to check in the undergrowth.

"Josh!" Dan cupped his hands and bellowed. It echoed faintly, 'osh, osh, osh.' There was no reply. Dan went up the trail without a word, and Pete trudged the other way. We could hear them both calling.

Wade, Claire, and I cautiously poked about in the undergrowth on either side of the clearing, calling out as we did.

"Josh, Josh—*Joooosh*!" Resounded up and down the trail.

Wade made his way back out of the crackling scrub above the path. "He must have gone for a bathroom break," he said.

A flash of annoyance flared in me at this inanity, but I didn't say anything. I was trying to hold down a bubble of panic. I eyeballed the scar the collapsed trees below the trail created and thought about how easily they'd fallen.

"Did he go before or after the trees went over?" I asked. "Would he have gone down there?"

My fear was reflected in the downward turn of Claire's mouth. We headed down to look. Wade joined us. A lot of the uncovered worms had disappeared back into the ground, but there were still enough visible to be uncomfortable.

A note of that strange, complex smell hung in the air. It was like a paint stripper in my sinuses. A clear trail of destruction led down the hillside. Upturned root balls, felled trees, and tangled branches made it impossible to tell if a small body was underneath.

"Jooooosh!" we all screamed. Nothing but the echoes came back.

Wade, Claire, and I had picked our way carefully and cautiously down either side of the flattened trees. The soles of my feet itched at the sight of exposed, tangled roots. I peered through fallen trees and tugged at branches, gingerly avoiding the dripping, squirming infestation.

I didn't want to look at the worms, but I had to; I couldn't help seeing the way they thinned and stretched, sniffing the air and then turning toward us. I checked my boots and trouser legs compulsively as we shuffled through fallen limbs and undergrowth. There was no sign of the missing kid.

We went farther than Josh could possibly have gone looking for a place to potty, but there was no trace of him. It was like the woods had eaten the boy. I had an increasing sense of incongruity, along with the revulsion backing up my nose; this couldn't be happening.

Gradually, we coagulated back into the clearing, all of us empty handed. The trees loomed around us with murderous potential.

"What the hell are we going to do?" Pete was leaning, hands on thighs, panting, having hiked rapidly back up the trail.

"We have to get going," Dan said.

"Yeah, we know, but how are we going to work it?" Claire said. "We probably need to look more on either side of the trail, right?" She turned to Pete. "How far down did you go?"

"A kilometer, maybe," he said. "I was checking along the sides as I went but I didn't see him."

"But if he'd fallen or something ... hit his head maybe, you may not have noticed him." Claire frowned.

"We're wasting time," Dan said. "He's gone back to the campground for the stupid dog." His lips clamped shut in a thin line.

Had the kid gone back? I could only hope he'd left before the trees had fallen, that he wasn't crushed beneath timber, wasn't pinned somewhere, his defenseless body pierced by needle-thin awfulness. Hope that he hadn't wandered off and fallen over a cliff, hadn't been eaten by a bear. If Dan was right, Josh was on the trail and couldn't have more than an hour on us. We had a chance of finding him, a good chance.

Josh would have heard us talking about the worms, but he didn't know what had happened to Mel. Now that I thought about it, he *must* have disappeared before we'd discovered the ground was unstable—he wouldn't have gone off alone if he'd known that, surely?

My innards felt full of squirming death, but I tried to focus on the positives. Provided he stayed on the trail, there was hope he wouldn't know how dangerous the trees were. If he wasn't panicked, there wouldn't be any reason for him to run between them. He might still be safe from worms if he didn't dig anything up. We could catch him. There was hope.

"We have to get out of here," Pete said, hitching his pack from the ground.

Claire raised her eyebrows at him. "We don't need to take our packs back down there." She pointed down the trail. "We can grab them on the way back, can't we?"

"We can't all go back." Pete's face was oddly rigid. "It's stupid. Dan can go back, but the rest of us should keep going. We'll send help as soon as we get out."

I checked Wade's face. "The kid can't have gotten that far; we'll have a better chance of finding him if we have more people—"

"No. We have to get out and warn people. You know we have to. It's too important. And we don't know how far he's gone. We don't even know how long he's been gone." Pete was shaking his head again. "We'll have a better chance of someone getting out if we stick together." Pete's eyes flicked to Dan. "As much as we can."

Claire nodded slowly, and I felt a little panic at the thought of us splitting up. There was a surreal quality to the discussion. Pete was right, of course, as someone had to get out and get help quickly. Warn people. I was knocked off kilter, though, when I thought that he could consider abandoning a child. I had trouble getting the shape of it to fit in my head.

"Okay," I said, nodding. "What if you and Claire go, and Wade and I can head back with Dan—"

"No. We all have to go look." Dan's voice was squeaky. "You have to come with us." He glared at Pete. "The more of us, the better chance we have of finding him."

Claire took a few steps up the trail, looking at Pete. "It'll be fine, we can do it—"

"No. No, no." Pete's voice rose as if he was on the verge of hysteria. "I'm not going back to the campground. After what happened to Mel. You saw what—"

"Pete," Claire hissed at him and nodded down at Dan standing sullenly on the trail.

"What?" Pete frowned.

Claire rubbed her hands over her face and turned back to us. "Look, I think Pete and I need to go on." She grabbed her pack and gave us an apologetic grimace.

"Goddamit, you've gotta come and help." Dan's face was red. "What if he's hurt and we have to carry him?"

Pete shook his head. "There's three of you, you'll be fine."

Dan stormed up the trail, barging Claire aside and getting up in Pete's face. "Listen, you jerk, that's my kid down there." He thumped Pete in the chest, knocking him off balance.

Not the best approach if he wanted the guy's help.

A second later, Pete found his footing, swiped back at Dan, and the pair scuffled.

"For Christ's sake!" Claire belted at both of them indiscriminately. "Stop it."

"Oh shit." Wade and I started up the trail toward them.

Arms and hands were flying everywhere. Pete was at a disadvantage with his pack on and Dan managed to land a blow to his cheek.

"Oww." Pete clapped a hand to his face. "Watch it, dickhead."

He wiped his cheek, looked at his fingers, and showed us a red smear. "You nearly had my eye out." Blood leaked from a line under Pete's eye.

Dan turned his hand over and frowned at his eagle pinky ring. "It's nothing," he said, a little defensively. "Barely a scratch."

"Fuck you," Pete said. He turned his back and started up the trail.

Claire shrugged, hoisted her pack, and followed.

"But you have to come and help," Dan whined after her.

She shook her head but didn't turn around.

"Come on, then. If we're going, let's go," I said. We were wasting time.

On the trail, Pete turned to wait for Claire. "You guys be careful!" he yelled.

"*Fuck off*!" Dan bellowed back at him with accompanying hand gestures.

"Hey, if we're going to find Josh, we should get going," I said, pulling on Dan's arm.

He shook me off and huffed over to where we'd abandoned our packs in the middle of the trail. I joined him, grabbed my water bottle, and left the rest since we'd be back this way once we'd found the kid.

I no longer had any sense of time; it seemed an age since we stopped, but if we hauled ass, I was sure we could catch the boy by sundown. If he was still alive to catch.

"Let's go."

The three of us headed down the trail, back over every painstaking step we'd walked up. Even though we were going the wrong way, giving up ground, I felt better. All around us was danger and terrifying death, and we were heading back into it, but I was doing something, helping. I tried to be as careful as possible, no leaning on trees or kicking up dirt. I kept a lookout for movement to either side of the path, but there was nothing, no sign of Josh.

"How fast could the kid walk?" I called ahead to Dan.

He shook his head and didn't break stride.

I looked back at Wade. As an ex-schoolteacher, he might have more insight into this than me.

"Who knows? If he was trying to be sneaky, he probably legged it as fast as he could."

Damn.

Wade leaned to yell around me at Dan. "Did he take his pack?"

I tried to think, had I seen Josh's pack?

"I don't know, maybe," Dan snapped back. "I can't remember."

Wade grimaced. "If he's smart, he took it. Food and water, yeah?"

I grinned. "Ha, he totally took it then. That kid wouldn't go anywhere without food."

Wade smiled back, but it didn't reach his eyes. "Let's hope."

Meanwhile, Dan had gotten the jump on us, and we had to scoot to catch him up. I tried to check the sides of the path as we went, but to be honest, in the thick brush, the kid could be ten feet from us, and we wouldn't know. The tall timber rose from the undergrowth around us like silent sentinels of an impenetrable maze. The woods were capable of eating a child whole.

About three miles down, we turned another switchback, and the trail was obliterated, wiped clean off the side of the hill.

Chapter 8

The trees we'd unleashed so far above had cascaded down the hillside in a massive landslip. Mud, rocks, and trees had poured down, destroying the trail and blocking any way forward. The scale of it was immense. A solid wall of tangled trunks and debris taller than a house barricaded the way forward, the path barred by the annihilation of the forest.

Looking at the destruction, I was amazed we hadn't heard it, but I guess we'd all been busy panicking and bellowing Josh's name. There was nothing now but a sheer wall of loose soil and rubble, with branches and roots poking out here and there. There was no way around.

We stood and stared. My nerves were a twisted ball of barbed wire. I could only hope Josh hadn't been on the trail when it happened. I squatted down and swore, a hand on either side of my head.

"Shit, shit, shit, shit, shit." Dan was kicking at clods.

Wade had given up on policing language; he merely nodded in agreement.

"What do we do now?" I asked. I was trying to think—was there another trail that would take us back to Harper's Meadow? The impossibility of trying to climb through the vast swathe of banked-up debris and filth, full of churned-up worms, swamped me.

"We have to find a way through," Dan said.

I could only stare hopelessly at the devastation.

"There's nothing we can do," Wade said.

I frowned at him, but his eyes were on Dan as the man explored the wild, tangled obstruction.

I gritted my teeth and didn't look. I felt like if I looked, I'd see something. A foot poking out or something. I couldn't look.

Wade shook his head, trying to make Dan understand. "There's no other way to get through from this side. We'd have to go right up around the rim and in from the other side. It'd take three days, maybe four." He pointed, but Dan ignored him. "It'll be quicker to go for help."

Plainly, that wasn't what Dan wanted to hear, but I thought it was sinking in for him that getting through wasn't going to happen. At least, I hoped he understood. We'd hit a brick wall. There was simply no way through. The foul smell was burning into my nose again.

Wade was scanning back and forth across the bank of fallen trees and muck. "All we can do is head to the pass and get search and rescue out here as soon as possible," he said, his tone flat.

"Shit," I said eloquently.

"There must be a way to get over it." Dan's voice cracked. He raised a hand uselessly at the blockage.

I pulled myself together enough to look closer, and Dan and I wasted a bit of time poking around, trying to find a way through. More debris fell from above us, and I got a bad case of creepy crawlies, especially regarding the sheer number of worms we could see and smell. Wherever there was exposed soil, there was movement, from the hint of a wriggle to heaving clots of dripping worms. The weird chemical trace in the air burnt my sinuses, adding to my growing unease.

I prodded about with a stick, but nothing was any use. I flung the stick away, wanting to smash something. I jammed my hands in my pockets.

If Dan tried to climb into that squirming mess, I would not be following him.

"Are you okay?" Wade tilted his head toward me.

"Yes." No. No, I wasn't ok. I kicked at a rock, stubbing my toes.

I'd wanted to find Josh to make up for lying to him about his mom. I'd wanted him to be safe, to make up for his mom being dead and his dad being a bit of a dick. It wasn't going to happen.

I was so angry I could barely stand myself. I guessed I'd always wondered how I'd react under real pressure. I supposed we all did, and we all wanted to think we'd be heroic and brave.

Well, it turned out I got irritable at everything and everyone. I scanned Wade's face and wondered how he could be so calm, and I was pissed at him for being so calm.

Eventually, we slogged back up the trail. The climb felt exponentially longer than it had going down, more than the slope could account for. On the way down, I'd had hope that I was going to find Josh, fix things, and save the day.

On the way back up, my emotions had flipped. I was tired, sad, and frightened. I was sick of looking at trees, wondering if the slightest breeze was going to bring a stand of timber down on us. I was sick of walking into the wet drizzle, sick of wondering whether Josh Taylor was alive or dead.

I'd been lagging behind when a shout from Dan sent a spark of hope through me.

"Over there."

I caught the sounds of crashing through the undergrowth as he left the trail, and I hustled to catch up to where Wade was peering after him.

"Is it Josh?"

"I don't know. I don't want to follow too close to Dan, in case the trees ... you know." Wade held up a palm indicating I should stay, then stepped cautiously off the path and around some scrubby trees.

I almost told Wade to stop, to wait, but I let him go. What if the ground collapsed again? What if he or Dan brushed against a tree and brought the whole lot down? The memory of the devastation below us lingered. I peered into the silent shadows and tried not to think about what was teeming beneath my feet. I tried not to think about one of these towering trees crashing down on me, crushing me, holding me to the worm-infested ground.

"Holy shit." Dan's voice came clearly through the brush, and I twitched.

"Oh no." Wade's voice wobbled.

"Is it the kid?" I stood on my toes, craning to see.

Neither jerk bothered to answer. To hell with waiting. I picked my way carefully toward their voices. My throat was full of dread, so I cleared it loudly into the silence and called again, "Is it Josh or not? Where the hell are you?"

"Over here." Wade was close.

Brush crackled beneath my feet. Behind a boulder lay a small, flat clearing. A bare space among the looming trees, carpeted with pine needles and filled with the sound of buzzing flies. Dan and Wade were still, staring at a shape on the ground. A dead body. Most definitely dead. I gagged and clapped a hand to my gob.

At least it wasn't Josh. This was a grown adult, a man with long grey hair and stubble. He looked like he'd been savaged by an animal, although ... I tilted my head, trying to work out what had happened. The man's shirt was half stripped off, and his one exposed arm was a gory, gaping mess of wounds.

There was a lot of blood. Smears ran over his arm and front, soaking into his damp shirt. I rubbed the back of my neck and tried to ignore my tumultuous stomach. A hunting knife, covered in clotted blood, was clutched in the man's other hand.

Dan extended a foot and nudged the body. The crawling, buzzing flies swarmed up in a cloud and I stumbled back a step.

"What happened?" Wade's voice was still wobbly.

"Poor bastard," Dan said.

I stared at the man's arm, unable to look away. "What the hell got him?"

A knife in one hand and defensive wounds on the other? Whatever it was had slashed his arm to shreds.

I tore my gaze away and scanned our surroundings, properly taking in the small clearing. A single yellow pack lay on the north side, torn open, contents strewn, a knife scabbard among the debris. It looked like he'd dug out the weapon in one hell of a hurry.

Dan knelt beside the body, waving aside a fat, blood-soaked fly. "I think he might have done this to himself."

My gorge churned again, and I tried not to breathe through my nose. I didn't want to take in the thick, coppery scent in the air.

"What? He killed himself." I tugged my sleeves down over my hands. "Like that?"

Dan grimaced up at me. "Look, those are knife cuts." He pointed to the man's hacked-up arm.

My eyebrows shot up. "How can you tell?" It all looked like revolting gore to me. The light drizzle had kept the blood wet, but it didn't look fresh. It looked ...foul. I tried not to notice the flies coating the wounds like a layer of living filth.

"It looks like a beginner's attempt to dress a deer, that's how."

I shuddered and redirected my gaze to the trees around us.

"How long's he been dead?" Wade asked. "Was he here when we went past before?"

Dan frowned. "We would have seen him on the way down if he'd been here, wouldn't we? I caught a glimpse of his pack from the trail."

I considered the boulder's placement amid the trees and scrub. "Maybe the rock blocked the view on the way down?"

"Jesus." Dan scanned the brush around us and rubbed at his head. "Josh could be anywhere, and we wouldn't know." He gestured briefly to the corpse.

"No. If Josh heard us, he'd call out, yeah? This guy couldn't," Wade said.

"You think he was already dead then, when we came past in the morning? Or just when we went back down?" I had that odd feeling of distrust again. Things like this didn't happen. It was the last straw of weirdness that pushed everything past surreal. I blinked away dizziness.

"Both, I'd say." Dan climbed awkwardly back to his feet.

"Should we see if he has any ID?" Wade asked.

"*No*," I said, a bit louder than I'd intended. I clenched my fists to stop my hands trembling. "I don't think we should touch anything. Like, in case he didn't kill himself."

As I spoke, a tiny quiver ran through the man's arm and my heart jumped into my throat. The coating of flies rippled, then resumed exploration, and my guts attempted to lurch from my throat to my mouth.

I tamped down puke. "We should get going."

"Yeah."

We looked blank-faced at each other.

"Yeah."

Wade led the way back to the trail.

We pushed on as long as we could, through dusk and into the night until it was almost too dark to follow the track. To either side of us, the banks of trees thinned, leaving shadowed tunnels to peer down. I tried to focus on the path, but my eyes flicked of their own accord, looking for movement. There was nothing.

I thought about how desperate I'd been to get away from my dull, every-day, heartbroken life. How I'd give anything now to be back there. I just wanted this to stop; I wanted the real world back.

The Australian couple had been so far ahead we didn't catch them again until we finally stopped for the night. Pete and Claire had found a good place to camp at least.

We'd come out of a closed-canopy forest and were making our way through dark open woodland when we reached a wide plateau of rock rising among the trees. It was a little bit rounded and hump-backed, but it was way better than sleeping on bare, worm-ridden terrain. I'd been dreading having to lie directly on the ground, where the infestation was. If we didn't have to risk trees falling on us in the night, it would be an added bonus.

The pair were seated beside a small fire and looked up as we crunched up the ridge of rock.

"Hi," Pete said, catching sight of us. He shot Dan a glower, and I remembered him and Dan fighting before we'd split up. I'd totally forgotten, as it seemed such a long time ago.

"You didn't find him then?" Claire peered up at us.

"We found a body," Dan said.

"Shit, not—?"

"Not Josh," I said quick, catching the shocked horror on Claire's face.

"Yeah," Dan said. "Just some old man."

Some old man? I shot Dan a look he didn't see. That man had been a person, a living, breathing human being.

"Sit down." Pete gestured to the fire in invitation, and we dumped our packs and pretty much collapsed.

"What happened?" Claire wrapped her arms around her knees.

I dropped my head. I couldn't say anything. I was tired to the bone. Dan ignored her and rummaged in his pack.

Wade sighed. "We couldn't get back to the campground. There was a landslide, and the trail's gone. There's no way through."

Pete stared at his feet and said nothing. At least it didn't look like the fuss between him and Dan was going to flare up, as the pair were ignoring each other. Good.

"Shit." Claire frowned. "Where did you find the body then?"

"Just off the trail. We caught sight of something on the way back—"

"On the way back?" Pete's head came up. "The bloke died while you were down at the campground?"

"No," Dan snapped at him. "He was a ways off the track, behind some rocks. I only saw him because I was looking around for Josh on the way back."

"We think he must have been dead for a while," Wade added.

"How could you tell? What happened to him? How did he die?"

Wade patiently explained about the man's hacked up arm and our idea that it was self-inflicted. Dan added gory details. I tried to tune it out.

"Why would he only cut one arm if he was trying to kill himself?" Pete asked.

Claire scrunched up her face. "What if he was trying to cut out a worm?" She made slicing motions over her hand and arm. "Like if he saw it go in, maybe he was digging for it."

Chapter 9

Oh God. I hadn't even thought of that. Wade and Dan wore the same disgusted realization on their faces.

It made horrible sense. The pulled-off sleeve, the hastily dug-out a knife, the cut-up hand and arm. I closed my eyes on the thought, as the sheer desperation of it was too much.

Dan's face was a pale mask across the fire. "He must have known what was going to happen."

"Did he get the worm, do you reckon, before he bled to death?" Pete asked.

My ribs felt too tight. I had to remind myself Pete hadn't been there, hadn't seen the mutilation, the blood. Or that little shiver running through the dead man's arm.

"He must have, eh? If the body was still there, hadn't been eaten?"

My gaze flicked back to Dan. "Maybe."

"I want noodles," Wade announced, pulling his pack open.

I blinked at him, noodle-like myself, before I understood what he meant. I was so tired and grossed out I was dizzy. Our packs were full of instant ramen, pretty nasty but light, easy to pack, and simple to make.

"Yeah, I could go for something warm," I said.

I dug around in my pack for the kidney-shaped aluminum tin we used to boil water. All I wanted to do was flop over and sleep, but I knew we should eat.

We all sat around the fire, Dan, Wade, and me, as a buffer between him and Pete. The solid stone beneath us was enormously comforting. I sat with my legs stretched out, palms flat against gritty rock, and was grateful I could relax.

Despite the circumstances, the mood eased and became a little brighter. We'd found a haven; the body was no one we knew, and, with luck, Josh would be alright.

Beside us, Pete and Claire had ripped open some pouches, and there was now a bit of rearranging as Pete made room on the fire for Wade's little pan with the turn-back handles.

"It shouldn't take us too long tomorrow and we'll be out of here," Wade said, ripping open a ramen pack.

"Too right," Pete said. "Then search and rescue'll find Josh." He turned marginally towards Dan. "This time tomorrow, we'll all be safe." He grinned at Claire. "Except me, of course, I've still got to sleep with someone's toxic farts."

"Oi." She did the swatty thing to his arm and I actually smiled. "Don't listen to him, he's the one with the lethal arse. Bloody crop duster."

I grinned and checked our pan, as it was taking forever to boil.

"It's not my fault," Pete said. "I'm lactose intolerant."

Claire glared at him in what I assumed was mock outrage because she was having trouble keeping the sides of her lips from quirking up. "Of course, it's your fault, you rampant arse-hat. You're the one who eats the shit."

For some reason, I was quite taken aback by her turn of phrase.

It was Pete's chance to look outraged then. "I don't eat shit."

"I swear to God." Claire shook her head at him. "Sometimes I wonder how closely your parents were related."

Up until then, Dan had been silent with an air of almost bravado, as if he'd forgotten about the worm disappearing into his hand. Now, it was like he wanted to join in the comradery. "We need a crop duster in here. Napalm the hell out of it."

There was a heartbeat of quiet, and then Pete said, "Mate, what we need here is a nuke."

Silence fell around the fire.

Dan glanced over at Claire. And, there it was again, the flick of the eyes to the young woman's chest.

I'd been feeling mildly sorry for the jerk, as he had to be worried about his son and himself, after all. The feeling that it was going to be alright, that we were going to get out of here, had overtaken me. Now, I stared at his stupid face, annoyed by him again.

The man's wife had just died in the most horrendous way, and he was still low-level sleazing. He had a fat pimple beside his nose, above his mangy stubble. His eyes skimmed back to Claire, and another spurt of irritation surged through me. I spent years watching my old man do this to my mother's friends and it never failed to piss me off, even if Mom was willfully blind to it.

Next to me, Wade took a drink from his water bottle and nudged me with the remains. "Here, you may as well finish it off."

I didn't know if he'd noticed me glaring at the arse-hat across the fire. I took a swig and tried not to be irked by Dan. Maybe he was in shock, or maybe this was some auto-pilot douchery he didn't even know he was doing.

The zit beside his nose looked red and inflamed. I screwed the cap back on the bottle and returned it. The water in the pan steamed, and all I wanted was for it to boil so we could eat and go to sleep.

I sat, gazing blankly ahead at Dan, and noticed the man's pimple had grown a little head of white puss. I glanced away and pulled my pack open. Wade and I would have to sleep on the bare rock. No tent, no sleeping bags. So, I figured I'd pull out every bit of clothing I had to put either over or under me. I was too grateful for the rock to bitch about sleeping on it, though.

Movement caught my eye, and my gaze snapped back to Dan's face. The flickering of the firelight, surely? I was riveted now, unable to look away, my pack forgotten.

Oh God, it wasn't a trick of the light. My breath came in a ragged pull as a tiny white thread broke through the surface of Dan's skin. What I'd thought was the head of a zit was a worm.

Frozen in shock, I watched as it squirmed out a bare fraction, the end revolving as if savoring freedom. I tried to say something, but I was suddenly drowning in saliva. I wanted to throw myself back away from the fire, away from him, but I was immobilized by the fact there was no safe place to go. Everywhere beneath the ground were worms. Nowhere was safe but on this rock.

Pete, across the fire, turned to look at me, his face concerned. Slowly I raised my finger and pointed to Dan. To his face. Pete looked.

"Oh God."

"Uuuh." Wade, on the other side of me, had seen it now too.

I wanted to cry.

How could Dan not feel it, the thing had burst through his skin. My head was full of horror. Claire was the only one brave enough to say anything.

"Shit, Dan, your face." She pointed at him then tapped the same place beside her nose.

Dan looked at her and frowned, tried to look at his cheek, wiped at it, then slapped at it.

"Shit, shit, shit—" he said, smacking and rubbing.

He smeared blood across his face. Dan looked at his hand, and I guessed there was blood there too.

"It was a bug, right?" Dan asked, his voice thin and panicky.

I thought he knew it wasn't a bug.

"Yeah, nah." Claire sounded like she barely managed to choke this out. "It wasn't a bug."

"It was a fucking bug, alright." Dan sounded angry, but his lower lip quivered.

"Shit." We scrambled to our feet and stood, looking down at Dan, who glared defiantly back at us.

"It's fine," Dan said. "It was a bug. Everything's fine." His voice didn't sound like everything was fine.

We all edged a little further together until Dan was on the other side of the fire.

His voice went up a couple of octaves. "It was a fucking bug, for fuck's sake."

I wanted to be as far away from Dan as I could, but I didn't want to leave the security of a good solid stone beneath me. Could we ask him to leave?

I turned back to Dan. "Why don't—"

Something white squiggled its way across the darkness of his pupil.

My chest seized up. I couldn't move, couldn't think. Dan's face was a ghost, his eyes red marbles in a sea of white. His jaw worked, but no sound came out. The world came rushing back with a gasp. Air flooded my lungs like I'd been underwater. My legs gave out and I hit the ground, boneless.

"Okay ... okay then. That's okay." Nothing was okay.

"What're you doing?" Wade hissed, grabbing my shoulder. "We need to get away from him. Now."

I looked up at Wade and gave him the tiniest head shake I could. We were safer here on this rock than we'd be on the trail. And we couldn't make this any worse for Dan. We couldn't run screaming and howling. I saw the moment Wade caught on.

I wanted to close my eyes and disappear, not exist, not see the naked terror on Dan's face. I was frozen in place now. Beside me, the others sat again and were still and quiet too. Us on our side of the fire, Dan on his, flames between us.

All I could think was, why had it taken so long? I'd thought Dan was okay. We'd all thought he must be okay. I remembered thinking how grossly unfair it was. Both he and Mel had been bitten, and only Mel had been affected.

My hands were shaking. I remembered Dan digging up and tipping worms into his palm. God damn it.

No one said much after that. We ate; we stretched out. We lay still.

The scream came a couple of hours after we'd all settled. I hadn't slept; I'd just lay there, awake, waiting. Even though I'd been expecting it, the first shriek was whiplash-inducing. Cold dread clenched a fist inside me.

I sat up and turned to peer at where Dan had stretched out. It was dark, but there was movement, thrashing. Around me, the others were waking to the wailing siren. Wade hauled himself upright, and the others were fighting their way out of their swag.

We stumbled over, flashlight beams waving about. The night was endlessly dark around us. We were so far from help I wanted to weep.

The four of us bunched, knelt, and squatted helplessly around Dan. He was in terrible pain. His bloodshot eyes bulged, caught in a glint from the flashlight. His body was arched, rigid in agony. His screams were macabre, high-pitched, piercing. A dentist's drill of sound bored through my head and skewered my brain.

I stared helplessly at the others, but there was nothing but blank, exhausted despair on their faces. Dan's body collapsed briefly, and deafening silence fell as his lungs heaved in air. Then the screaming kicked off again. It went on and on. Five minutes? Ten minutes? I had no idea, as time was intensified and elongated. It was so much worse than with

Mel. Now we knew what was happening. Every second we knew what was going on inside him.

Eventually, Claire scrambled to her feet and thumped me on the shoulder. I looked up at her in the gloom. There were no moons or stars; she was in a dark shape against a dark sky.

She pointed to the other side of the rock, over past where the smoldering campfire glowed, then grabbed Pete, and the pair of them retreated. I squinted after them, and Claire beckoned to me. My stupefied brain caught on eventually, and I stood, nudged Wade, and urged him up. We staggered over to Pete and Claire, black silhouettes by the fire.

"What is it?" I asked. "Do you have an idea?"

Claire grabbed a stick and stabbed viciously at the embers. "We have to kill him." Her voice was shaky.

We all stared at her. Orange coals were reflected in her eyes. From behind us, the screaming stopped. Then started again.

Pete's eyes were so wide they seemed to bulge from his head. "What the fuck?"

Claire's breathing came heavily through her nose as if she'd run a race. "We can't let him suffer. Not like his wife did."

I couldn't believe what I was hearing, didn't want to believe it, because I knew then, she was right. And I *so* didn't want to know that.

In the flickering light of the fire, Wade's face went rigid. He shook his head back and forth as if unable to stop. "No, no, no—"

"We have to do something." Claire smacked him on the arm.

"We don't have a gun," I said, grasping at straws.

"Bloody Americans." Claire scowled at me. "You don't need a gun to kill someone."

I didn't know why, but I was shocked. "What, you want to bash his head in with a rock or something? Stab him? Jesus fucking Christ."

Pete clutched his forehead and looked at his girlfriend like he'd never met her before.

"No." Claire's lip quivered slightly. "Smother him with a pillow."

"Oh, dear God." Wade looked like he was about to hurl. "You're going to suffocate someone?"

"I'm bloody not," Claire lashed back. "All of us have to do it."

We all turned back to where Dan lay, flailing.

"Come on." Claire moved to head back toward him.

"Wait." Pete grabbed her arm. She jerked at it but couldn't pull free.

"I slept in their tent last night." Her voice was shaky again. "Think about it. What if ..."

Pete's hand dropped as if a string had been cut. Claire was shaking.

"I don't want that. If it's me next, I don't—" She broke off and had trouble swallowing. "Fuck." She flung away and threw herself down beside Dan.

I stood frozen. Beside me, Pete was a statue, his mouth hanging open. Wade squatted on the ground behind us, his head in his hands. I wanted to go to sleep and stay there for a thousand years.

Pete and I could only stand and stare at each other. No one went after Claire. On the ground, Dan screamed as he floundered, a shrill, high-pitched, ear-shredding shriek.

Claire regained her feet and came back around the fire to us. Pete and I backed away slightly, back to where Wade was still crouched, to try and avoid the inevitable. As Claire returned, I briefly regretted the four of us leaving Dan alone even for a few minutes and wondered if one of us should stay with him. Then it hit me again that we could do nothing for him.

Dear heaven, except for the one thing we could do for him.

Chapter 10

Wade pulled himself off the ground, and we formed a huddle, trying to ignore the howling. We looked at each other, our faces pale and tense, before Claire said what I knew she was going to say.

"We have to do it." She gestured between the four of us. "Together. All of us." Claire squared her shoulders and repeated. "We have to do it. Smother him."

There was a brief lull in Dan's screams, and my idiot heart sparked with the thought, 'Maybe he's better.' Then, of course, he started again.

"We don't have a pillow!" I bellowed, stupidly, above the sound.

Claire shook her head at me. But maybe it wasn't so stupid a statement. Wade and I had blow-up pillows. I could never be bothered with mine, but I didn't think anyone had an actual pillow. You couldn't smother someone with a blow-up pillow. Or maybe my mind was searching desperately for anything, any reason not to do what we had to.

"No." Wade shook his head like he couldn't stop, little shakes, almost like trembling.

"We have to," I said as if it clarified everything.

"I can't do it." His face was blank with a sheen of sweat even though the night was cool. "Thou shalt not kill."

I wanted to hit him. I couldn't believe he was doing this. I was so close to the edge I was scared he'd pull me over with him, into refusal, into cowardice.

"What the hell, man? You want to leave him like this?" Pete was incredulous.

"I can't. I can't. It's wrong." Wade's voice was panicky, hitting high notes.

"Wrong? Fucking wrong?" I was so furious I shoved him, thumping the heel of my palm into his shoulder. I wasn't proud of myself.

Claire had slipped away again and was over by Dan. She'd grabbed his sleeping bag and was folding it up, wadding it into a ball. The man was screeching with an ear-splitting wail now, his body arching off the ground again in tormented spasms. When I turned back, Wade had retreated a few feet from us. In the dim light, he shook his head again.

"You piece of shit," I said to him. Yeah, not proud of myself.

I turned to Pete. Agony filled his face. He was panting slightly, gaping. He nodded though. "Right," he said.

Queasiness lined the back of my nose. We both turned and headed over to where Claire was kneeling beside Dan's tortured body. As we stepped up, Claire was talking, raising her voice, trying to be heard over the screams.

"Dan, Dan, can you hear me? We're going to help you. We're going to try and make it stop. Can you hear me?" Claire raised her arm and swiped her eyes with the back of her wrist.

I hunkered down on the other side of Dan, across from Claire. She shot me a glance as Pete moved to kneel above Dan's head. Part of me couldn't believe what we had to do. Things like this didn't happen, couldn't happen.

Interspersed with the flailing, Dan had those shuddering tremors in his limbs that Mel had. He gaped wide to suck in air and there was the strange chemical odor. I detached a bit then. My head literally could not process what was going on inside his body.

"We have to do this," I said. I couldn't believe I was psyching myself up to kill a person. Like, *could not* believe it. It wasn't possible we had to suffocate someone. It was just something we had to do. A task which had to be done. We had to make the screaming stop.

Claire was wiping her eyes again. Pete reached over, grabbed the sleeping bag, and wadded it up all over again.

Dan paused for a great sucking gasp and Pete said into the quiet, "Are we gonna do this?"

I nodded. I couldn't stop swallowing.

"Let's do it," Claire said.

Dan was thrashing and flailing, so getting the bag in place wasn't easy. Pete tried a couple of times and Dan threw his head about horribly, as if he knew. Dear God, as if he knew.

I reached in and grabbed my side of the bag, thrusting it down, pushing it down. Across from me, Claire shook her head as if she'd woken up, then joined her hands to ours. The three of us bore down, pressing the bunched-up, plasticky fabric into the man's face.

It wasn't easy. At first, he wrenched his head away, and we had to clump up the sleeping bag again. Eventually, we all managed to push in the right place, and it felt secure enough that I could look up, away from my hands, so I wouldn't see what I was doing.

Grief, like a physical pain, flooded my body. I looked down again. I noticed Claire's nails had the remains of dark polish on them. Under my hands, I could feel Dan's struggle. His limbs were still jerking, but his head was immobilized. We held the fucking bag there. We held it there forever.

At last, Dan went still. I focused on Claire's blank face. Her eyes were closed, and her lips kept pulling down spasmodically, her chin quivering. I turned to Pete. He stared straight ahead. He was looking into the distance, yards away, years away.

Claire opened her eyes. "Do you think...?" she said.

We all let go; it was almost reflexive. I knew I didn't think, only pulled back, collapsed back onto my haunches, and looked down at the still body. There was no movement. I was hollowed out, gone inside. Claire pulled the sleeping bag away gently, reverently.

Dan took a great shuddering breath.

"Oh God," I said.

"Fuck. Fuck, fuck, fuck." Pete collapsed backward onto his ass and beat his hands against the rock beneath him.

I don't think Claire said anything. I couldn't hear if she did because the agonized squealing started again. Broiling anger flooded through me. All that horror, all the angst, all the anguish, and we hadn't fucking done it?

Dan went still briefly, then made those grisly, grunting noises again. The relative quiet was almost a relief.

"Come on," I said and bundled up the sleeping bag.

Claire closed her eyes briefly, then opened them and nodded at me. I checked Pete, but he was shaking his head now as Wade had done.

"I'm sorry. I can't do it again."

"Come on, you've got to," Claire looked at him beseechingly. "You know we have to..."

Her voice quivered. I remembered my fear when Wade had chickened out: that he'd pull me down with him.

"Fuck him," I said to Claire. "We can do it." She had to help me. I couldn't do it on my own. I couldn't.

"Pete. Come on." Claire's voice was clear and hard now, over Dan's groaning noises.

"I'm sorry, I'm sorry." He'd scrunched himself into a ball, rocking back and forth with his arms looped around his shins. His hands grasped his wrists in a mad, twisted monkey grip, as if to ensure they couldn't be used. "We had a fight, I can't kill him, it's—" He broke off into strangled sobs.

"For fuck's sake," Claire said. "Bloody time us then. Make sure it's long enough. Do something useful."

Claire and I pushed down. Dan didn't fight as much this time. I must have gone away a bit in my head then. I didn't feel him struggle. I didn't feel his legs and arms spasm as his body tried to pull in air. I didn't feel his head try and thrash back and forth beneath my hands. I didn't feel Claire lose her grip and then press down again. I didn't feel every fucking last thing.

We did it right then. Waited until Pete told us it'd been long enough. Definitely long enough. Claire had to remove my hands when it was time. My arms were locked in position, and I could no longer feel my fingers.

When we were sure, we wrapped the heavy, limp body with the Taylor's tent and left him there. There was nothing else to do. I didn't know anything could be worse than the night with Mel Taylor, but I was wrong. I had a new worst night of my life.

Afterwards, we sat, dazed, by the fire. I wanted to sleep, desperately, wanted to shut down, shut out what we'd done, what I'd done. Even though it was the right thing to do, and we'd done what we'd had to, I was clogged with anguish. There was a blistering bubble of it inside me. I could feel it in my head. There was no room for anything else, not even sleep. Yeah, I'd had better nights.

I didn't know whether I actually slept a bit or zoned out, but I became aware of an intermittent rustling noise. The sound hit my frayed nerves like nails on a chalkboard. My skin prickled, and my muscles tensed. I *really* wanted to yell at someone.

It was Dan, or to be exact, Dan's body. Those obscene internal twitches. Sporadic tremors as what was inside feasted. Gorged and burrowed for more.

I turned over and tried to get comfortable. Now it was all I could hear. I bunched my fists over my ears, but it didn't help. I heard every rustle, every spasm. I glanced around and couldn't believe everyone else was asleep. How could they sleep with these sounds?

I hauled myself to my feet, deliberately making as much noise as I could, I was so pissed. How could they be sleeping? I stomped over to where Dan's body was burrito-ed in tent fabric. Every now and again, there were disgusting little ripples in the flickering remains of the firelight.

I gagged a bit but bent and grabbed an end of the bundle. I had hold of where his feet were, and I pulled at it, intending to drag him down the trail till he was far enough I wouldn't be able to hear those rustles, hear him being consumed.

I pulled at the fabric, feeling the dead weight inside. Either I was exhausted, or Dan had gotten heavier. I'd made it halfway to the trailhead, followed by the slither of fabric across rock, when his hand came out the end of the bunched tent.

"Aaauugh." I dropped the bundle and couldn't help but stagger a few steps back.

His fingers were moving. I went blank. Not simply odd twitches but actual movement, the fingers drummed against the stone. That was impossible.

Was he still alive? That was impossible. We'd wrapped him with his hands beside his sides. How had his hand gotten out? The air stopped in my mouth as if held by a wad of cloth. I reached out and tried to flip the tent away from him, my fumbles frantic. It was caught around him and I had to tug hard and pull to the side to free his head and shoulders.

One arm was raised above his head. The hand that had moved. It was totally still now. I peered at Dan's face in the dim flicker of the flames. His eyes were closed, the lids sunken. His lips were ajar. Inside was movement. Something vicious squirmed. It shone white-yellow in the firelight then resolved itself into several winding, twisting somethings.

A surge of sharp revulsion ran through me. I crouched on the ground, hunched over in disgust. I was making odd keening noises and tried to stop.

"Come on, come on mate." Pete was there beside me. I didn't know he was awake. He put his arm around my shoulders. "What are you doing?" he asked.

I took a deep breath and tried to dry the wetness under my tongue. "I couldn't stand the noise," I said. "I was going to take him down the trail." I sucked in another breath. "Then his hand ... his hand came out. Like he was reaching—"

As I said it, another of those spasms ran through Dan's body, twitched his arm. His hand flopped. The tent made a God-awful rustling noise.

I choked a little.

"It's alright," Pete said, patting me on the back. "His hand's come out because you were dragging him by his feet. That's all."

I braced myself and nodded. Another of those slithery, tent fabric sounds began.

"Give us a hand." I thought Pete was talking to me until I saw Wade standing beside us. Pete patted my shoulder again. He was pale and strained. "Go on," he said to me. "We'll take him down the trail."

I left them to do it. A part of me was glad Wade was forced to do it, to feel Dan's dead weight, the spasms. I staggered back to the campfire, sprawled beside it, and tried to block out the sliding noise as they hauled him down the trail.

Claire was sitting there, silent. I had a quick flush of anger that she could be okay with this—how the hell could she be okay with this? Then she raised her head. She was not okay.

I must have slept eventually, dozed at least, without awareness of rest. When I opened my eyes again, I was slumped by the fire, and it was morning, or near enough morning. I felt ancient and brittle. It was another grey day; it felt like I'd never see the sun again.

We were quiet, sullen. The embers of the fire glowed, but no one stirred them. I really wanted coffee but wasn't willing to stay there for the time it'd take to boil water. I guessed the others felt the same—we all wanted to get out of there. I certainly did. It should only take us half a day to reach the pass, if everything went well, and I wanted out. I wanted to be as far away from there, as far away from Dan Taylor's body as I could get.

Nobody said much as we stumbled around, doing what had to be done in the morning. Every time I saw Wade, I choked with anger. So, I tried not to look at him. Eventually, everything of ours was packed and ready, and the four of us gravitated to Dan's belongings. We stood staring down at the pack, random tent poles, Dan's shoes, and Josh's sweater.

"We should probably take the food and water," Wade said.

"Yeah, nah. I'm not touching the water." Pete was still strained and pale beneath his straggle of beard. "Food might be alright, but we won't need it, will we? We'll be out of here by midday."

Meanwhile, I was seething. "So," I said to Wade, "You're okay with thieving, but not murder, is that it?" Even as I said it, I knew I was being absurd and irrational, but I couldn't stop. "Isn't there a fucking commandment about stealing, like there is about killing? Do you get to pick and choose then? I'll obey this one, but not that one?"

It wasn't really Wade I was angry at, or maybe it was a bit. I kicked Dan's pack. I wanted to smash something, hit it, break it, obliterate it, so the pain would go away. I kicked at the pack again, hard. Gave it all I'd got and connected with something solid, cookware, from the rattle.

"Fuck." I danced around, rubbing my damaged foot against the back of my other leg. Sometimes I was a prize idiot. "Fuckity, fuck, fuck."

Wade watched me, blank-faced. Maybe he kind of got it because he didn't say anything at first, only shook his head at me after a bit.

We ended up taking Dan's packaged food, which was sealed, and we knew would be safe. Pete had been a bit optimistic, assuming we'd get out of here by midday, as we still didn't know if the pass would be clear.

We trudged back onto the trail, back among the trees that now included the odd mountain ash, rowan, and birch, carefully looking for signs of falling timber. The air was wet with mist again, the sky dull.

The four of us spread out: Pete was first, then Wade, Claire, and me. We were spaced out to be away from those we were annoyed with. I was already regretting that I hadn't made coffee before we left camp.

We'd barely been going half an hour when there was another gunshot.

Chapter 11

*B*AM— Again, there was no way to tell where it'd come from.

Pete stopped, and we caught up with him. "What d'you reckon it is?"

We looked at each other wordlessly.

"Was it louder than last time?" Claire asked.

I have to admit, I didn't really care. I was preoccupied, wondering whether I could bear to scoop a spoonful of instant coffee and creamer powder into my mouth while we were stopped.

"We're closer to the rim now, so it might sound louder because of the echoes around the cliffs?" Wade said.

Whatever it was, there was nothing we could do.

"Let's go then." Pete grabbed his pack straps to adjust it, shot Claire a look, and then headed up the trail.

She looked down and waited until Wade strode off between her and Pete.

"You guys alright?" I asked quietly as the others moved off.

"Yeah, I guess," she said. "I'm cranky with him, you know." She shook her head. "I notice you're not talking to your mate."

My sleep-deprived brain took a second to realize she meant the Australian 'friend' definition of mate, not the wild kingdom variety.

"Yeah, I guess," I said, echoing her reply. "Yeah, I'm kind of cranky with him too."

We moved on.

It was a lie about being cranky with Wade. I wasn't cranky with him, I was furious with him. I was enraged, incensed. I didn't have enough words for how angry I was with him. And I knew, part of it was anger at myself for what I'd done, for what I'd had to do, but also, at Wade for making me fucking do it alone. Well, with Claire and Pete but, you know, they weren't my childhood friends.

We'd done the right thing, but it didn't make it any easier to bear. I could still feel the shape of a desperate man's face through a sleeping bag. It felt like my heart had been blackened. Claire was angry with Pete in the same way, but he'd tried at first; at least, he'd tried.

By mid-morning, I was struggling. The certainty I'd had before, that we'd done the right thing, and we'd had to do it, kept slipping away. It slithered through my fingers like slick tent fabric. What if there was something we could have done to help Dan? What if we could've gotten him out? We hoped to be out by midday. What if there was something, anything...? After all, we knew nothing about the damn worms, nothing at all.

I should have stopped thinking then. I should have beat my head against a rock because then I thought, what if it wasn't about worms slipping through your skin? Or not *only* about that. What if the worms began small enough, so we couldn't see them? Like spores. We knew nothing about them, nothing. What if everything was affected, not just the ground? The water, the air, every damn thing we touched could be killing us. We could all already unknowingly be tainted. Waiting for the first inkling something was wrong. We could all be ... incubating.

The blank devastation this conjured wiped everything else out of my head. There was no room for grief, rage, or regret. Was it wrong that my anguish about Dan was pushed away and became a vague background to this all-encompassing fear for myself?

I tried to talk myself down. To keep walking through the terror, one step after another. I tried to think, breathe in, breathe out. I'd seen the worm whip itself into Dan's palm, actually seen it. Mel had told us the same thing had happened to her.

I tried to focus on that. None of us had been ... I hesitated between 'bitten' and 'infected,' as neither seemed right. My moron brain offered the word 'infested,' and I made an involuntary noise of disgust. I wanted to actually smack my own mind up the back of the head.

In front of me, Claire turned around. "You, okay?"

No, I wanted to say, no, I wasn't okay. I'd never be okay again. I could still feel Dan's face under my hands. "Yeah."

She dropped back to walk beside me. "You don't look okay."

I couldn't bear to tell her what I'd been thinking about, so I offered up something else which had occurred to me in the godless small hours.

"Do you think we'll be charged with murder? For Dan?"

Claire's mouth dropped open, and she gawped at me. "Oh, get fucked," she said, eventually.

Fair call, and I'd kind of gotten used to her style of eloquence, but I tried to expand on what I meant.

"What if they don't understand? I mean we know, we saw what happened to Mel, but out there." I pointed unnecessarily. "We'll tell them about it, and they'll have to come here with, like, protective gear, hazmat or whatever. But they're not going to see what happens." I nerved myself to continue. "Hear what happens. They're not going to *know*. What if they don't understand why we ... why we had to ..."

Our pace had slowed now, and we'd lost sight of Wade and Pete. It was okay, though, because it felt like this should be a private discussion between Claire and me.

She frowned. "Don't be stupid," she said bluntly. "They'll do autopsies on the bodies. Him and his wife, what's-her-name. And that man you found. When they see what's inside, they'll understand all right." She hitched her pack up a little and kept walking.

Autopsies. Why hadn't I thought of autopsies? I chased after Claire.

"Do you think they'll be able to tell they were still alive when the worms ..." I trailed off, not wanting to say it or think about it.

"Mate. You're starting to piss me off." She frowned back at me. "They'll be able to tell."

She huffed on up the trail.

"I'm not sure they'd be able to tell. What if, by the time they've recovered the bodies, there wasn't enough to tell by?"

"Piss off, fuck-knuckle."

For some reason, I found this vaguely comforting.

After an hour or so of trudging up the trail alone, I came across the others who'd stopped for a break. An outcrop of rock had supplied a place to sit away from the wormy ground, and everyone had taken advantage. I settled myself, trying not to show I was breathing heavily. I wondered, guiltily, if they might have stopped to let me catch up.

Pete had dug out a snack bar and was chowing down. Claire sat next to him. The trees around us had thinned out more, clearing the space further to either side of the trail. More boulders and rocks appeared around us. I'd plainly come in on the tail end of some conversation which continued now.

"I resent that," Pete spoke around vigorous chewing. "I'll have you know, I have the voice of an angel." He paused, brows furrowed in righteous indignation. "I strangled it."

"You really are impossible to underestimate," Claire said, but she grinned as she said it.

Pete's face took on a faraway look of great thoughtfulness, and he nodded slowly. "I've always suspected that about myself."

"Pfft." Claire swatted him with the back of her hand.

Something inside me unfroze a tiny bit. I pulled my water bottle from its netting pocket and took a swig. I should probably say something to Wade, but I had no idea what.

There was a flutter of wings, and a crow landed a few feet up the trail from us. It was the first one I'd noticed in ages. I hadn't seen any birds at all since we'd been back at the Harper's Meadow campground.

Looking at the thing, I wondered again whether it was a crow or a raven or what? Wade would probably know. I coughed to catch his attention, my eyes fixed on the bird. It was doing some desultory pecking at the ground to the side of the trail now.

"Is that a raven or a crow?"

Wade glanced over at me as if to check who I was talking to. I raised an eyebrow to query him.

"It's a raven. See the beak's curved, with a little tuft? Crows aren't as big either." He kind of smiled a little.

It was a start. I was still furious with him, but it felt like we could maybe be alright. Pete and Claire turned around to look now as well. Pete broke off a piece of his granola bar and flipped it toward where the bird was foraging. The raven cocked its head at the offering but didn't approach.

"Bugger you, then," Pete said.

The bird did a little hop toward the food.

There was a burst of black feathers, a squawk, and it was gone. Where the raven had been, sludge sprayed up like a miniature shell had exploded.

Wet mud rained down with a familiar heavy plopping noise. We were all on our feet in a second.

"What the fuck?"

"Holy shit."

The bird was gone. It hadn't flown away, but it was gone. Eaten by the ground.

"What the hell was that?" What had I seen? I checked the others, wanting someone to say something, to explain this, to make it normal.

"Did something just come out of the ground?" There was disbelief in Claire's voice.

"It looked like another bird," Pete said.

Yeah, that was almost what I'd thought too. Almost. Something like a filthy, dirt-encrusted bird had burst from the ground like a damn shark and grabbed the other one. Skewered through it. Then slid back underground as easily as if the surface had been water.

My teeth felt like they were made of ice. I clenched them together and hoped they wouldn't splinter. I was having trouble processing. It was impossible, literally impossible. I scanned the shocked faces around me.

Eventually, Wade said, "Mel Taylor said she saw something else in the ground. Besides worms, I mean."

I frowned and tried to think. I had a vague memory of her saying something along those lines, I hadn't really been paying attention at the time. But I remembered a couple of other things too. One was the flash of something black among the exposed roots of the sapling I'd accidentally toppled. The other was the noise of the mud falling when the raven vanished. It was the same odd little sound I'd noticed repeatedly back in Harper's Meadow, yesterday morning after Mel had died. Was it only yesterday?

I closed my eyes for longer than I should have. What the hell was going on? What the hell was beneath us? I shuffled my feet, then told the others what I'd remembered.

"You mean this has been going on the whole time?" Pete sounded almost accusatory.

"I don't know." I shook my head. I knew nothing.

"Maybe that's what the worms grow into." Wade's voice trembled. "What if it wasn't a bird that came, you know ... up from underneath." He made a shark-like motion with a shaky hand. "What if it was what they become? The worms."

I'd honestly believed I couldn't be any more freaked out and horrified than I already was but, yep, that did it. I felt like I was armpit high in the ocean and my legs had just been swept from under me. I'd previously wondered if the worms might start smaller, but I'd never considered they might grow into something else, something bigger like the worms were some kind of larvae.

"Think about it," Wade said.

I couldn't come up with anything I wanted to think about less.

"The thing couldn't have been a bird," he went on. "It was too strong. A bird can't pull another bird into the ground. It had to be something else."

The woods around us were eerily silent. Whatever had taken the bird was gone, and there was no sign of life now. Nothing was moving above ground but us.

"What if they grow bigger than that?" Claire said, glancing between us. "I mean if that's what the worms grow into, how do we know if it was fully grown?"

Beside her, Pete made a little involuntary 'hnk' sound.

I wished Claire hadn't put that idea into my head. Things were bad enough as they were. The way the thing had leaped from the ground, as if it were water, was hair-raising enough without picturing it getting bigger than Jaws.

"Fuck, Claire," Pete said.

"Well, think about it. If the worms grew to worm size in what, two days? How do we know how big they'll get?"

One by one, we stepped and scrambled up to stand on our rock seats instead of the ground.

"We have to get out of here now," Wade said.

I goggled at him. The world's biggest Captain Obvious stood on his boulder like a lighthouse on a rock. Tell me something I didn't already know.

"Before they get any bigger," he said, frowning back at me.

Oh, crap.

The four of us exchanged tense glances. Nobody wanted to get off their rocks; it was like the grossest game of 'The Floor is Lava' ever.

We wasted maybe ten minutes discussing what to do. Not that there was any point talking about it; we had to get out of there; we couldn't all perch lighthouse-like forever.

I didn't think anyone wanted to be the first to put their feet back on the ground, I certainly didn't want to. The thing had punched through a bird the size of a damn chihuahua like it was nothing. Could it do the same to my boot? I'd rather not find out.

Eventually, it was Wade who led the way. I got a sense maybe he wanted to make up for last night, for letting me down the way he did. I didn't know.

He extended a foot cautiously then put his weight on it. Leant half-on, half-off his rock for a while, scanning the ground and listening. At last, he stepped fully off and put both feet on the ground. The rest of us all held our breath. Nothing happened.

Wade quirked a lopsided grin at us. "One small step for man…"

We all carefully climbed off our rocks, but nothing happened. We put our packs back on, and still nothing happened. We filed back up the trail, this time Pete, then Claire, Wade, and me.

We were all quiet, heads swiveling. I estimated we were an hour, perhaps an hour and a half from the start of the pass. The trail was getting steeper and rockier with less vegetation, and the path dipped and turned around occasional boulders. I found myself assessing each one for climb-ability as we approached it, getting anxious when it fell behind, and we moved back onto bare patches.

Luckily the further we went, the stonier the terrain got. We were approaching the foothills of the rim, the encircling cliffs created when the ancient caldera had collapsed. Most of the dirt in this area had been washed away millennia ago, and I couldn't tell you how relieved I was by that.

We were nearing where the trail to the pass began when we came over a little rocky ridge and found a wide dip, bare of stone. It was almost a mini plain, as it tipped over and ran back down the hill in a sweep of sparse, grassy scrub.

Shit.

With unspoken accord, we all stopped. I had zero memory of this place from the hike in, even though I must have walked across it.

"What the hell is that?" Pete pointed.

Throughout the open space, there were traces of … disturbances. In some places, the ground looked like something had whacked it from below, little hummocks of freshly turned soil here and there. In some places, it looked almost like scored lines across the ground. We all stood and took in the width of those odd traces.

NAMELESS THINGS

Beside one was a single shoe.

Chapter 12

We all fixated on the shoe.

Pete and I had fetched up together, and I nudged him. "Is that a shoe?"

Pete snorted. "Yeah, it's definitely a shoe."

"Do you think someone dropped it, out of their pack?" I tried to imagine how that might actually happen.

"Maybe."

"What else then?"

"Maybe they were running so fast it came off?"

"Hmm, maybe."

We all ogled the shoe some more, then checked out the disturbed ground before inexorably refocusing on the shoe.

"It's probably fine," Wade said. "We walked all the way up the trail before we even knew there was anything ..."

He trailed off, and we looked at each other before turning back to the shoe.

"Is there any way around?" Claire checked over her shoulder.

Wade struggled out of his pack straps. "I don't think so," he said. "But let me check the map."

He dug the map out and we crowded around. Nope, and it was a big nope; this was the only way to get to the pass. The pass was the only place to get out on foot, as the other paths were marked as requiring rock climbing equipment. Wade put the map away and struggled back into his pack.

"It's probably fine," he said again.

Pete was scanning the expanse, his eyes shaded by a hand even though it was overcast and grey.

"Looks okay now, I guess," he said. "Should we go one at a time, do you reckon? Or like normal?"

We all turned to Wade as if he'd somehow become an expert. He shook his head helplessly.

"We're probably making a fuss about nothing." Claire pushed her sleeves up then clutched her pack straps. "If this is the way we have to go, then we have to go."

She stepped off the solid stone beneath us and onto the weedy grass. We stared at her. She walked on steadily, a pack with legs, from the rearview. Pete flicked us a grin and then followed. Both of them carefully skirted the shoe.

Wade and I stood and waited as the pair made their way across the span of grass. Nothing happened. First Claire, then Pete, reached the bulge of stone across the way and climbed up the curve of it.

They'd done it easy enough. I nudged Wade. "You want to go together?"

"Yeah, okay, let's go," he said, taking off.

Wade jumped off the rock and walked fast, as if he'd had to psych himself up to do it. It took me by surprise, and it was a second before I followed him. When I stepped off, the rock on the other side of the plateau suddenly appeared twice as far away, like I was looking down the wrong end of a telescope.

I picked my way, trying to check all around me at once, avoiding stepping on broken ground. The bird disappearing into a feathery bomb replayed over and over in my head. All I could think about was the sheer power of whatever it was that took it.

I caught a flicker of movement out of the corner of my eye. I turned, and it took me a second to understand. Stupidly, I paused mid-step and gaped in shock.

There was a shrill, screamed chorus from the safety of the rock. "*Ru-uuuun*!"

Across the ground, streaming straight for me was a moving hummock.

It was so fast, *so fast*. I'd previously heard the term 'bowel loosening' but never experienced it. I didn't actually shit myself, I was far too busy for that, but I understood the feeling of your guts suddenly turning to water with nothing to clench.

It took me what felt like years to lumber into a run. My pack was a dead weight, slowing me down and pulling me down, but there was no time to drop it. I'd never tried to run with a pack on before, so thank God it wasn't full, and thank God we'd ditched the tent.

I tried to will my feet into speed as whatever it was tunneled toward me. Wade was well ahead of me, going flat out.

"Run, you *fuck-wit*!" bellowed Pete.

I glanced back, and the thing had halved the distance. Fuck, it was fast.

At last, I was moving. I thrashed across the space, screaming my head off, "*Faaaaaaaaaaaaaaark*." Not my finest hour. I should have saved my breath to run, but some things were totally involuntary.

Wade reached the slope of stone, and I pounded on towards him. I felt like I was in slow motion, my legs made of lead. I couldn't look back again, had no idea how close it was.

I lunged for the rock, feet slipping. Wade and Pete's hands locked onto my arms, yanking hard. BOOM! The ground erupted behind me. I flinched, tucking and rolling. My legs scrambled, desperate to get away from whatever the hell that was. I got a split-second flash of some-thing—then grit rained down, pelting my back.

I scrambled up the rock. "That's got to be bigger than a bird. That was bigger than a bird, right? No way that was a bird." I was trying to make myself shut up. "That was *soooo* not a fucking bird." Seriously though, it was bigger than a damn bird.

I got as far up the rock as I could before I collapsed, panting.

"What the heck was that?" Wade's face was contorted.

No one said anything. It wasn't a damn bird; I knew that much. I pulled at the straps of my pack, wanting to get it off, but my hands were shaking too much.

"It was brown," Claire said as if this were the most confusing thing about it.

"You saw it?" I asked.

"I don't know, it ... I saw something. I think it was brown; it was hard to tell with the dirt. It wasn't the same as last time." She looked stunned.

I wanted to grab her and make her tell me what it was—how could she not know? I tried to calm down and think rationally, but I was fizzing inside. I managed to wiggle out of my pack and dug out a water bottle, as the one in the outside netting pouch was empty.

I sat there, panting and shaking, reliving those last few minutes again and again. What the hell was that? What the hell had we gotten into? I couldn't tear my eyes from the ground below us, at the humped-up pile of rumpled soil directly where I'd been.

My eyes locked on the slope, heart pounding. Part of me was scream-ing to look away, to run, to forget this whole mess. But I couldn't move. Couldn't blink. *Come on, you bastard. Show yourself.* My fingers dug into the rock. Sweat trickled down my back. A thousand miles suddenly felt way too close.

"Are we safe up here?" Wade voiced exactly what I was thinking.

We all checked each other's faces.

"Mate," Pete said with some emphasis. "If whatever that was could've followed you up here, you'd be cactus."

That was strangely encouraging, and I decided I'd take it. I couldn't move anyway, as my legs were limp noodles, sprawled out before me. Was it possible my feet were shaking?

"It was big. Whatever it was, it was way bigger than before." Pete shook his head slowly. "How big are these bloody things gonna get?"

That was less reassuring. No one wanted to get going again. We were all pretty wobbly, so we sat silently for a while.

Then Claire said, "How big *can* these things get? I mean, what are they eating?"

Us. Hysteria bubbled inside me.

"The birds," Wade said. "Have you noticed there's hardly any birds left?"

I nodded.

"And there's other wildlife in the park too. Bear, mule deer, coyotes. Maybe mountain goat. Beaver ..." Wade trailed off.

"So, you're saying there's plenty here for whatever it is to feed on?" Pete looked faintly nauseated.

"Then there's all the little stuff too," Wade continued. "Squirrels, chipmunks. Rats and mice—"

"Yeah, you can shut up any time." Pete pulled a face.

"And people of course..." Wade stared into the distance.

"Let's go," Claire grabbed her pack and yanked a pocket zipper. "We can't sit around here all day."

True, but I could have used a few more minutes to cower on my big, safe rock. We all got up, grumbling and groaning.

Thankfully, the trail was mostly over stony ground for the next half mile, or places where we could jump from boulder to boulder. I was still shaky. We stopped and considered a few cupped sections carefully, but they were nothing like before. Nothing like that stretched-out, dug-up field.

Eventually, we reached the area composed of boulders and chunks of black basalt, which meant the start of the pass. We took a quick break and pulled out our water bottles. I shook mine and frowned. There wasn't much left.

From where we sat, we had a bird's-eye view of the park spread out below us, rocky scrub down to thickening tree line. I could see miles and miles of sloping woods, even a glimpse of the lake at the bottom of the vast basin, slate grey to match the sky.

The great plume of smoke still rose from where the meteor had hit. It plainly hadn't scored a direct hit on the pass, which was a massive relief, but it sure had come close. Less than a mile from where we were sitting, the enormous, grubby grey column rose upwards, dark against the paler grey sky. I either couldn't smell the smoke or had become so accustomed to it as not to notice, which was odd, given we were so close to it now.

"Is that normal?" I asked.

"Mate, none of this is normal," Pete said with the quirk of a grin.

"No, you dork, the smoke." I gestured with my water bottle.

He shrugged and turned an enquiring face to Claire. She shrugged. Wade shrugged. None of us knew.

The water hit my throat, cool relief. I eyed the steep incline ahead. The pass. Our ticket out. Almost there. The thought sent a ripple of energy through my tired muscles. I slumped against the rock, half-sitting. Wade caught my eye. The air between us still felt thick, words coming out forced and awkward. Dan's face flashed in my mind. My jaw clenched, a familiar heat rising in my cheeks. The memory of what he'd made me do ... it stung like hell.

I screwed the cap on my water bottle with a click. We trudged on, boots crunching against rock and gravel. Then—voices. Distant but unmistakable. My head whipped up, neck muscles twanging. Ears straining, I froze mid-step. Just like Rover back home, catching that telltale rustle of his treat bag from clear across the house.

"What was that?" The noise might have come from above us on the pass, but I couldn't be sure.

"What was what?" Wade lifted his eyebrows.

"Shh—" I said. "I heard talking."

The four of us stopped and listened intently, but there was nothing.

"Maybe it was us? Our voices, echoing?" Wade suggested.

I narrowed my eyes at him, as I knew he thought I was losing it, hearing voices. I'd felt slightly safer up here among the rock, but I was still strung out, jumpy. Not, I hoped, jumpy enough to start hearing voices, however, and none of us had been talking when I'd heard it.

Everyone listened some more. Still nothing. Maybe it'd been a trick of the wind, as there was a slight breeze up here, little gusts every now and again.

"Maybe it's help?" Claire said.

Chapter 13

A knot tightened in my gut as we continued forward. I refused to let myself believe it could be help. We slogged on, each step a battle against hope and exhaustion, until we rounded a bend in the path.

Suddenly, figures appeared ahead of us in the distance.

A shiver ran down my spine, and my fingers instinctively twitched toward the knife at my belt, ready for anything this godforsaken place might throw at us next. Three of them, all male, and none of them looked helpful. They were young with short, over-styled haircuts and barely any stubble. I was suddenly, acutely aware I was filthy, unwashed, unshaven, and greasy-haired.

When they stumbled to their feet, I realized they were younger than I'd first thought.

"Shit. Hiya, hello," said the one closest to us.

They quickly scanned us.

We stood dazed, adjusting to the idea that other human beings still existed. Everything had gotten so bizarre and alarming that it felt like we were the last people in the universe.

"Are you trying to get up the pass?" The same dark-haired boy spoke again with a sharp, clipped UK accent. "Cos it's blocked. There's no way out."

Well, shit. I'd been holding a bubble of hope deep inside, and it punctured. As it deflated, dread seeped in.

"Bloody poms," Pete said under his breath.

We all introduced ourselves and met Aaron, Hassan, and Declan in turn, and, yes, as Pete had said, they were English. We were quite the multicultural group, but I guessed that given the park was a tourist attraction, it wasn't too unusual.

Hassan and Declan were pleased to meet us, but Aaron seemed quieter. We wriggled out of our packs and hunkered down. We had the same discussion we'd had with everyone else since the meteor. Where they'd been when it hit and what they'd seen, which was nothing, only the smoke billowing up in the aftermath.

"Was it you shooting earlier?" Wade asked them.

"No, we did hear a couple of shots though." Declan nodded.

"What do you reckon about the worms?" Pete asked them. "D'you think they're from the meteor?"

Their expressions were blank.

"You know, in the ground?" Pete's eyebrows performed a complicated tango.

"Um, no?"

My companions and I exchanged slightly goggle-eyed glances and more eyebrow eurythmics. How could they not know about the worms? However, now, explaining the worms, what they did, and our theories on them felt like too big a can to open.

The same thought was reflected on the faces of the others—all we cared about now was getting out. A nasty clenching seized my chest; all I could really think about was the trail above us. "So, what's the trail like?" Wade asked, voicing my thoughts. "Did you have a good look?"

"It's totally blocked; there's no way through," Hassan, the one with the dark hair, said. "The rockslide, it's all ..." He raised a palm to indicate a complete stop.

I tried to sort these kids out in my head, to evaluate the chances they knew what they were talking about. They appeared twelve to me but had to be older. The sandy-brown buzz cut with geometric edges was Declan, and the shorter, pasty-faced boy who looked like he was in shock was Aaron. They didn't look like they could fight their way out of a paper bag, let alone find their way out of here.

"We should probably go and check it out," I said to our group with an apologetic grimace to the three newbies. I didn't want to offend them, but I had to know for myself. "To be sure?"

Hassan and Declan both nodded, not bothered by this at all. Aaron just stared at us with his red, watery eyes.

"Sure, if you can find a way out, come back and let us know, yeah?"

"Of course," Wade said.

We hauled our packs back on. The kids shuffled up to get out of our way, and we all did an awkward do-si-do around each other to get past. I winced again at how badly I stank.

Up and around a sharp hairpin, about a hundred yards further on, we came to a complete dead end. A massive rockslide had blocked the trail. I was reminded of the landslip that had obliterated the trail back to Harper's Meadow, although that had been mud, trees, and plants.

Here, boulders and stones had collapsed onto the trail, some as large as small cars. It created a sheer face of jigsaw-like rock, hanging above us. It might have been an optical illusion, but it almost seemed to overhang us at the top.

Well, shit. The towering wave of rock loomed, blotting out the sky, ready to crash down on me. My diaphragm hurt as air came in short gasps. This was our way out, our escape.

"There's no way we can climb that," Wade said, pointing this out in case we hadn't noticed.

"It doesn't look stable enough to sneeze on," Claire said.

My hands trembled slightly as I gripped the straps of my backpack. I clenched them hard, willing my breathing to steady. The others glanced my way, and I forced a nod, hoping they couldn't see the cold sweat beading on my forehead. The urge to bolt surged through my legs, but I planted my feet firmly on the ground. I inhaled deeply, the crisp mountain air filling my lungs, and exhaled slowly, trying to push out the panic with each breath.

"No wonder they," Pete flipped a thumb to indicate the boys back down the trail, "went back down there. I'd have gone even further; if that lot comes unstuck, we're nothing   but jam."

Almost in answer to his comment, a trickle of pebbles fell from above, and we staggered back, like that would help if the Everest of rock collapsed on us. As if on cue, more scree skittered down from above, pattering around our feet. We stumbled backward, our bodies reacting before our minds could process the futility of the movement. The towering wall of boulders loomed over us, immovable and indifferent. My eyes locked onto its surface, scanning desperately for any sign of weakness, any hint of a way out. The sheer impossibility of our situation pressed down on me, making my feet blocks of lead. The air felt thin, my joints tight, as the truth of our predicament slowly sank in.

Eventually, Wade had to pull at my arm.

"Give it up, man," he said. "One touch and the whole lot'll be down."

He was right, but I couldn't think straight anymore. I hadn't understood how much I'd been banking on getting out today. Not only getting to safety but getting to someone who'd tell me I'd done the right thing by Dan Taylor, someone who'd help take this burden off me. Until I saw that great pile of rock and knew we weren't getting out, I hadn't even known what I was expecting, hoping for, and desperately needing.

"It's alright," Wade said. "They'll send help. When the park service realizes what's happened, they'll get us out."

He wanted to be reassuring, but a wild flash of anger raced through me again. I shut my eyes in a slow blink. Everyone had pulled out their phones when I opened them, checking for reception, even though we knew there'd be no chance. But this was the highest spot we would likely reach, so we had to try. I had hardly any charge left, so I didn't bother doing the stupid, 'raise it above your head and pray to the magical signal' dance everyone was doing. There was no point.

I followed the others back down the trail in a daze. The other hikers acknowledged us as we reappeared, completely unsurprised. To their credit, none of them said, 'I told you so.'

After a quick discussion, we decided to move further down the trail. The spot we were at might or might not be out of the path of any further rockfall, but it wasn't big enough for seven of us to sit in any comfort and certainly not to sleep if we needed to.

We trooped back, single file, talk filtering back and forth. The English kids were touchingly pleased to have met us, as if they thought we were adults and could somehow make things better—the fools.

"You're here on vacation?" Wade asked.

"Yeah, gap year before uni," Hassan said from behind Wade. "And we wanted to do some walks while we're here."

Bad luck for them.

"We were supposed to do Yosemite next." Hassan's lips twisted, and his head dropped down, his eyes on his feet.

"So, when the meteor hit, you were down in the basin?" I asked over my shoulder, trying to remember what they'd said earlier. I hadn't been paying attention, as all I'd been focused on was the pass, the way out of this mess.

"We were on the bottom trail below here when it hit," Declan said. "We'd been heading back anyway, so we came up to see what'd happened and, yeah, the whole pass was blocked."

Thankfully, it wasn't long before we found a place with enough room for everyone to sit, stand, and lie down. We called a halt and Pete and Claire parked themselves on a little rock ledge. Wade and I collapsed on the stone shelf near their feet. I was still wobbly with the knowledge we were trapped in here. The kids sat across from us.

We had nothing to make a fire with. There was no timber, no kindling up here, only rock and no one offered to head back down and look for wood.

"What do we do?" I was still holding the tide of panic at bay.

"There's nothing we can do." Pete bounced his heel against the rock.

"So, what, we sit here and wait?" I glanced up toward the pass, where the English boys had been sitting and waiting.

"What else can we do?" Claire looked as exhausted as I felt, and I wondered if she'd had the same secret hope for reassurance.

"We could try and get to one of the other passes, see if we can get out." I had to get moving again. The constant motion had given us a sense of purpose, a feeling that we were heading towards something. Each step forward, no matter how small, had felt like a step closer to safety. The logic behind it was flimsy at best, but rationality took a backseat to the comforting illusion of progress. Our movement had been a lifeline, a way to keep the creeping despair at bay. Now, standing still, that thin veil of hope began to unravel.

"They all need climbing stuff," Wade said.

"Well, yeah, but..." I looked at him.

"But what?"

"We could try."

"But someone'll come get us, won't they?" This was Aaron, the one with the red-rimmed eyes. His gaze flicked between us, as all three new-comers had been following our conversation.

"Yes, but we don't know how long they'll be," Wade replied. "And we don't have too much water. Well, I don't." He turned to me. "Mike?"

I shook my head, as I didn't have a lot left either. "How much do you guys have?" I asked the boys, hoping they might be topped off.

"Yeah, not too much."

There was an odd silence before Hassan said, "There's Malik's bot-tles."

"No way. I'm not touching his." Declan shook his head.

Aaron made an odd choking noise.

"Who's Malik?" Claire asked.

Hassan rearranged his feet, tucked them beneath him, and then coughed nervously. "Our friend. He ... uh. There were four of us, you know, but ..."

"Malik got sick." Declan's voice broke in, hard and flat.

Hassan shook his head. "There was nothing we could do."

"What happened?" Wade asked.

"We don't know." Declan clenched grimy hands together. "We couldn't wake him up at first. You know, he was burning up and shaking like he had a fever." He plaited his fingers. "Then he started yelling and kicking around. I don't know ..." Declan was noticeably pale. "Then he, then he ... died."

The word 'died' echoed in my mind, but it felt hollow, insufficient. Images of our recent horrors flashed before my eyes, and a sickening realization settled in my gut. Malik's fate suddenly seemed all too clear, all too familiar. The pieces fell into place, forming a picture I desperately wished I could unsee. My nostrils flared as I connected the dots, the truth too grim to voice aloud. "Had he been digging in the ground at all?" I asked.

"What?" Declan's face twisted, his expression indicating I'd lost my mind. "I don't know. Why?"

"I told you," Aaron chimed in, breaking his silence.

"Oh shit." Declan turned on the kid, his voice savage. "Don't bloody start again."

"I saw it." Aaron's lower lip jutted out, but his eyes were still watery. He was maybe a year younger than the other two.

"What did you see?" I asked, not sure if I wanted to know.

"Fuck," Declan spat. He got to his feet and stomped away to the edge of the flat rock, hands stuffed into his pockets.

Aaron stared after him, then turned back to me. His hands were trembling, and he pushed them beneath his thighs.

"Mal's body." Aaron was having trouble getting it out. "After he died. He … His body tried to kind of … When he was dead, you know? It was like he was trying to claw at the ground." Aaron's face crumpled as if saying it hurt.

What the hell? These kids *really* didn't know about the worms. I scanned Wade, Claire, and Pete, and the same understanding was mirrored in their expressions. Aaron had seen the twitches and spasms caused by the worms feasting inside, and had mistaken it for movement, the same as I had. The other two hadn't seen it and thought he'd lost his marbles.

So, I tried as best as possible to explain the worms. I told them about the Taylors, about what had happened to them, how Mel had been … bitten, then Dan. I didn't mention the dead body, as we hadn't seen that guy bitten and couldn't be certain what had happened. And these kids looked freaked out enough.

I couldn't go on, so Wade took up the tale, saying we'd lost Josh Taylor and stating that Mel and Dan had died. By tacit agreement, none of us said exactly how Dan had died.

Instead, he told them about Mel, that first horrible night. Aaron and Hassan got real intent when Wade got to the bit about Mel screaming.

Declan was still sulking by the ridge behind us, but I guessed he was listening.

Aaron's face stayed frozen in sullen blankness, but Hassan's brow crinkled when I told them about the next morning. About the worms, about Mel being eaten from the inside, about the movements in her body.

Then their expressions moved to skepticism, then doubt. It was obvious they didn't believe me.

Logically, I understood. If I hadn't seen what I had, I probably wouldn't have believed it either, but not being believed pissed me off.

"That's bollocks."

"What?"

Declan had returned and was standing behind me. "Bollocks," he said.

I had some trouble with his accent. "Buttocks?"

"What? No, bollocks, you melon. Balls."

I stared at him; I honestly had no idea what he was saying. Pete and Claire were grinning at me.

"Bullshit?" Pete offered.

Declan nodded in confirmation. "Yeah, bullshit."

They all turned to me. "What*ever*," I said. I sounded like a teenage mallrat, which only irritated me more. "This is serious, you bunch of—" I hunted for something understandable in whatever lame-ass language they were all using. "Wankers."

"Woo-*ooo*." To my annoyance, Pete and Claire joined in the amused hooting at this.

Jesus Christ. I could only stare at them, dumbfounded. *Look, I get it. When shit hits the fan, you gotta let off some steam. But come on, read the room.* Their snickering grated on my last nerve, reminding me why I'd always hated group projects in high school. Teenage boys—walking hormone bombs with the emotional intelligence of a potato. And yeah, the irony wasn't lost on me. I used to be one of those little shits. Didn't make it any less annoying now.

I leaned back, and the ground met my back with an unforgiving thud, every pebble and lump making its presence known through my worn-out clothes. Staring up at the indifferent sky, I let the others take center stage with our batshit crazy meteor theory. Their audience wasn't exactly receptive—faces twisted in disbelief, eyebrows shooting up into hairlines. Couldn't say I blamed them. A week ago, I'd have laughed any nutjob spouting this crap right out of the bar. But after the week we'd had? Even the most out-there explanations were starting to sound like cold, hard facts.

"That's bats," Hassan said about the worms, or whatever they'd become, and how we believed they were growing and breeding underground into something bigger and more threatening.

"Are you mental or what?" Declan said, about whatever the hell had chased Wade and me across that wide strip of grass.

After this, they went quiet and exchanged a few side eyes. I couldn't tell if it was worry they'd fallen in with a pack of lunatics or genuine concern. Aaron, the younger one who'd seen his friend's body move, might have gotten it. He didn't talk as much as the others, but he might be thinking about it.

"Okay," he said, eventually "But even if there *was* something down there, how do we know it's still there?"

Chapter 14

The question hung in the air like a slap to the face. Wade's jaw dropped, Claire's eyes widened to saucers, and Pete froze mid-scratch. My brain short-circuited, struggling to process what we'd just heard. The only sound was the wind whistling through the rocks, as if nature itself was waiting for one of us to break the stunned silence.

"Where are they going to go?" Wade asked, bemused.

"Mate, if they'd grown wings, we'd have seen them." Even Pete looked incredulous.

"No," Aaron said. "I mean, like in *War of the Worlds*. The planet turns out to be toxic—"

Declan slapped him on the arm. "Cut it out, would you? Could you be a bigger dork?" He grimaced at Aaron. "These guys are serious."

I pressed my lips together, hard. I got it, Aaron was poking fun at us, but I answered anyway. "I don't think anything will be toxic to these things. They pretty much filled the entire basin in a day and then practically doubled their size overnight. God knows what's down there now."

Pete was red behind his beard. "You think we're making this shit up?"

"No, I think maybe ..." Hassan paused, embarrassed.

"Maybe what? That all four of us are crazy? Batshit?" Pete bristled.

"Oh, come on. I'm not trying to piss in your chips, but you've got to admit it's a bit out there." Declan grinned at us.

Pete said nothing at first, then hauled himself to his feet. "That's it. Get up."

We all gawped at him.

Declan frowned. "Ah look, no offence—"

"We're bloody going down there, and you can see for yourself." Pete stood above us, hands on hips, and glared. "Now get up before I stick my hand up your O-ring and turn you into a meat puppet."

We staggered to our feet and followed Pete as he strode off. I didn't think anyone wanted to be left alone or made into a meat puppet. I certainly didn't. Pete stalked ahead of us, but I guessed he'd calmed down somewhat, or at least he'd stopped threatening people with bodily harm. We left our packs and filed back down the trail.

The thought of backtracking all the way to that grassy plain I'd sprinted across earlier made my skin clammy. Luckily, we stumbled upon a sweet spot—high enough to keep our distance, but with a clear view of the ground below.

The rocky slope gave way to a patchwork of scrubby grass, dotted with clusters of yarrow and cattails standing sentinel. An eerie stillness blanketed the scene, broken only by the scraping of feet. Dewdrops still clung to the grass blades, catching what little light filtered through the heavy air. The whole tableau seemed suspended, waiting for something to break the unnatural calm. We stood and looked at it.

Nothing happened.

"What are we supposed to do, sit here till a bird lands?" Declan sounded petulant.

We craned our necks, checking the empty grey sky, and nothing moved but the plume of smoke still rising from the meteor strike.

"I haven't seen any birds in ages." Wade shaded his eyes and looked up again. The sky was a luminous light grey, glary even if overcast.

We waited on the rocky edge of the trail, focused on the hillside below us. Nothing moved.

"How far are we from water?" Claire asked abruptly, bending to look further down the trail.

"I don't think there's any this side of the big grassy bit where we ... you know," Wade said.

"Shit."

"Yeah."

Racking my brain, I tried to conjure up memories of water from our frenzied dash across the terrain. Nothing came to mind—no babbling brooks or even the smallest rivulets over stone. Then again, my recollection was about as reliable as a sieve. Pure adrenaline had been coursing through my veins, my focus narrowed to the singular goal of not becoming worm chow.

The others seemed to have kept their wits about them a bit better. Me? I'd been bringing up the rear, scrambling onto those boulders like my life depended on it—which, come to think of it, it probably had. Being the last one to reach safety wasn't exactly a badge of honor I was proud to wear.

Hassan and Declan hunkered down on the edge of the trail. Aaron was leaning back against the rock behind us. My legs tensed, ready to bolt; sitting felt like inviting disaster when we were this close to potential danger zones.

A quick glance confirmed I wasn't alone in my paranoia—Pete, Wade, and Claire were all on their feet too, eyes scanning the scrubby patch of ground as if it might detonate at any second.

"What, we're supposed to wait here all afternoon?" Declan asked.

"What else were you planning to do?" Claire shot back.

"It heard us," Pete said. "Before." He waved back down the trail. "When it happened. It heard our footsteps."

"I'm not going down there," I said, then cleared my throat. My voice had come out way squeakier than intended.

"I didn't mean that, dipshit," Pete said with a grin. He turned and hunted around on the trail till he found a decent fist-sized rock. "Here we go."

He stepped up to the edge and tossed it underarm. It hit rock below us with a crack, then bounced and rolled, thudding down the grassy area.

Nothing happened.

We all waited, watching intently.

Still, nothing happened.

"Bugger." Pete turned to find another rock. The two seated lads scrambled around themselves for stones and found a few, mainly pebble-sized. The air suddenly filled with the clatter of stones raining down on the scrubland below. I found myself in the midst of a makeshift artillery unit, as my companions transformed into overzealous, rock-hurling maniacs with all the restraint of sugar-charged toddlers.

Stones and pebbles rained down onto the slope. I stood warily, eyes scanning the area. Around me, it became a game for the rest of them to see who could find another rock, who could throw it to hit the right spot below us. Everyone was up, hunting around, pulling out bits of stone.

I stayed where I was. None of these morons had been the last one chased to safety over the grassy plain. I couldn't tear my gaze away from the area below us.

A geyser of soil spurted from the ground, spraying grit and debris in all directions like nature's fireworks.

"Oh fuck—"

"Holy shit."

Everyone went quiet. The air of fun evaporated instantaneously. Nobody moved. We all waited, breathless, scanning backwards and forwards, eyes peeled.

Nothing happened.

"Throw another one," Hassan said to Pete, who still had a rock in his hand.

Pete quirked an eyebrow at Claire, who pursed her lips.

"Go on," I said.

He swung his arm back and then forward, releasing the rock. All seven of us tracked its arc till it hit the ground, then flinched in unison when it disappeared in a great churn of dirt and gravel. The spray of falling soil pattered down.

"What the hell was that?" Hassan turned to us as if we knew, as if we had answers.

Aaron drew back his arm to throw another rock.

"Don't." Declan reached out and stopped him.

"Screw you," Aaron said. He jerked his arm away and threw his rock as hard as he could out over the space. He flung it like he was angry.

Everyone watched. It landed further down from the others. A split second later, a hummock rose a few feet away and raced towards where it had come down, exactly like it had behind me as I'd run earlier, fleeing for my life.

The thing slammed into the rock with another subterranean blast, offering a split-second glimpse of something—a flash of brown, perhaps a claw?—before vanishing in the shower of dirt. Ice flooded my veins, memories of that nightmarish chase crashing over me like a tidal wave. My limbs trembled as if my body was reliving every terrifying step of that near-miss. The phantom sensation of the creature's presence prickled at the back of my neck, a stark reminder of how close I'd come to becoming its prey.

Below us on the slope, a couple of other hummocks appeared and disappeared, streaming under the surface, lifting the scraggly grass and scree before it fell back, leaving a hollow trail. Like something was cruising, waiting, more than one 'something.' A queasy feeling began deep down inside. We shuffled back away from the edge of the trail.

"I think we should go back. Up," I said, pointing up the trail, up towards solid rock.

"Yeah, I reckon it might be a good idea," Pete agreed.

The boys were a lot quieter on the way back, thoughtful. It was coming on to dusk by the time we got back to our packs. The first thing Declan did was pull out his phone and fiddle with it. God knew what for; it wasn't even worth trying for a signal here, but the kid couldn't leave it alone.

"If I'd known there was no reception here, I wouldn't have come," he said.

Aaron glared at him. "Seriously? That's your problem?" He was red in the face now instead of pasty white. "That's your problem with this trip? No bloody phone reception? Malik's dead and—"

"You think I don't know that?"

I think it had finally sunk in that things were bad, that we weren't a bunch of wandering lunatics telling ghost stories.

We stumbled around for a bit, picking out places to sleep and getting organized to stay for the night. It was early, but there was nothing to do; we didn't even have a fire to poke.

Of our new group, Aaron was having the most trouble. He was beside me, muttering under his breath as he rolled out his sleeping bag. He plonked himself down on it and looked at me blankly.

I'd noticed, with envy, that all three newcomers still had their sleeping bags. I tried not to think about mine, what state it would be in by now under Mel Taylor's body. I wasn't looking forward to trying to sleep on this rock, but I figured if a sore back was the worst thing that happened, I couldn't really complain.

"Are those things aliens?" Aaron asked, his tone oddly casual, as if he was commenting on the local wildlife.

"*No*," I said, then frowned at him.

A general silence fell on the group around us. I turned this idea over in my mind. I knew we'd thought, speculated, the worms had come from the meteor, but it hadn't occurred to me to think of them as 'aliens.' Or call them that. Aliens were little green men with flying saucers and ray guns. Or with giant battlecruisers and shit. Not worms. Worms were ... worms.

"Well." I turned to Wade and the Australians, but blank faces responded. I guess none of us had thought about it like this. "I don't know, they looked like worms."

"Who knows what they look like now though," Claire said.

I remembered the flash of what might have been a claw. My mouth felt full of moth dust.

"'Cos if this was a movie, someone would say how they're the most efficient killing machines or something." Aaron appeared entirely serious.

A nagging doubt crept in, whispering that maybe the gears in his noggin weren't meshing quite right anymore.

Declan threw a balled-up pair of socks at him. "Shut up."

The air between Aaron and Declan crackled with tension, their interactions laced with the subtle hostility of two cats forced to share the same cramped cardboard box.

"Yeah, I don't think that's too helpful, mate," Claire said.

Aaron frowned at her. His face was pasty. I wondered how long he could keep it together.

"You don't get it, you're the 'Final Girl,'" he said.

Claire's head jerked back slightly, her face a mask of bewilderment as if she'd just been asked to explain quantum physics in pig Latin.

"What the hell are you talking about?" Declan scowled at Aaron.

"In horror movies, there's always one girl who survives. It's a thing, the Final Girl."

"This isn't a movie, you dumb twat!" Declan snapped.

Hassan leaned forward. His interest was fair enough, as it was a distraction from the situation, and at least it appeared Aaron wasn't losing his mind.

"The rest of us are going to die then, are we?" Hassan asked him.

"No, they'll be okay too." Aaron gestured towards Wade, Pete, and I. "Old, straight, guys. They'll be fine."

"We will be too then. See, nothing to worry about."

"No, you don't get it. We're college kids. The college kids always die because they're into drugs and sex and stuff."

"Bruv, you've never had sex with anyone but Mrs. Palm and her five daughters," said Declan.

Hassan broke into a thunderous snort-laugh that could've startled nearby wildlife, while Aaron blushed so hard he almost glowed. "Shut up," he said at last.

Frustration bubbled over, and the words tumbled out before I could stop them. "I'm gay."

"What?"

"You heard me. Gay." My finger jabbed the air, pointing between Wade, Pete, and myself. "Your little theory about us living because we're 'old, straight guys'? Yeah, not so much."

The word 'old' stung more than I cared to admit, but I pressed on. "So, correction: I'm not your stereotypical 'old, straight guy.' I'm an equal-opportunity pain in the ass, thank you very much."

For some reason saying it gave me a tiny feeling of taking back control. This was my world, and this was the way things were. Hassan and Declan looked at me with blank indifference before Declan hitched a shoulder. "Whatever."

Aaron's face twisted into a mask of exaggerated horror, like I'd just confessed to kicking puppies for fun. A weary sigh escaped me. *Here we go.*

"Oh man," he blurted, his voice a mix of pity and morbid excitement. "You're totally screwed. The gay guy *always* bites it. It's like, horror movie law or something."

"*Shut up,* Aaron." Declan reached across and clouted him on the arm.

Chapter 15

Sleep came in fitful bursts, consciousness bobbing up like a stubborn cork every time I started to drift off. My spare clothes, meant as a makeshift blanket, ended up wadded beneath me in a futile attempt at cushioning. Trying to get cozy on a pile of rocks, comfort remained an elusive dream, always just out of reach.

In the morning, I laid and looked up at the lightening sky. I decided to convince myself I was hopeful. Surely, someone would come find us today. How long had it been? Three days since the meteor hit. God, was that all?

After Aaron's movie comparison, I thought about how I'd always scoffed when characters said, 'It all seems *soooo* long ago' when it had only been a day or two. But it genuinely felt like *soooo* long ago. A different world. God, I was one giant sleep-deprived cliché.

An hour after everyone else woke up, it dawned on us that sitting around all day wasn't going to work. I'd perched myself up on the little ledge of rock, sitting and looking out across the basin. Pete sat next to me with Claire beside him. I'd been trying to work out whether a mile or so to the right, there'd been another landslide or whether it normally looked that way. I hadn't heard anything in the night that sounded like trees crashing, but it may have happened during the thirty seconds I was asleep. I asked Pete what he thought.

"Dunno," he said.

Hmm, helpful. We fell back into silence. At our feet, the others were spread out across the rock shelf, Aaron rooting through his belongings, his stuff sprawled everywhere. Everyone else was staring into space.

"Watch it, Flower," Declan said as Aaron had upended his pack, cascading dirty clothing over Declan.

Aaron recoiled as if slapped, his face contorting into a mask of indignation. "Don't call me that!" he snarled, snatching up a grimy T-shirt like it was battle armor against the offending nickname.

"You don't complain when Mum says it."

Declan and Hassan sniggered, and Pete snorted.

"Cut it out; he can be a flower if he wants to," Claire said, smacking Pete on the leg. "What kind of flower are you?" She raised her eyebrows at the kid.

Aaron's face was instant tomato. "It's just something Mum says. It doesn't mean anything."

Pete snickered and Claire turned innocent eyes on him.

"Never mind, petal, you're *my* flower.' Her words dripped with saccharine sweetness as she reached out, ruffling Pete's hair with the same patronizing affection one might show a particularly dim puppy.

Pete's gaze slithered sideways, his face a mask of mock innocence. "What kind of flower?" The words squeaked out, barely above a whisper, as if he were a timid mouse daring to question a cat.

"Oh, definitely a blokey one." Claire grinned. "Like, one of those pitcher plants in the jungle that eat insects and stuff. Little frogs even, you know, a manly type of flower."

Pete appeared to consider this before his eyes narrowed. "Hang on a second, don't those flowers smell like shit?"

Claire stifled a smile, and Pete glared at her like a mad shrimp. "Are you calling me a poo-flower?"

Claire's face was deadpan. "Well, you have to admit, you don't always smell like roses."

Pete flourished outraged eyebrows. "A *poo flower*!"

Claire collapsed in giggles.

The water bottle found its way to my lips, more out of habit than thirst. A pointless sip, really—just a feeble attempt to fill the awkward silence with something, anything other than words.

"A fine state of affairs. My girlfriend saying I smell like—"

"Shut up, you idiot!" Claire threw her empty water bottle at him.

Pete couldn't dodge quick enough, and it bounced off his head with an audible 'donk.'

"Ow." He rubbed his head before his face became a picture of confused innocence. "What was that for?"

Claire grimaced at him. "Drop kick."

Pete sat back up trying to keep a straight face. "I'm not angry," he said, gravely, shaking his head. "Just disappointed."

"That'll teach you to stick your god-awful snoz into things."

I choked a little on my water and checked out Pete's nose. It didn't look that big to me. I leaned forward to look quizzically at Claire.

"That bit at the end," she said, pointing. "See. Where it looks like a penis."

I examined Pete's nose again. There was a touch of Owen Wilson about it.

"Oi," Pete said with great indignation.

Claire poked her tongue out at him. "Shut up, dick-nose."

Yeah, a whole day of this wasn't going to work.

A half-hour later, we were packed and ready to go, but a consensus on where we were going was another matter. Technically there weren't a lot of options. The pass above us was blocked, and if we followed the trail back the other way, we'd eventually come to the grassy field where Wade and I had been chased by whatever lurked beneath us.

The thought of a repeat performance made my skin itch, especially considering the possibility of overnight growth spurts for our subterranean nemesis. Pushing the image aside proved about as easy as herding cats. My mental 'do not think about' list had ballooned faster than a marshmallow in a microwave, each new entry more unsettling than the last. We'd have to go off trail, either towards the Angels' Pipe climb, or further down where we could try to reach the high rim trail, which might lead to Dante's Crag.

The bickering washed over me, each proposed route blending into a meaningless cacophony of what-ifs and maybes. My feet itched to move, to leave behind this carousel of indecision and the relentless parade of thoughts it fueled. The words 'Let's just draw straws' teetered on the tip of my tongue when a sharp crack made us all jump.

Everyone shut up and looked around, trying to figure out where the gunshot came from. We all swiveled our heads, but it was no good. The echoes from the basin made it impossible to tell. About the only thing we knew for sure was, it hadn't come from outside of the park. If it had come from the other side of the pass above us, the sound wouldn't have ricocheted around the basin like that.

"How many is that now?"

"Why do we keep hearing that?"

We'd heard a few shots now, but my brain was too fuzzy to count. We just needed to get going.

"Well, it definitely had to come from below us," Wade said.

"So?" I said with a bit of a huff.

"So, if we go down the trail, we might find whoever it is?" He managed not to roll his eyes at me.

"Oh. Right."

"Do we want to find whoever it is?" Aaron asked. "What if they shoot us?" A wild gleam had crept back into his eyes, his demeanor teetering on the edge of unhinged. Stress etched deep lines across his face, a roadmap of barely contained panic. Clearly, this mess was wearing him down like sandpaper on bare nerves.

"Us Americans don't all go around shooting each other you know," Wade said, his gaze narrowed slightly. "It's probably someone trying to get attention."

In the end, it was decided we'd go down the track as far as we could, then turn off to try and find the high rim trail. If we met with anyone before we turned off, all was well; if we didn't, then we wouldn't wait around. There was probably no point anyway, as there was nothing we could do to help anyone.

We got moving at last, a bare hour after we'd begun discussing which way we'd go. At this rate, it would take us a week to reach Dante's Crag, not two days. Pete and Claire led the way as usual. Their giant packs were the heaviest, so the theory was they'd be the slowest, therefore, if they set the pace, no one would be left behind.

I didn't say anything; I was definitely the slowest, even though there wasn't a whole lot left in my pack and certainly not a lot of water.

The Aussies might as well have been fresh out of diapers, probably a solid decade younger than yours truly. Even Wade had a few months on me, the smug bastard. Suddenly, my bones creaked with the weight of centuries, like some ancient, cranky wizard surrounded by eager apprentices. These damn whippersnappers ought to show some respect for their elders.

"Holy crap." Ahead of us, Pete and Claire had reached the spot where we'd hurled rocks yesterday. We stumbled to a halt behind them and stared over the edge of the trail.

Below the grassy, scrubby slope, the ground had given way, the few trees now flattened. Above it, though, was what took the eye. What had been grass yesterday was now completely churned up, dips and hollows among ridges. My leg muscles tightened. The scale of the disturbance was staggering.

"Do you think we pissed it off with the rocks?" Aaron's voice sounded wavery and he tried again. "That we threw. Yesterday, I mean …"

The thought skittered away like a roach exposed to sudden light, too grim to entertain. Instead, attention shifted downward, where the toe of my boot traced idle patterns in the gritty debris, as if the scattered pebbles and twigs held answers to questions best left unasked. Whatever it was had happened with such violence that dirt had been flung all the way up here.

"They must have grown," Claire said. "It's the only thing that explains …" She pointed to the torn-up landscape below us.

My scalp twitched. "Should we go back up?" I checked around the group. "You know in the movies when they say 'I've got a bad feeling about this'? Well, I've got a fucking bad feeling about this."

Pete snorted.

Yeah, I hadn't meant to be funny.

"I don't know. We're going to have to find water soon," Wade said, looking further down the trail. "It's more likely down there."

Hassan turned to us. "We should be okay if we stay on the stone though, right?" As if we had any idea what was going on.

"Maybe," Claire said.

Pete nodded slowly.

"We'll have to be careful," Wade said.

A herculean effort of willpower kept my eyeballs from performing an Olympic-level gymnastics routine in their sockets.

We shuffled off again, heading down. Everything around us was still and quiet, the air damp with moisture that wasn't quite a drizzle. It was another dull, grey day. Would the sun ever come back? Occasionally, as we twisted and turned down the trail, I caught sight of the plume of impact smoke, still reaching to the sky. It was thinner now, or maybe it was my imagination.

There was no sign of whoever had fired the shots. Not a single bird above us either. Even when there was a view out across the basin, there were none. I wondered if whatever was down there was getting hungry. Then I really wanted to not have wondered about it.

After another ten minutes or so, the trail broke up into earthy sections between rock. I recalled jumping from boulder to boulder on the way up yesterday, still freaked out about whatever it was that'd chased us.

Eventually, we came to another halt. A ways to either side of us, rocky ground still showed, but below us, the trail led back into more grassy areas. If we followed it for a few more minutes, we'd be back at that wide stone-less expanse.

"D'y'reckon we should try and get across now?" Pete asked. He was standing on the highest point of the rock, looking away to the right of us.

"I don't think there's any point going down more," Claire said.

Pete nodded solemnly. "Said the actress to the bishop."

Claire frowned at him in exasperation but was too far away to swat him. "You're a tool."

Pete nodded again. "That's what *she* said."

We turned off the trail. Oddly, it felt like leaving safety. We leaped and scrambled through an area of tumbled boulders, grey, lichened, and stained. The rocks here were bigger, and we had to climb up and over them. Little bits of ground showed between odd angles. There was no path, as no one was expected to hike through here.

I kept thinking we'd come to something too big to climb, but we managed to keep going for an hour. Even if we hadn't gotten very far distance-wise, it felt like forward movement. And we were away from wide, bare areas. Safe I hoped, from whatever squirmed underneath us.

I was having trouble believing the outside world still existed. It was bizarre to me that out there, people were going about their everyday lives, completely unaware of what was going on here. Ben, my ex, was probably enjoying his day without the slightest thought of me, unaware I was probably about to die a revolting death. It was dreadfully unfair. Ben was like a little paper cut I couldn't help picking at, the price of trying not to think about the last few days.

After a particularly steep part, we stopped for a break on the top of a broad, domed rock. A spill of smaller basalt lay below us, which led to a shallow gully of grass before it curved back up to rock.

We sprawled out, trying to get comfortable. I didn't bother taking my pack off. I flopped back on it and tried not to make it obvious I was panting after the last climb. We all stared at the landscape below us, eyes peeled for any sign of movement.

"Do you think if the things have grown, we'd be safer on the smaller bits of dirt?" Claire asked.

"I'm not bloody trying it," Pete said.

"Not there," she waved a hand at the dip. "I mean the little bits, like where we jump across?"

No one offered anything to this, and we lapsed into silence.

"Can you hear water?" Declan sat up and tilted his head. "I think I can hear water."

We perked up and did the meerkat swivel.

"Yeah, over there?" Wade pointed down into the gully.

"You think?" I listened but there was nothing.

"I can hear, like, trickling." Declan stood and moved to the edge of the stone.

Wade moved over to join him. "Look, there." He pointed. "It could be water?"

Following his outstretched finger, eyes squinted against the glare, revealed nothing but a slightly darker patch on the sun-baked stone. If this qualified as water, it was less an oasis and more nature's cruel joke—a microscopic tease of moisture on parched rock. "We should check it out?"

"Mm-mm, I don't think there's any way to get there," Wade said.

We traced the gap with our eyes, sheer rock to either side with the only way through being the grassed gully. One rounded stone poked up in the ground about a third of the way across but there was nothing beyond it for several yards. It was too far to jump.

"Let me check it out," Declan said.

He scuttled down off our stone and onto the patch of tumbled rock above the gully.

"Be careful," Hassan said.

Declan jumped from stone to stone, then across onto the final rounded protrusion and stood, wobbling as he looked about. He was altogether too close to the dirt for my liking.

"If there was one more rock, I could get up there," he called back up to us, pointing to the damp patch. "Do you think there's actually anything under here?" he added, inspecting the ground.

"Don't—" I think practically all of us said it, like a chorus.

"All right, I'm not going to." Declan frowned at us. "Pass me my pack."

"Why? What do you want?" Hassan bent to grab it.

"No," Declan said. "I can use it to stand on." He pointed downwards. "See, across here."

Hassan had hoisted Declan's pack and was picking his way back, precariously. It was actually a pretty good idea. If there was anything under the gully it would be blocked by the pack. Declan could use it like a steppingstone.

I turned to Wade and lifted a brow. He screwed up his nose in return. Pete and Claire looked non-committal too. Worth a try, I guessed. In my defense, I thought we'd all gotten a bit complacent. Jumping safely from stone to rock all morning had pushed back the memory of the churned-up ground. There was a good covering of grass here too, without any of those dimples and scars that were evidence of something below.

Hassan had reached the gully now and stretched across to pass the pack to Declan where he stood on the last humped rock. He wobbled a bit as he took it and we all pulled in a breath as he caught his balance. He flashed us a big cheese-eating grin before he shuffled back around to face the ditch.

Declan bent carefully at the waist, swung the pack and let go. It landed with a whump, pretty much halfway between his rock and safety on the other side.

Nothing happened.

"Nice shot," Aaron said.

We all waited, scanned the gully, and listened.

Nothing continued to happen. Declan shifted his weight backward and forward on his feet, readying to jump.

"Whoa," Hassan said suddenly, and a little spark ran through me. "Hang on."

He was holding out a water bottle to Declan. I snorted; yeah, that might be helpful.

"Oh shit, right." Declan grabbed it and wobbled back around. "Okay, here goes."

He jumped.

Before he even hit the pack, something burst through it from below.

Chapter 16

L ike a razor, the thing slashed through the pack and propelled Declan upwards. The sheer power of it was incredible.

Declan let out a high-pitched shriek and searing panic burst through me. Instinctively, I reached forward even though I was yards away.

By chance, the kid fell back towards his rock. He clutched at it and Hassan clutched at him. The pack was gone now, vanished into the ground along, temporarily, with one of Declan's feet.

I hadn't blinked since Declan had leaped; I was frozen with horror. There was a mad scrabble below us. Declan screamed again and kicked frantically, managing to pull his foot out of the flourish of dirt. It came out without his shoe. Another thrash of mud burst upwards, but Hassan took hold of him and pulled.

The pair scrambled up among the tumbled boulders, and the rest of us knocked heads in reaching down to haul them up. We got them, yanking them up in panicky, desperate pulls. At last, we had them clear of the gully, and they sprawled beside us on the domed surface of the rock.

"Shit, shit, shit. Keep going, keep going." Declan stumbled to his feet, staggered across, and flung himself over to the next rock.

A flicker of movement in the ditch below snagged my attention. The ground seemed alive, writhing and splitting as if possessed. Unseen forces carved channels through the soil, quick slicing motions pushing up mounds of dirt in erratic, humped trajectories. Each crack and shift sent my heartrate skyrocketing, my breath coming in short, ragged gasps.

Declan's words echoed in my skull, suddenly crystal clear—distance from this underground horror show couldn't come fast enough. Spinning around, it slapped me in the face—I was bringing up the rear again. The others had already transformed into sure-footed mountain goats, scrambling up the rocks and vanishing from sight. Meanwhile, my brain was still fumbling for the ignition switch. Damn it.

Dread and quivering muscles conspired to propel me upward, each handhold a desperate grasp at safety. The frantic scramble blurred into a haze of ragged panting and burning limbs. Finally, hauling myself over the last crag, I emerged onto a stone shelf like a bedraggled sea creature flopping onto land. The others sprawled around me, a tableau of exhaustion, their heaving chests a chorus of relief and fatigue. For a horrible moment back there, I'd believed they were all going to disappear without me, so I collapsed beside Wade. *Dignity be damned—let them hear the full orchestra of fatigue.*

Across from us, Declan was maggot-white and shaking. He sat with his legs out in front of him, the trouser leg of his shoeless foot hauled up.

Memory flashed to the English kids' footwear choices—those flimsy excuses for hiking shoes that had seemed laughably inadequate. Now, a grudging respect crept in. Those lightweight sneakers might've just saved Declan's hide. Stranger still was the intact sock on his foot, a tiny island of normalcy in our sea of insanity. I shook my head, marveling at how quickly 'sensible' had become a moving target in this living hell.

What really drew my attention was the state of his lower leg, directly above his ankle. Declan had pushed his sock down and was staring at his leg. His hands trembled above the marks as if he couldn't bring himself to touch them.

Growing on either side of his leg were deep, swelling bruises, like he'd been grabbed by an enormous nutcracker with tremendous force. Or hit by the bumper of a car, on both sides, at the same time. I went cold all over. Blood welled from superficial scratch marks on one side, leaving dribbles down his ankle and into his sock. I was pretty sure it'd been pure luck he'd gotten away, that whatever it was had taken his shoe instead of his foot.

"That didn't bloody work, did it?" Claire broke the silence.

Declan snorted at this, hiccupped, and then began to sob in deep, heaving grunts. I couldn't say I blamed him.

"Oh shit, sorry." Claire reached over to pat him on the shoulder, but he flinched away.

We decided to stay where we were for the rest of the afternoon, spend the evening there, and start again in the morning. We'd found the highest point of rock we could. Everyone was shaken and shocked, and it probably wasn't safe to go on in this state.

Declan had nothing, no pack, no sleeping bag, no food, no water, and only one shoe. We sat around and stared at Declan's leg, at the damage.

Finally, someone said it. "What in the name of arse dandruff *was* that?" Pete asked.

Okay, not exactly how I would have put it, but what we all wanted to know.

Pete turned to Declan and Hassan. "Well?"

Declan's mouth made wobbly shapes, but nothing came out.

Hassan shook his head. "I didn't see."

"How could you not see? You were right there." Pete's voice ran a few notches up the scale.

"I don't know, okay? It was so fast. And, you know, Declan was between—" Hassan circled a hand to indicate his view had been blocked.

"Did you see it?" I asked Declan.

He was still dazed. "It was so strong. It was like being hit by a truck. I don't know, I don't..." He shook his head, as if trying to shake something loose. "It cut right through my pack like it was nothing." The kid looked close to tears. "It just happened, I was there, and then—" He stifled a sob and fell quiet.

Curiosity nagged at me, pulling my thoughts to the others who'd clung to the higher ground. Had their vantage point revealed anything we'd missed? The question tumbled out. "Did anyone see?"

Claire considered. "It was under the pack. So, I couldn't, no." She sounded both regretful and thankful for this. From Wade, Pete, and Aaron there was nothing but head shaking.

"It wasn't a bird, that's for sure," I said.

"You what?" Hassan said. He and Aaron both frowned at me like I'd grown a second head.

I had to remind them of what Claire, Pete, Wade, and I had seen on the trail up to the pass before we got above the tree line.

"Oh, right. Yeah." Hassan's expression was blank but he nodded.

Yeah, back when they hadn't believed a word I was saying.

"Well, whatever it was, it wasn't a bloody bird," Declan said, his voice still shaky.

I tried to review what I'd seen, over and over in my head, to get it clear, to make sense of it. I'd seen something, but I didn't know what. I didn't know how to begin to describe it to the others, so I kept quiet, worried they'd ask questions I couldn't answer.

For a fraction of a second, I'd seen something come through Declan's pack like punching through water. But it wasn't even that, it was like it came through empty air and reached through the pack like it hadn't been there. It was brown-black and thin, like a pipe or a tube. Maybe an inch in diameter? Knobby, organic, like ... an enormous feeler?

Saliva flooded my mouth, a physiological betrayal of mounting dread. That fleeting glimpse had unleashed a torrent of gruesome scenarios, each more vivid than the last. Forcing my mind blank proved as futile as herding cats. The thought of fielding a barrage of questions made my skin crawl. No, better to keep this horror show locked behind clenched teeth. Some nightmares were best left unspoken.

The thing was, I had another idea I kept to myself. This one was worse, and plainly it hadn't occurred to anyone else. Declan's foot had been underground. It was only for the barest instant, but still, what if it was enough? Enough time for one of those worms to whip its way into his skin.

Around me, the others were recovering some composure.

"Well, it's one way to lighten your load." Hassan grinned at Declan. "No more complaining from you about how heavy your pack is."

"Very funny." Declan was a bit less wobbly now. "How am I going to get out of here with only one shoe?"

"You can have my plimsolls," Aaron said.

His what? Aaron dug around in his pack. It turned out plimsolls were white canvas tennis shoes, light enough to be brought along, to have clean shoes when not hiking. Well, Aaron had brought a pair at least, neither of the others had thought it necessary.

"It'd be alright if you didn't have those great flippers." Declan waved derisively to Aaron's feet.

Aaron grinned at him. "You know what they say about men with big feet."

"Yeah, I do, bloody big flipper shoes, that's what."

"Do you want them or not?"

"Yeah, alright then." Declan reached for the shoes. "Oh shit, my passport, it was in my pack."

I wasn't sure what connection of thoughts led to this realization. Then his head came up, his face a mask of complicated distress. My head jerked back—had he felt something in his leg? Had he felt something move? *Eat?*

"Fuck," Declan said. "My *phone*."

Suddenly, absurd laughter bubbled up from some hysterical corner of my psyche. Shock, probably—the brain's last-ditch attempt at sanity in a world gone mad. Bewildered frowns from all directions sobered me quickly. Desperately, I morphed the ill-timed chuckles into an unconvincing cough, as if that could erase the flash of inappropriate hilarity.

A half an hour later the sun came out. It wasn't hot but the gentle warmth felt like a blessing on my skin. Everyone flaked around our ledge of stone and soaked in the rays, in the joy of being safe, still alive. Only a flag of sky was visible, but it was blue.

I laid back with the sun on my face and tried not to think about anything. Especially not what it would feel like to be eaten alive by worms, or how it would feel to be smothered with a sleeping bag. I tried to let go of the knot in my soul.

Later, I sat propped against the rock, my legs in the sun and my head in the shade, barely awake, following a conversation between Pete and Declan. They were comparing swear words, or at least that was what

I assumed they were doing. There appeared to be some crossover in vocabulary and some divergence. The kid's voice was still shaky, and I guessed Pete was trying to distract him.

"Bastard?" suggested Pete, gravely.

Declan nodded slowly and responded in a tone of reverent agreement, "Bastard."

There was a brief silence then it was Declan's turn. "Bell end?"

Pete wrinkled his forehead as if savoring the term. Nodded slightly. "Bell end."

His turn again. "Knob-jockey?"

Declan blinked, and then his lips formed a circle. "Whoa. Hang on." He jerked his head in my direction. "Isn't that a bit, you know? Not PC?"

I pretended not to notice.

"What?" Pete was plainly confused until he caught the nod. "Yeah nah, knob-jockey, like—" He mimed using a jockey's whip on his flank with one hand and choking the monkey with the other. As the whip hand's enthusiasm crescendoed, its partner accelerated to match, transforming the hapless victim into a macabre jack-in-the-box, bobbing up and down with grotesque vigor. To finish off the performance, he flung his monkey-strangling hand away in a sweeping motion as if scattering something to the wind. "You know."

Ah, that kind of knob-jockey.

"Ohhh." Declan shook his head. "You are so wrong."

More silence.

"Cockwomble?"

Consciousness returned with a jolt, dragging me from a twisted dreamscape where Declan's fate unfolded in grotesque detail. In this nightmarish vision, worms had made a gruesome feast of his lower leg, leaving the rest of him horrifyingly intact. His agonized screams pierced the dream-haze as the voracious horde inched upward, consuming him bite by excruciating bite from the ragged stump of his former limb.

Rubbing my eyes, I checked and there he was, thankfully still in possession of all his limbs. Paranoia whispered in my ear, prompting a silent vow to scrutinize his every move, twitch, and grimace for the slightest hint of impending doom. If there were worms inside him, incubating, then there were worms up there with us, mere yards from me.

Evening brought a curtain of clouds, smothering the sun and ushering in another bone-chilling night. Dawn revealed a world glazed with heavy dew, a cold comfort for stiff joints. Sleep came in fitful bursts, each waking moment a stark reminder of the unyielding stone beneath. Yet, that very hardness offered a perverse solace—a barrier between vulnerable flesh and the nameless horrors lurking below.

Come morning, gratitude warred with discomfort as protesting muscles screamed their objections to the night's accommodations. It took a while for my bones to organize themselves into the right position. I felt about a hundred years old. The lack of coffee might have had something to do with it too.

Down along the rock, I found a private spot. Sadly, sound carried in the still morning air, so nothing was particularly discreet. Returning, I sat back down and tried not to listen as everyone else took turns trying and failing to be discreet. Oh, what a glorious morning.

No fire again, no boiling water, no coffee. We had very little water left altogether. We sat around in the early morning light, everyone filthy and dazed.

Around us towered a bastion of solid, damp rock, lichen blooms showing stark against the gritty, grey surfaces. I knew today we'd probably have to risk leaving this nice, safe stone, if we wanted to get across to the high rim trail, and I had little squiggles of panic at the idea.

Digging out another protein bar, I checked how many were left and promised myself I would never eat another one of the damn things again once we were out of here. In the future, I would avert my eyes in that aisle of the grocery store.

"Do we keep going this way?" Wade asked the sullen circle of faces.

Claire frowned at him. "What else would we do?"

"We could go back, try and get up to Angel's Pipe?" He scanned, checking expressions.

"I thought it was too dangerous?" said Aaron.

"It's a bit bloody dangerous this way too, in case you hadn't noticed." Declan was recovering some of his bravado.

Claire nodded. "Yeah, maybe we should give Angel's a go." She turned to Pete as if he might argue. "If we can get out there, it should be quicker."

Pete nodded. "Yeah, I reckon."

I didn't say anything. These were all the same things we'd said before when we'd decided to try and reach the high rim trail instead of the Angel's Pipe climb; we were simply too frightened to keep going now. I was so relieved, my guts felt like water.

Chapter 17

We set off again, back the way we'd come. And yeah, I'd been so desperate I put a couple spoonfuls of coffee-creamer mix into my water bottle and shook it hard with the splash of moisture remaining. It was every bit as revolting as it sounded. I chugged it down, anyway. Thankfully I had another bottle tucked in my pack.

Declan's leg pain was evident despite his efforts to hide it. His plimsoll flippers couldn't have been much fun either.

You'd think retracing our steps, undoing all the effort we'd put in yesterday, would be demoralizing, but instead, it was comforting—the appeal of the familiar. It felt like running back home and hiding. It was no such thing, but I thought we all felt like we were returning to safety.

The morning was slow going, although not as slow as when we'd come the other way. Going back, we mainly managed to retrace our steps, though without an actual path, it was difficult to be certain.

Pete and Claire were in the lead again when there was another halt.

"Hey, you blokes!" Pete's shout carried back to us. "Come and see this."

The Australians had stopped on a flat heel of stone.

I was the last to arrive. "What are we looking at?"

"Over there." Pete pointed. "See, that's someone's pack, yeah?"

Perched on a knob of rock across a gully was what looked like a hiking pack, dirty orange with a lot of black straps.

Pete cupped his hands to yell through. "Helloooo?"

I scanned the pack's surroundings. Unless someone was hiding down among the crevices of the rock, there was no one there. It was just that little bit too far to jump across and find out.

"Why would someone leave their stuff?" Beside me, Hassan eyed the stretch of ground between us and the lonely pack.

Following the direction of his gaze, I worried at a bit of loose skin beside my thumbnail. The ground was a churned-up mess. "D'you think whoever it was tried to get across there?" Hassan pointed.

"Why would they leave their pack behind?" Pete rotated on the spot, looking around. "Maybe they're coming back?"

"Shame we can't reach it," Declan said, also inspecting the gap. "There might be some better shoes in there."

Pete frowned at him. "That's someone's stuff."

"Yeah, but they're not here now." Declan had a point. "And there might be water in there."

More water would be great but the memory of Declan trying to cross a gully was fresh in my mind. No one volunteered to try, likely considering the same thing. It was too far. Tantalizingly, just too far.

Eventually, we gave up calling and moved on. I tried not to think of someone slipping and tumbling down into that bare dip. Of something ... organic, clawing up and taking them.

We reached the pass trail by late morning. I had a wash of relief when we found it, and I thought everyone's spirits picked up; it felt like the tiniest tinge of normality.

"Should we keep going?" Pete was in the lead again.

"Yeah, let's get further up before we take a break." Wade waved him on.

An impromptu stop happened when we reached the place we'd thrown rocks and stones before. It was difficult to tell if there'd been any further disturbance since we were here yesterday.

"D'you think they're still under there?" Declan said.

He was crouched down, rubbing his leg. I remembered the scratch marks there, the claw marks. Yeah, on reflection, I didn't think what I'd seen was roots or a stick.

"Hopefully if we leave them alone, they'll leave us alone," said Claire.

"Now there's a motto to live by," said Pete. "Or how about 'remember kids, they're more scared of you than you are of them.'" He grinned.

Nobody laughed.

"Alright then," said Pete. "What about 'don't feed the animals'?"

"Ugh, stop it." Claire swatted him on the arm before turning back up the trail again.

We all shuffled after her, break over, I guessed. We'd gone maybe twenty yards or so up the trail when a great splatter of dirt sprayed out from behind us.

We froze and listened to it hit the ground like hail. It was loud, much louder than the earlier 'plopping' sounds I remembered. We stood like statues, goggling statues.

Was this it? Was this something that was going to crawl out and come up the rock after us? My gut roiled, although it might have been the curdled coffee/creamer mix.

"What was—"

SPLUCKK— Pete's words were drowned out by a loud pop. It was almost like a detonation but ... wet. Like torn fabric bursting.

The faint hail of something scattered fell in the aftermath, unlike anything we'd heard before. Catching a whiff of the chemical taint, I sucked in air. We stood in horrified silence, absorbing the scene. "What was that?" I asked. As if any of us would know.

"It sounded big," Declan said quietly. "Way bigger than whatever it was yesterday." He was a bit quivery about the lips, couldn't say I blamed him.

"Yeah, way bigger," Hassan said. "I don't think..." He broke off, his eyes on Declan's foot.

"Definitely. Or maybe they're changing somehow?" Claire said.

"Do we want to go look?" Wade asked and hitched the straps of his pack.

"No. No, I don't think we do." For once Pete's face was dead serious.

We hustled on up the trail. I thought everyone was moving a bit quicker, even though it was steeper and more difficult going. I listened hard to the sound of panted breath and boots scraping on stone but didn't hear the sound again.

We had a short break for lunch. Once again, I pulled out a protein bar with the opposite of enthusiasm. We left the trail, this time to head in the reverse direction, around the rocky perimeter of the caldera. It felt safer the further up toward the rim we went, but maybe I was kidding myself.

Part of me was wildly curious to know what was happening beneath us. Another part, the biggest part, wanted to get the hell out of here. Maybe read a few headlines after they napalmed the bejeezus out of this place, or read some details in some scientific journal, in a few months. Yeah, I could live with that when it became a dangerous, natural oddity—one that happened far away and to other people, like Ebola or Nickelback.

We set off across the rocky slope and, by pure luck, stumbled onto the marked trail to the Angel's Pipe by mid-afternoon. Going with rough steps cut into the stone was much easier than random tumbled boulders and basalt. There were even some wooden guardrails on some steeper parts. It felt like civilization. A half an hour later, we got our first glimpse of the Angel's Pipe.

We all stopped. I didn't know what I expected, but it wasn't this. The rim still loomed above us, but a great slanted crevasse ran up through it, far deeper than I'd anticipated. An immense rift slashed down through the stone like a scar, less of a pipe than two bare cliffs facing each other across a gulf.

The reclining side, rather than the overhanging one, was the one we'd have to climb. It began sharply, almost vertical, before it tilted further up into more of a slope. That was as much as I could make out as the rest twisted out of sight.

Stupidly, I hadn't expected it to be so steep. My legs wobbled, and my hands trembled as butterflies did frantic, ill-advised swoops inside me.

"We'll have to get up closer to see properly," Wade said.

I sighed. I supposed it was true—we couldn't tell from here if there might be handholds or little ledges. Even if there were, I wasn't looking forward to trying to get up there. I wasn't *bad* with heights, but I wasn't great either.

By the time we reached the bottom of the Pipe, we were in shadow. The cliffs above us stretched forever into the sky. They loomed. I pulled at the collar of my shirt and turned back the other way.

The day was hazy again, but even so, I could tell the sun had dipped below the western rim. A panorama of the basin was spread out before us, cast into shade. The great plume of smoke from the meteor impact site still rose like a column. It was thinner now, but it was still burning or smoking, whatever it was.

Everyone else was focused on the sheer Angel's Pipe above us. I tried not to look at it. We got as close as we could walk, then dumped our packs. There was a little flat patch that appeared to be used as a base camp for climbers. I expected there to be one of those little info boards with a diagram and details, but there was nothing.

From there, it was a short clamber over more tumbled rock, and then we were inside the Pipe. The dim space had a musty, stale smell. The name made much more sense here.

As I looked up from inside, the back of the crevasse was round and practically vertical all the way up. Stained rock wrapped us in an enormous, leaning pipe. My butterflies had escaped my stomach and were partying in my chest.

"Does anyone have any climbing experience?" Wade asked.

Hmm, yeah, maybe we should have considered this before. I got a grip on myself and looked up, then up some more. Some of my butterflies might have vomited.

No one said anything for a while, then Aaron offered, "I went on a trip once with school, doing climbing."

Hmm. Nobody said anything to this thrilling information. To this point, I'd been sure we'd be able to get out, confident the specified need for equipment was over-caution, that if we were desperate enough, and God knew we were, we could climb it. I was quickly revising this assumption.

The English lads were already assessing the rock, searching for handholds and places to climb. Declan stood behind the other two with his hands on his hips. "How am I supposed to get up there in these bloody shoes?"

Everyone stopped what they were doing and focused on his giant, Krusty the Clown flipper shoes.

Yep, that wasn't going to work.

"Take them off?" Aaron suggested. "Go barefoot?"

"You go bloody barefoot."

I inspected the sharp edges of the rock, where it split and razored, supplying what holds I could make out. Bare feet were not a good idea.

"We should probably wait till the morning anyway," I said. "It'll be getting dark soon."

"No way." Aaron turned from his examination of the rock. "I'm getting the hell out of here."

He and Hassan focused back on the stone. "What do you think?" Aaron pointed. "Up there?"

"Yeah, look, you can see where people have put climbing stuff there before. And there."

The pair conferred while the rest of us stood back. I could kind of tell where they were pointing, but I had a dizzy wobble and focused firmly on my feet.

"I'm sorry, but I'm not climbing up there in the dark," I said. I hoped this sounded a bit more composed than blurting out, 'Mother of God, there's no way you're getting me up there.'

Declan made the 'pfft' noise. "It won't be dark for hours."

"We don't all have to go," Hassan said. He grinned at me like he knew what was going through my head. "We only need someone to get to the top and see if there's phone reception, yeah?"

Why didn't I think of that? Panic was probably scrambling my brain. I might be a bit worse than 'not good' with heights. Some of my butterflies wet themselves in a nice warm flush.

"I'll give it a go," Pete said.

Claire swatted him. "No."

Pete turned to her. "What? Why?"

"'Cos, you're clumsy as fuck, bigfoot. That's why."

Now Pete made the 'pfft' noise.

"I think I can do it." Aaron was still tracing a path with his eyes. He pointed up. "See, if I can get to the bit there, I should be able to reach the ledge."

I had no idea what he was talking about, as it looked like sheer rock to me. Sheer, terrifying rock that, thank God, I wouldn't have to climb.

"Okay. I'll come too," Hassan said. "We might need two people to, like, get up places."

He pointed upwards, and my stupid eyes followed, causing my stomach to try to get up places all by itself.

It was decided that Aaron and Hassan would climb while Declan and I stayed below, in the bottom of the pipe. Wade, Pete, and Claire headed back down to the base-camp area. From there, they would have a better view of the upper reaches of the Pipe.

Declan and I would try to point out handholds for Aaron and Hassan if they got stuck lower down. The others would look further up if needed. Yeah, madness, I knew, but at least it gave us a feeling of being helpful. I expected they'd get nowhere fast and have to come back down.

Instead, I was surprised at how high they got and how quickly. Aaron went first and was soon well above my head, edging up a slanted split running through the rock like a knife slash. I focused above him, where his hands were searching for holds, and tried to keep control of my knees.

When I glanced back to the ground, I couldn't believe how far the kid had gotten. Then I peered up into the Pipe. It was only a fraction of the climb, and my insides made a queasy roil again. I bottled the wetness on my tongue and tried to be positive. They'd have a good chance if they could get to the place where the pipe tipped over and the slope shallowed.

Aaron had managed to get about thirty feet up when he stopped. He clung with one hand, the other fumbling over the rock, searching.

Then he slipped.

Chapter 18

Aaron skidded a couple of feet down, clutching madly to try and stop. His fingers clawed at the stone, scraping for purchase as he slithered.

He caught a toehold, and I gasped, relief flooding through me. He was okay, but this was too dangerous; maybe I should tell them to stop.

Before I could say a word, the rock Aaron's toe rested on broke away with a crack. A rattle of falling debris cascaded down as he slid again. Desperately flailing, he scraped at a fold on the cliff, but it was too late.

He smacked into Hassan and knocked him clean off the rock.

Something hit me as the kid fell; it might have been the side of his shoe. It slugged me across the cheekbone and tipped me sideways. Fire burst through my face.

Hassan hit the rock beside me with a wet thud and a sickening crack. Staggering to keep my balance, a sharp pain sliced through my cheek. Dizzying, stabbing disbelief washed over me as I looked down.

No, no, no.

Hassan was a broken mannequin. Declan was beside him in an instant. I collapsed down next to them and tried to think around the agony in my face. Declan's hands hovered over the kid's torso, afraid to touch him, and they made little patting movements in the air. A puddle of blood spread out around Hassan's head in a red halo. I could smell the sharp, repulsive tang in my nostrils. I stared at it in frozen dismay.

"Jesus, Jesus, come on." Declan's voice was a high-pitched tremble.

There was no response, no sound. He grabbed at Hassan's shirt, and shook him gently, tentatively. The kid groaned; eyelids fluttered. *Dear God.* My heart clogged my throat.

"Mum—" Barely a word, more of a sigh. Blood bubbled over his lips as they fell open and trailed out in a frothy gush.

Warmth seeped through the fabric at my knees before I noticed the pool of blood had reached them. Denial throttled me into silence. Rocking back onto my heels, I tried to avoid the encroaching red tide. A gust of air and a thud broke the silence as Aaron climbed down from the Pipe above us, jumped down the last few feet, and stumbled to lean over us.

"He's okay, isn't he?" Aaron's voice was a quaver of disbelief.

Declan turned anguished eyes to me. "Do something."

God, I wish I could.

Wade was suddenly beside us, panting from scrambling back up the rocks. "Oh no."

He folded himself down beside us, trying to avoid the red pool. There was too much blood, though; it was everywhere. Wade grasped Hassan's wrist.

Wade, Declan, and I were lined up beside Hassan's body, three not-so-wise men praying. Wade tried to find a pulse and failed.

I became aware of a choking, hiccupping noise behind us and turned to find Claire and Pete. Claire was hunched on the ground behind us, hands to her head. I wondered how she could see Hassan's body with the three of us crouched there. Then I understood: she was staring at the slick of blood spread out under our feet, dripping down the rock. Pete stood behind her with a hand over his mouth. He was the one making the noises.

"You stupid fuck." Declan pushed up to his feet. He was shaking, his face red. "This is your fault, you stupid—" He lashed out and shoved at Aaron where the kid stood, white-faced and unmoving.

Blood from Declan's hand smeared across Aaron's shoulder and up the side of his cheek. I wanted to collapse, sit backward onto my ass, and put my head in my hands like Claire, but I couldn't, as all around and beneath me was wet.

"It should have been you, you stupid bastard." Declan was shrill, hitting and slapping at Aaron, who stood there frozen and took it. "Stupid, *stupid*—"

Wade broke them up. He shoved Declan down the trail away from Hassan's body. Declan broke into great rending sobs.

I stood, managing to push up awkwardly without putting a hand on the ground. Aaron was still immobile, a graven image against the rock. Pete and Claire came hesitantly over to where I was. They looked down at Hassan's broken body as if to confirm he was dead, or was it to pay their respects? I didn't know. They tried not to step in the spreading blood, but there was no way to avoid it. A great wave of despair rolled over me.

"What are we gonna do?" Pete turned to me as if I'd know.

Shaking my head, I pointed back down towards the staging area, desperate to escape the overpowering smell of blood.

"We're just going to leave him here?" Claire's hands were clenched.

"What else can we do?" I could taste copper.

"We could ... we should cover him."

I didn't know what to say then, but Pete woke from his daze and struggled out of his filthy overshirt, pulling it off with shaking hands. He and Claire draped it over Hassan's face.

Aaron made an odd hiccupping noise as wetness instantly soaked through the material.

I grabbed him then and chivvied him into movement. Out of the pipe, away from his dead friend and the blood, which was almost black in the dusk, an oil slick across the rock. We left Hassan's body where it landed. There was nothing else we could do.

Somehow, we got our shit together and stumbled back down to where we'd left our packs, where Wade stood with a hand on Declan's shoulder. The kid sucked in gulps of air and wiped at his face before turning to us.

"Is he dead?" Declan choked out the words like he'd forgotten how to speak. His lips trembled, and I knew he'd only asked the question out of desperation.

"Yes. I'm sorry."

He crouched into a ball then, his face in his hands.

"Are we going to stay here for the night?" Wade asked, scanning Claire, Pete, and me. Aaron was vacant space.

"No!" It shot out of me.

The thought of being within earshot if scavengers came made my skin crawl. I fell silent, queasy at my thought processes. What was wrong with me?

"I think we should get going," Claire said.

"Yeah, let's go." Pete grabbed his pack. "There's no point staying here, as there's no way we can get up there anyway."

No one else said anything. We were leaving. I had to remind Aaron to grab his pack. His face was a blank page, but something must have seeped through because he reached for it. I put my pack on, then dragged Hassan's over to where Declan was slumped. He had none of his gear left, after all.

There was a brief hiatus as Declan refused to take Hassan's pack. "No, no." Shaking his head. "I don't want it."

"Don't be stupid. Take it." I shoved it at him.

"No!" he almost screamed.

Aaron stepped forward. "I'll carry it." I handed it to him, noting his pale, pasty face with its slight sheen of moisture. Not good.

We set off, found where we'd met the trail earlier, and left the track, back to scrambling over trailless, rocky terrain. I was numb inside like everything was fuzzy. I tried not to think about whether this was worse than Dan's death or Mel's. With Mel, we hadn't known what the hell was going on. Then ... Dan, that'd been a drawn-out torture. The sudden, brutal violence of Hassan's loss was like an ambush.

It was soon clear Aaron couldn't manage with two packs. With an odd sense of incredulity, I realized I was pissed at Declan for not carrying the pack, as if that was the problem here. I called a halt, wriggled out of my pack, then shoved it at Declan.

"Here, carry mine; it's light." I tried not to sound snippy, but I probably did because he took it without a word.

"Give it to me," I told Aaron and took Hassan's pack from him. I yanked it up and slid my arms through the straps. It was heavier than mine, way heavier. The weight of a life became startlingly clear. It was a wonder how Aaron managed to haul it along with his own. Then, we set off again.

We took a different path at some point, heading back around the rim to the pass trail. I didn't know if it was actually harder going, but it felt like it. Pete and Claire were in the lead, followed by Declan and Wade. Wade was trying to comfort Declan, as he wasn't doing too well. Aaron and I brought up the rear.

Aaron was quiet, pale, and putty colored. I'm pretty sure he was in shock, but I didn't have the bandwidth for it. I just tried to make sure he kept moving and didn't walk off any drops.

We'd fallen behind a bit, and it was almost full dark when a shout came from ahead. Relief washed over me, hoping it meant we were stopping for the night. The thought of dealing with anything else felt unbearable.

"Come on," I said to Aaron. "We're almost there."

I nudged him forward, and we finally caught up with the others. They'd found the pass trail again, close enough to where we'd left it. As I climbed down the last boulder, the group stood huddled and uneasy on the track.

Jumping down the final few feet, I glanced back to ensure Aaron was still with me. Ahead, the stocky figure of a heavily bearded man in dirty hiking gear stood on the path.

"Hi, I'm Bill," the man said.

I goggled at him, then leaned a little forward to see if there was anyone else with him.

"Um, hi," I said. "Are you by yourself?"

Aaron slipped, skidded, and fell down the rock beside me, landing in an awkward sprawl on the trail.

"Bollocks," he said from ground level, which effectively broke the ice.

It was good to have something new to focus on. Someone new. Even if it was a hairy guy who looked like Sasquatch. I squinted at him in the dim light. I don't know how long it'd been since this guy last had a haircut and a shave, but it had to be way before the meteor hit.

"Um, are you headed this way?" I asked, pointing up the trail, the etiquette for meeting complete strangers in the middle of a shitstorm temporarily abandoning me. "We're going to find somewhere to stop for the night."

Swiveling around, I searched the faces of the others, hoping for confirmation. In the dim light, I caught a few nods, a silent agreement that matched my exhaustion.

"Yeah, let's go." Claire's voice was flat, tired.

Bill smiled, his teeth gleamed yellow through his beard. "Mind if I tag along?"

I raised a shoulder. No one else said anything, and I guessed that meant Bill was joining us. We shuffled single file along the trail till we found an open space large enough for all of us to sit and lie down in.

By then, night had fully set in, making it pointless to continue. Besides, curiosity about Bill offered a welcome distraction from Hassan's fate. We all seemed eager to focus on something else, to pretend the tragedy hadn't occurred. I sure did. The loop of that horrible, cracking thud replayed endlessly in my mind.

By the time Aaron and I shuffled in, followed by the newcomer, everyone was already picking the best spots and flopping down. Aaron chose a spot as far from Declan as possible. I ended up next to Bill.

The man had barely wriggled out of his solid pack when Wade jumped in. "Are you here alone?"

Bill's beard twitched. I didn't think he was going to answer, then his head went down, and he fiddled with his pack straps. "Yeah."

Uh oh. "Did you start out by yourself?" I asked.

Bill focused on me for a second then his eyes slid away. "No."

Ah. I waited to hear more, but he said nothing. Okay, not a talker. I likely didn't want to hear whatever awful thing had happened to his companions. Trying to muster some understanding, I realized I was all out of sympathy; something terrible had probably happened, but I couldn't take any more.

Or maybe it was everything building up to swamp me. Hassan, Dan, Mel. What had happened to them was still so big, so raw, I couldn't fully grasp it, like I was standing too near a movie screen watching something giant and incomprehensible.

Dan, though, I couldn't escape the feel of his face under my hands, of thinking about how his body had been trying to claw its way out of the tent fabric. Strangely, I didn't think too much about Mel Taylor now.

Her death was from another world. It had happened 'before,' back when normal existed.

I rubbed my face and tried to get out of my head. The group was talking about the meteor and what was beneath us again. We talked about it a lot. When I tuned back in, Wade was asking Bill if he'd managed to get a look at whatever was below ground.

"No. Haven't seen much. Not clearly."

It was difficult to tell in the dark, but Bill's face twisted beneath his rampant facial pelt.

I needed a drink, but Declan had flopped over, using my pack as a pillow, and his eyes were closed. From the *glug* of Hassan's pack, I suspected there was a fullish bottle in there. Declan had refused his friend's belongings and Aaron was uninterested. Did it mean I inherited them?

My hands trembled as I unzipped Hassan's pack, fingers brushing against fabric and metal. My eyes burned at the reminder of what these items meant. Clothes still smelling faintly of his cologne, sealed snacks he'd never unwrap. I pulled out a water bottle, its surface cool and reassuring.

I sank to the ground, the bottle cradled in my lap. The night cloaked me in darkness, the knees of my trousers blending into the shadows like a pair of black voids. I stared at them, my mind slow to recall the reason before I remembered. I'd knelt in Hassan's blood. Fatigue weighed on me like an anchor, every muscle screaming for rest.

Beside me, Bill was digging through his things. He had a full pack and a lot of food, so maybe he hadn't been here very long.

"Where have you come from?" Wade asked. He was probably wondering the same thing. "I mean, where abouts were you when the meteor hit?"

"Over by the western campground." Bill took a long pull from his water bottle.

"Wow, that's a long way. You came all the way across the basin after it hit?"

"Yeah."

"It's such a lot of ground to cover, what with everything ... you know, the worms and everything. I'm just, well, how did you get right across there?"

"Just lucky, I guess." Bill took a big bite of an apple, crunching loudly in the night air.

"Huh. I mean, we only came from Harper's Meadow, and when we started, it was only worms, so I think we got up onto rock before things got ... bigger."

Wade's voice droned on, his words a desperate attempt to keep the looming dread at bay. I folded my lips, wishing for silence, but I knew he needed the noise to cope.

"But all the way from over there ... whoa." Wade shook his head.

Bill said nothing, taking another cracking chunk out of his apple.

"Were you waiting for us?" That was an odd question, but it occurred to me it was a bit of a coincidence he'd been right there on the trail.

Chapter 19

Bill crunched some more before speaking. "Yeah. I heard your voices, so I thought I'd wait and see if you were coming this way." It was the most he'd said since we sat down, so maybe he was human after all.

"Huh. Right." It made sense.

"Where were you folks coming from?" he asked.

The wet thud of Hassan's body ambushed my consciousness, a gruesome echo from the recent past. With a mental slam, I shoved the memory back into its dark corner, refusing to let it take root.

"We went to see if we could get up the Angel's Pipe climb." I waved a hand back the way we'd come. "We don't have any equipment though." I left it at that.

No one else said anything either.

"No, you won't get up Angel's without climbing gear. I did it a few years ago. Dante's is a possibility. Maybe," Bill said.

My spine snapped to attention, muscles tensed as if preparing for action. A quick glance revealed Pete mirroring the sudden alertness, his posture a carbon copy of heightened vigilance. "You're here climbing? Do you have equipment?"

"No, it was a while ago I used to climb, so I don't have any gear with me."

Well, shit.

"But you know how to climb, right?" Pete asked.

It was a good point. Having experience would surely be helpful. Someone who knew what they were doing. Maybe we'd have a chance after all. The tiniest bubble of hesitant hope bloomed in me. I'd been dreading trying to climb again, having someone else fall, having it be me.

"We're going to try Dante's Crag next," I said. At least, I assumed we were, as there hadn't been any discussion about it, but what else was there to do? I left out how we'd headed that way previously, then chickened out. "Can you tell us anything about the climb there?"

"Sure, I guess." Bill finished his apple and threw what was left into the darkness with a flick of his wrist.

A reflexive flinch rippled through my body, accompanied by a silent prayer for the apple core to find purchase on unyielding rock rather than vulnerable soil. Though bare earth seemed scarce at this elevation, the nagging possibility of exposed patches gnawed at the edges of certainty.

"Be easier for me to explain when we're there," Bill said. "If you don't mind me coming along?"

"Sure, yeah, of course." Someone who knew about rock climbing, who'd done the climb we needed to make? No way I was letting him out of my sight.

"I'll see you right," Bill said with an unexpected grin.

It was nice to have a tiny bit of reassurance. I fought for sleep, though, fought hard, swimming against a tide of blood spreading across rock.

Around about the thousandth time I opened my eyes, I found the sun had deigned to join me in my wakefulness. Or at least show it still existed behind the banks of cloud. I rubbed grit from sore eyes, taking in the bodies sprawled around me like shipwrecked flotsam.

"Morning."

"Ugh." I creaked around like a rusty weathervane, trying to locate the source of wisdom that was Bill. There he was, perched on his throne of gravel like some disheveled mountain guru.

My brain was taking its sweet time to boot up. Between the all-night insomnia party, dying of thirst, and oh yeah, watching people get munched like chips, my head felt like it was stuffed with cotton balls.

"You don't look too good."

Rich, coming from a guy whose face looked like a massive drain clog.

"Ugghh." I rubbed my eyes again. "I need coffee, is all. No chance of that."

"Ah. I don't drink coffee. Caffeine's not good for you, you know."

I narrowed my eyes at him. "Your ridiculous opinion has been noted."

Bill snorted laughter, then reached down for his pack. When he opened it, I couldn't help but notice how much food was in there. Like a *lot*. Bars, packets, sachets. Ration packs. He dug about a bit, pulled out a little tetra pack, and looked at the label.

"Heads up." He tossed the thing to me.

My hand shot out, snagging the airborne object. The corner of the carton dug into my palm, a small price to pay for potential caffeine salvation. Flipping it over, I squinted at the label. Iced coffee, thank the caffeinated gods. Some off-brand number I'd never seen before, probably concocted by forest elves or desperate hikers. Suddenly my eyes were doing their best Niagara Falls impression.

"You sure?" I croaked, trying to sound casual and failing miserably.

"All yours. I'm more of a wheatgrass kinda guy," Bill replied, his grin cutting through the facial wilderness like a machete through under-growth.

"Thanks." My brain was doing somersaults while my mouth just hung open like a broken garage door. Nothing said 'thank you' quite like gawping like a stunned fish.

Instead, I popped the little straw through the foil dot and sucked in heaven. Sweet coffee-flavored bliss fleetingly filled everything, and I closed my eyes to savor it.

It tasted like home, like safety, like normality. Just for a second, with a gulp of coffee, I time-traveled back to the real world. It was incredible that this could exist alongside such bizarre danger and unspeakable death.

I opened my eyes to find Bill smirking at me. His pack was still open between his knees. When he caught me looking, he stuffed a sweater in on top and quickly closed the flap. I wondered if he suspected I might ask him for something else, food, maybe or water. He needn't have worried; I was good. I had a warm glow of thankful well-being. I had coffee; cold, sweet, long-life-milk-tasting paradise.

Later, the others grudgingly returned to consciousness. It was possible my turbocharged slurp-fest, sucking every last drop up the little straw, might have been hard to sleep through.

We had our usual debate on what to do.

"Maybe we should stay here." Declan turned his face upwards, up the path to where the boys had been camped when we found them. Where Hassan had been alive.

Would he still be alive if he hadn't come with us?

"We could find water and come back. Like, wait here for someone to come." Declan's tone was lifeless.

"What the hell for?" Aaron said. "No one's coming."

I focused on him. He was still pasty and pale this morning. Honestly, I was finding it difficult to care about anyone but myself—bad, but there it was. It was better to be callous; that way, it wouldn't hurt as much when the next person died, fell off a cliff, or was eaten by... I blew out a coffee-flavored breath and tried to think of anything else.

Declan still thought we might be rescued, but Aaron disagreed. I tried to focus on this and considered it from a few angles.

"We don't know no one's coming," I said in answer to Aaron's comment. I did some rapid math in my head. Yeah, never my strong suit, even when not sleep deprived and living in constant fear of being eaten by—*Damn it.*

I frowned and tried again. "I mean. It's been four days. It'd probably take them a couple of days to realize something's wrong, right?"

Tired faces stared back, a collection of human wreckage held together by spite and desperation. Who was the real sucker here—them for buying it, or me for selling this load of bull? Either way, we all looked like we'd been run over by the exhaustion express.

"Then what, another day to get organized and get out here? Okay, then they find the pass is blocked, they have to go back and organize something else."

"It's been long enough then, hasn't it?" Aaron said. "Where's the bloody helicopter? Where's the rescue team?" His voice trembled.

"They may not send a helicopter," I said. Not entirely sure where I was going with this, I paused to think. Aaron was looking at me like a dog waiting for someone to throw its ball, but someone with a history of fake throwing, as his face bore disbelieving, expectant hope.

"They might send climbers?" I suggested. "Like a team of climbers. To find whoever's in here."

To my surprise, Wade nodded. "It'd be a lot cheaper," he said. "And they wouldn't know anything was wrong in here besides the trail being blocked."

Could it be? Maybe I wasn't the only one wondering where the hell our chopper-riding knights in shining armor had fucked off to. For once, my paranoid brain cells might be onto something legit.

"What if those shots we've been hearing are the Park Service, the rescue team?" Wade said.

My eyes locked onto him like he'd just announced he was secretly Batman. This half-baked theory lit up my brain like a Christmas tree, logic be damned. If those noises were our so-called rescuers, they were probably enjoying the same five-star apocalypse package we were. *But hey, misery loves company, right? Even if that company's just as royally screwed as we are.*

Beside me, Bill twitched. He leant across me and checked down the trail but didn't say anything.

"You alright?" I asked him. *Stupid question in our current circumstances, but everything's relative.*

"Yeah, I just want to get out of here," he said.

Didn't we all.

"So, what are we going to do?"

Pete's voice hit my ears like a ghost deciding to start a conversation. The guy had been doing a world-class mime impression ever since Hassan died. Hearing him pipe up now was like witnessing a statue suddenly ask for directions.

"I think we have to keep going; we'll be out of water in a day," Wade said. "How much does everyone have?"

"We could find some and come back here," Declan said, ignoring the question.

"What bloody for?" Aaron snapped at him, then slumped back down and pulled his sleeping bag over his head.

Moving on sounded like the best plan. Sitting around twiddling our thumbs was a recipe for disaster, with Declan and Aaron ready to fight at the drop of a hat. One more round of their bickering and I'd be tempted to introduce their skulls to each other, up close and personal. That might not win me any popularity contests with the rest of our ragtag bunch, but hey, sometimes you had to take one for the team. Whatever kept us from killing each other before the worms got a chance.

"Well?" Wade said, looking each of us in the eye in turn. "Who's got water?"

No one spoke. I guessed no one wanted to admit to what they had, as none of us wanted to share.

"I've got a bit less than a bottle," I said at last. And by that I meant the half bottle in my pack, which Declan may have already finished, not Hassan's bottles.

Eventually, everyone else chimed in, reluctantly confessing to what they had. Bottom-line, we didn't have much water. We were going to have to find some soon.

So, we set off, back the way we'd been before, but probably fifty feet higher up the slope than where we'd turned off last time. In the end, there'd been virtually no discussion on finding water and coming back. We'd all packed up and moved out, and Declan had to follow. He didn't say much either; he kind of huffed a bit and kept his distance from Aaron.

We had to zigzag up and down to find our way. There was no trail, so we wasted hours climbing only to find the way blocked and had to backtrack again and again. It was frustrating, but we had to keep on rock, where it was safe. I tried to take as few sips from Hassan's water bottle as possible, but my tongue felt like sandpaper.

Eventually, we worked out a system. One person would scout ahead to check if a route was workable. If it was, they'd call back, and the rest of us would follow. If it wasn't, they'd come back, and someone else would try a different way. It was painstaking, but it helped conserve energy, water, and tempers. We meant to take it in turns, but in the end, Bill ended up mostly doing it and said he preferred it. It was a stroke of luck running into him.

Early afternoon, we were propped and sprawled about, waiting to hear from Bill, who'd scrabbled up a straggling staircase of columnar basalt. I was looking at the steepish climb, vaguely hoping he'd come back and say it was a no-go, when Bill shouted, "Hey, Mike! Come and look."

I grumbled into movement, wondering why I was the one who had to climb up and see, but I owed him for the coffee, if not the scouting. I tried not to be annoyed, but if we couldn't get through, then we couldn't get through. *Don't make me climb up there.*

Wade followed me, as if he considered he ought to be consulted instead of me. That was a fair point; Wade knew more about hiking stuff than I did. He grinned at me, but I wondered if he was a bit piqued Bill had called my name, because he cut across in front of me and set a scrambling pace up the slope.

We found Bill outlined against the sky on a rocky pinnacle above us.

When we arrived below him, he scowled, his face flushed pink above his beard—plainly not a happy camper. I had to squash down annoyance again that we'd probably come up here only to be shown a dead end.

"You can get up over there." Bill pointed to where we could scramble up the side of his boulder.

Wade made it up first.

"Oh, no."

I followed in Wade's footsteps, saw what he was looking at, and then snorted at his carefully restrained language.

"Shit, we're fucked." This deserved swearing.

Below us ran a wide ribbon of weedy scrub that went all the way to the rim—a great peninsula of bare, stoneless ground running up to the cliffs above us. The tumbled rocks had blocked our view of it before, but now there it was in all its grassy, earthy, wormy assholery.

Even though Bill had found the narrowest point, it was still too wide to get across. The other side was tantalizingly close, but we'd had a lot of practice jumping between rocks by now, and I knew this was too far. Just the tiniest bit too far.

There was nowhere jumpable. I peered up the slope, with my heart in my boots. It would take hours to get up and around, maybe even a day.

"Well, come on, we have to tell the others." Wade blew out a gust of air and flapped his elbows, his thumbs hooked through his pack straps.

But Bill squatted at the stone's edge, looking across the gully. His head turned and his eyes flicked back and forth. What the hell? The guy was strong and agile, but there was no way he could make it across there. Was there?

Swiveling around, I gave the chasm in front of us another once-over. You know, just in case it had miraculously shrunk while we weren't looking. Spoiler alert: it hadn't. Still too wide for any sane person to consider jumping, unless they had a death wish or suddenly sprouted wings.

Hassan clinging to the cliff came flooding back. The memory hit like a sucker punch to the gut. That instant of seeing him fall, the sickening realization of what was about to happen ... No way in hell I was letting history repeat itself. Once was more than enough to drill home the lesson that some risks just weren't worth taking, no matter how desperate we got.

"What are you—?"

Bill raised a hand to cut me short. "I'm trying to work something out," he said. "I have to get it just right."

I checked again. Get what, right? There was nowhere to cross. What the hell was he doing? I raised my eyebrows at Wade, who rolled his eyes back.

"What's going on?" Claire called from below us.

Bill twitched at her voice, and I had an urge to grab him and drag him away from the edge. He was okay, though, so I leaned over to see the others had caught us up, probably gotten bored of waiting. It wasn't very nice when you didn't know what was going on, where the path led, whether there was even a path.

"Don't move." Bill's voice was hard and blank, expressionless.

"What?" I turned back.

There was a gun in his hand.

A jolt crisped through me, frying my nerves; the end of the barrel was an icy black dot. Look, I was about as far from a gun aficionado as you could get. Sure, I'd seen 'em in movies, and there was that one time as a kid when my buddy's dad thought it'd be a great idea to let us play junior Rambo at the range.

But ask me to identify the piece Bill was holding? You might as well ask me to recite pi to a hundred digits. Handgun, check. Beyond that? Your guess was as good as mine. Could've been anything from a peashooter to a hand cannon for all I knew. All I could focus on was the sudden dryness in my mouth and the way my tongue felt like it was trying to glue itself to my teeth. Funny how staring down a barrel could make you hyper-aware of the weirdest things.

"You." Bill waved the weapon. Was he pointing to me?

"Whoa, now." Wade stepped forward; hands raised in the universal 'calm down' gesture. Wade knew about guns and had one at home, and maybe that was why he stepped forward. I didn't know.

"You'll do," said Bill.

He *had* been pointing at me then. What the hell? He waved me away now, and I backed up a couple of steps, not all the way. I didn't know what I could do, but I didn't want to get too far away from Wade.

"Take your pack off," Bill said to Wade.

My forehead was apparently trying to fold in on itself, and the resulting headache was making its presence known. What was this guy's deal, anyway? He could have whatever he wanted if he'd just leave us alone. But no, he kept eyeing Wade's pack like it held the secrets of the universe.

If he thought he could use it as some kind of magic bridge, he was in for a nasty surprise. Last I checked, backpacks weren't exactly designed for crossing monster-infested ravines.

"Here, take it," Wade said, echoing my thoughts. He grappled his pack off and held it extended.

Bill shot him.

Chapter 20

B LAM. The sound engulfed the world. For a heartbeat, nothing else existed but that explosive roar. Then, with a whiff of cordite, I was suddenly a kid again, back at that shooting range twenty years ago. Just for a split second, I was somewhere safe, somewhere this cataclysm couldn't touch. Frantic disbelief poured in, drowning out everything else. This couldn't be happening. But it was. Real life came crashing back like a tidal wave of ice water.

Wade spun towards me, and there was an obscene little hole in the front of his T-shirt. Red bloomed, blotting it out.

Wade looked down, gasped, then met my shocked gaze. "Fuck," he said.

He folded, almost gently, to his knees. His arms flopped, lifeless, beside him like a broken puppet. He was dead before he fell forward onto his face.

The world tilted on its axis, warping around me. My limbs were made of lead, yet somehow weightless at the same time. Blood rushed in my ears, drowning out everything but the echo of that gunshot.

Without conscious thought, my body lurched forward. One step towards where Wade had fallen, then another. It wasn't a decision, just pure instinct driving me towards the impossible scene unfolding before me.

"No you don't." Bill pointed the gun at me again, and I froze. My heart was full of disbelief. "Back up." He waved the gun, and I complied. I was numb. My head was stuffed with cotton wool. Wade was dead. Dead. My brain kept refusing to believe it; it wasn't possible. All I could see was the hypnotic black dot of the gun's barrel.

Bill gestured with the weapon again. I caught a gasp from behind me as Claire appeared. We both flinched as Bill pointed to each of us in turn.

"Stay back." He reached down then and grabbed Wade's body by the back of his belt.

I boggled at him. Was he going to try to help Wade now? The bastard had shot him, killed him. Instead, Bill dragged Wade's corpse to the edge of the rock. He turned the weapon back on us like he was going to shoot me. My ears thudded with my pulse.

Then Bill reached down, still training the gun on us, and shoved Wade over the edge of the rock and onto the ground below. The body tumbled down to the lowest point, rolling like a bag of laundry. I couldn't believe the bundle of limbs was my friend, had been my friend.

Bill launched himself out across the gap with almost balletic grace. He landed on Wade's body briefly, then rebounded up the other side.

My lips gaped open, but no air came to my lungs, as if a violent wind had snatched it from my mouth.

Almost the exact second Bill's foot left Wade's back, something sliced up from below, in a violent spray of dirt. It had to be big, but my eyes were full of dirt. I flinched as another vast spray flew upwards. Behind me, Claire squeaked. I spat dirt, tried not to think of worms, and swiped at my eyes. Wade's body was gone. Wade was gone.

Bill was gone too, disappeared among the tumbled boulders on the other side of the gap.

With badly coordinated steps, I stumbled right to the edge of the rock for a closer look. I had to know. If I looked, Wade would be there. He would be alright, and I'd reach down and grab him, pull him up.

Another wave of dirt sprayed from below. My hand came up automatically to protect my eyes as soil spattered my body, hitting like hail. Then, it was quiet. I peered over the edge, my heart a melted mess inside me. The surface between the rocks bubbled obscenely, heaved, and then sank down to leave a hollow.

There was nothing there.

Claire stepped cautiously to the edge beside me. She, too, knelt to see down into the gully, then up across the rocks on the other side, as if Wade might have somehow followed Bill up there. "Fucking hell."

Pete, Declan, and Aaron crowded onto the rocky promontory behind us.

"What happened?"

"Where's Wade? Where's Bill?"

"What's going on?"

Words failed me, trapped behind a wall of denial. Speaking would shatter this fragile illusion, force me to confront a fact too brutal to face. My body moved on autopilot, turning away, legs carrying me through the group as they huddled at the edge, peering into the gully below. Each step felt like wading through molasses, the world moving in slow motion around me.

"What happened, mate?" Pete reached out to me, but I shook my head. I scrambled back down the way we'd climbed up and collapsed onto flat stone below.

My friend had been murdered, and his body taken by whatever foul obscenity was beneath us, and yet stupid things kept going through my head. Like, we came here in Wade's car. It was his car out in the Park

Service's lot, and the keys were in his pocket when whatever it was pulled him into the ground. What the actual fuck was wrong with me?

My hands clamped over my ears, a futile barrier against Claire's voice. Her words seeped through anyway, each syllable a dagger as she recounted the nightmare we'd just lived through. Bill's name cut sharper than the rest, a reminder of betrayal layered on top of tragedy. I wanted to drown it all out and rewind time. But the truth kept hammering away, relentless and merciless.

"Bloody tip rat," Pete said, so loud I registered it through my hands.

Desperate for silence, I jammed a fingertip into each ear, pressing hard enough to hurt. The rest of my hands curled into fists, clamping down over my ears like makeshift earmuffs. The world muffled, but not enough. Words still filtered through, distorted but unmistakable, each one a reminder of the horror we couldn't escape.

No, no, no.

We retreated down the slope until we found a place further away from the gully. The others guided me and treated me like I was made of glass, but I barely noticed. Shock, I guessed, that, and my mind kept repeating what had happened.

Reviewing the events in my mind as if watching a movie, I beat myself up for doing nothing. I was a fucking idiot. Why hadn't I done something? At each step of the movie, I thought, if only I'd stepped in then, if I'd done something there, I could have stopped it. Wade would still be alive, but instead, I'd done nothing, nothing.

It hit me like a landslide at one point: this was how Aaron and Declan had felt yesterday. I thought I knew how they felt. I'd been shocked and horrified by Hassan's death, too, but it wasn't the same. It wasn't anywhere near the same as when it was your friend, someone you'd known forever. It wasn't the same. I sobbed a bit then. I wanted to bawl like a kid.

Eventually, I became aware of a squabble among the others. I tried to focus on that instead of seeing Wade's face repeatedly, how he'd looked down at his wound then back up to me. It was the first and only time I'd ever heard him swear.

Pete was up on the steep, slanting rock between us and the gully, arguing with Claire. Aaron was sitting, his arms wrapped around his knees, his face blank, but Declan joined in the discussion occasionally.

It felt like I was listening to them from the end of a long tunnel. I stared at Pete and tried to understand what was going on. Tried to focus on him, on this, to think about anything but Wade.

"Hey," Pete said when he noticed me looking up at him. "There's a dead tree down there."

Following his gesture, my eyes traced down the slope to the gully's edge. There, jutting from the surface like skeletal fingers, stood a cluster of dead branches. They were remnants of something larger, their surfaces bleached and scored by time and weather into ashen streaks. The stark, lifeless forms stood in eerie contrast to the surrounding landscape.

"So?"

The world felt distant, unreal. My thoughts swam through a fog of shock and regret. Why had I frozen? Why hadn't I stopped Wade from stepping forward? Bill's call echoed in my memory—he'd wanted me up there with him. The weight of 'what ifs' pressed down, each possibility a new twist of the knife.

Pete frowned at me. "If we can get it and get some branches and stuff, we can make a fire."

"It's too dangerous," Claire said.

"I reckon I can reach it," Pete said.

Declan's head came up then. "Yeah, Aaron reckoned he could reach stuff too." His tone was harsh.

"Shut up. Bloody shut up." Aaron came out of his hunched coma. He sounded manic, like he was barely holding it together. A flicker of empathy cut through the haze. The guy was barely holding it together, a feeling I knew all too well. My grip on sanity felt about as secure as a house of cards in a hurricane. Thank whatever gods were left that Declan finally got the memo and clamped his gob shut.

"Okay, okay, everyone calm down." Pete raised his hands in benediction. "I think we'll all feel better for a fire and something hot to eat."

Claire threw up her hands and shook her head at him. Pete jumped down out of sight, heading toward the tree. I was surprised when Declan hauled himself up to follow. At first, I didn't pay much attention, as I was still frozen. Disbelief fought with guilt in my head; this wasn't real. None of this was real. Bill had chosen me to be his stepping stone.

Then a stick hit me on the head. It hurt. *What the hell?*

"Hey, watch it." Without a second thought, my hand snatched the stick. In one fluid motion, fueled by a surge of pent-up frustration, I hurled it back towards Pete and Declan. The action was pure instinct, raw and unfiltered. A fleeting sense of satisfaction coursed through me as the stick sailed through the air, a physical manifestation of all the words I couldn't say.

"Oy, dickhead!" Pete bellowed back. "We're trying to collect that shit."

Oh, yeah, right. I stood up to see properly. The dead tree was lying, gawkily twisted, out in the gully. Pete must have jumped to it from some low protruding rocks, and he was snapping wood off and chucking it back toward us.

Claire had climbed over to help collect the twigs and sticks he was throwing. She and Declan had a small pile, but Pete threw at an awkward angle. Dead kindling was going everywhere.

"Don't throw so hard," Claire called, missing a catch. "They're going down between the rocks, and I can't get them."

"If I don't chuck them hard enough, they bounce off and end up in the gully." Pete paused in thought. "Tell you what, chuck us my pack."

"What?" Claire frowned. "Oh right, hang on." She turned and climbed back up.

"Empty it first!" Pete yelled.

Claire paused to roll her eyes at me dramatically before calling back to him, "Well, durr!"

She wrenched open Pete's pack and then upended it. A great rain of dirty clothes, food packets, and camping equipment rattled out.

"Hey, careful, woman," Pete called over the gap at the sound of everything being roughly disgorged. "Mind the valuables."

"What, your crusty derps?" Claire shot in return. She turned the empty pack upside down with a flounce and patted at the larger pockets.

"Come on, that'll do. I'm not here to fuck spiders." Pete waved her back.

I guessed they understood each other. Sometimes I had no idea what they were talking about.

Claire, Declan, and I went closer, stood at the edge of the rock, and watched as Pete broke up branches and twigs and stuffed them into the pack. It worked pretty well, although there was a bad moment when he hauled it up to thread his arms through the straps. He wobbled precariously for a breath-catching second.

He was going to fall into the gully. That woke me up all right, sending a sharp spike of fright through me. Pete caught his balance and then grinned at us. I let the air out of my lungs and watched him climb carefully back toward us.

Then he slipped, dropped with a thump, and the ground exploded.

Chapter 21

It was so fast my brain didn't process what'd happened. Pete's leg vanished into the ground, into the spray of dirt. One moment, he was there; the next, he was down, like he'd stepped out into the air. He was whipped away in a second.

His body jarred to a stop. One leg had disappeared, and the other was skewed, crumpled above, and he was stuck, his pack wedged between the outcrop of rock and the hump of a small boulder.

Pete's scream was closer to a roar. It was a harrowing sound, worse than anything that'd come out of Mel Taylor's mouth on the horrendous night of never-ending screams.

We lunged forward, grabbed at him and pulled. I had a hand in the strapping of his pack and hauled as hard as I could. Beside me, Declan and Claire knocked into each other as they grasped at Pete. Claire caught at his pack as well. Declan managed to get a hold under his arm. Wood and sticks had fallen everywhere.

It'd happened so fast. We all pulled, collapsing back onto the stone slope in a tangle. Pete's lips parted soundlessly, and his gaze slid sideways.

Then it hit me: blood, literally, a spraying wall of blood. His leg was gone from the hip. Everything got a bit weird in my head then. Human bodies didn't look like that; whole legs didn't disappear, and they didn't spurt great gouts of blood. Under my hands, Pete shuddered.

"Pull, get—" I didn't know what I was saying. My voice was drowned by a great howl from Pete. Declan had leaned over and was pushing his hands to where Pete's leg had been, trying to push down and put pressure on it. Everything was bloody, red, and warm against my skin, horribly warm.

A sudden jerk on Pete's body snapped my attention downward. The ground spewed another spray of soil, and something emerged from beneath. My brain struggled to process the sight; eyes fixed on the impossibility unfolding before me. Time stretched, and the universe deformed, as I gawked at the ... thing ... now visible. A clump of mud hit my face, and my idiot brain informed me this was bad, that we shouldn't let dirt get into Pete's wound.

Then he was gone. The sheer strength of what grabbed him was overwhelming. He was torn from our hands, slipping through my fingers like water. I had an image of his face stuck in my head, eyes and mouth round gaping circles, but he was gone. A flare of dirt, grassy clods, and pebbles rained onto us, onto the swathe of blood left behind on the stone. Pete disappeared.

At the foot of the rock where it'd happened was a collapsed hollow. There was blood everywhere, pooling in the dirt and smearing across the stone, but no Pete.

Beside me, Claire was making strange choking noises, as if she couldn't pull in oxygen. I stared stupidly at my empty, shaking hands, unable to process the force that had ripped him away. The power of it was unbelievable.

"Get up here." Aaron was pulling at me, shaking Claire. "Get, get—"

Adrenaline finally kicked in, coaxing a few precious feet of movement up the gully's slope. Aaron focused on Claire, while Declan had already clawed his way to higher ground. Flopping onto my front, I felt a sudden surge as my previously unresponsive limbs sprang to life. Instinct took over, hands and feet finding purchase on the rough stone as I scrabbled upwards, mind blank save for the primal urge to escape.

Exhaustion hit like a tidal wave, and I crumpled against the unyielding stone. The rough surface bit into my cheek, grit and gravel scraping skin raw. I pressed harder, welcoming the physical pain as a distraction from the anarchy in my head. Each shallow breath came faster than the last, barely keeping pace with my racing heart. Somewhere in the background, voices rose in a cacophony of panic and confusion, but the words blurred into meaningless noise.

Pete was gone, dead. No one could survive that. Over and over, I felt him torn from my hands, saw the flash of his face, shocked mouth and eyes. I saw what had taken him.

Someone grabbed me, pulled me further up the rock, and I tried, automatically, to help. To get as far away as I could from what had happened, from what else I'd seen.

Because what took him was the other thing seared behind my eyelids, the other thing that flicked behind my eyes again and again.

My surroundings swam back into focus as I struggled to sit up. My body rebelled, trembling like a leaf on the wind, but somehow, I managed to drag myself upright. My legs sprawled awkwardly down the rock face, refusing to cooperate fully. As the world steadied, I realized we'd climbed higher than I'd thought. The dreaded edge now lurked further below, a small mercy in this dystopia.

Beside me, Declan had his head in red hands. "Shit-shit-shit-shit-shit—"

"Shut up." Words croaked out, but they were lost in the turmoil. Not that it mattered—it wasn't him I needed to silence.

A God-awful howling pierced through everything, relentless and raw. My hands clamped over my ears in a futile attempt to block it out. Claire, of course. It had to be Claire. Curling into myself, I pressed my eye sockets against my knees, trying to shut out the world and the horrific sounds filling it.

A desperate longing for normalcy washed over me. Yearning for a world where the biggest worry was whether Starbucks had run out of my favorite Danish. Where 'adventure' meant trying a new takeout place while settling in for a night of gaming. Where the most annoying thing was the inconsiderate upstairs neighbor stomping around at all hours.

Those mundane times now seemed like a distant paradise, something I ached to reclaim. This couldn't be real. It just couldn't be. Hunched over, I lost all sense of time as existence and nightmare blurred into one. Each fragment of thought stretched endlessly, even as every sensation screamed otherwise.

Declan snapped out of it first. He dug out his water and swigged, then came and collapsed beside me, giving me a nudge.

"Here," he said.

He was offering a drink, and it occurred to me that my tongue was bone dry. My hand froze midway to the water bottle, the sight of dried blood caking my skin jolting me back into focus. Wet crimson still lurked beneath my nails, a grisly reminder I couldn't shake. I glanced at Declan, only to find his hands equally stained with gruesome evidence.

"Here," he said again, pushing the water at me.

I guzzled and finished it. "Shit, sorry..." The bottle shook in my grip, a feeble rattle confirming its emptiness. The hollow sound seemed to mock our predicament, echoing the void of hope we faced.

"It's alright, it was yours anyway." Declan took the empty container back, but his hand was shaking too.

The question burned on the tip of my tongue, begging to be asked. Had he witnessed the same impossible thing? Part of me yearned for him to dismiss it, to tell me I was losing my mind, that what I'd seen was a hallucination. But fear sealed my lips shut. The possibility that he might confirm it, that he'd seen it too, was too terrifying to face.

After a while, it was quiet. I twisted around to look for Claire. She was sitting further up, swathed in someone's sleeping bag. Maybe hers, maybe Aaron's. She was shivering, her face a blank, white mask, eyes open but looking at nothing. Shock, I assumed. I hoped it was. I hoped shock had cradled her mind in soft pink cotton candy and she wasn't here with us. Aaron sat beside her, looking helpless, hopeless.

After eons, he broke the silence. "Nameless things," he said.

My head whipped around. What the hell was he talking about?

Aaron's voice was shaky, and I thought he was rambling, babbling. Then he went on, "In Tolkien," he said. "Nameless things. In the dark, under the ground, there are nameless things that gnaw on shit. Worse than Sauron, worse than all the—"

"Shut up." Declan flailed at Aaron. He looked like he was on his last nerve. "I swear to God, if you don't shut up with that Witcher shit, I will come over there and—"

"What?" Aaron's face went red; he got so angry so fast. "Are you serious?" He staggered to his feet, enraged. "Are you taking the mick? Are you so fucking stupid..."

Aaron's lips worked, and he loomed, fists clenched, forming words I could barely hear till he found his voice again. "Fucking Witcher?" He was spitting, his face contorted and red. "Lord of the Rings, you fucking Muppet." He launched himself at Declan. Battering at him. "You stupid—"

"Get off—" Declan smacked back, defending himself, and they wrestled and whacked at each other.

I sat and watched them dazedly until I realized I was waiting for Wade to break them up. He was always the peacemaker. Eventually, I hauled myself up and separated the pair, mainly by plonking myself between them. I couldn't be bothered doing anything else.

Things quietened down, and I pushed Aaron back up the slope, indicating he should sit with Claire. After he'd flung himself down, I saw it may not have been the best idea, as he was covered in Pete's blood. But we were all covered in Pete's blood.

Claire began to rock backwards and forwards ever so slightly. There was a splash of dried blood across the left side of her face. I hoped wherever she was, it was nice. I hoped there were fucking rainbows and unicorns.

"What are we going to do?" Aaron looked at me like I'd know.

Anger welled through me. If I had a dollar for every time someone had asked that stupid question since all this began—

"What are we going to do?" I spat. "We're going to get the hell out of here. That's what we're going to do." I was probably as red in the face as Aaron had been before, but I didn't care. I was so furious.

He looked at me. "I meant, do we go back to the pass and wait, or do we keep going?" He looked at Declan and then back at Claire. No one had any answers.

The anger slipped out of me as quickly as it had built. What the hell were we going to do? Wade was dead, Pete was dead.

Would it be better if we got moving? Would I feel better and stop thinking about what had come out of the ground? Stop thinking about what else might be down there? I closed my eyes and saw it again and again. It wouldn't work. Nothing would blot it out. I opened my eyes and looked at Aaron.

"Did you see it?" I asked.

"See what?" He shot back.

How could he be so calm? "Don't give me that. You know. You must have seen it."

Aaron looked down, quietly saying, "I don't know what I saw."

"Horseshit." No way, I wasn't having it. I found myself shaking my head back and forth and forced myself to stop.

Aaron's eyes swam, pleadingly. "It could've been anything—"

"It could've been," I said with a sneer, "but it wasn't."

There was silence before Declan said, "I saw it." He ignored Aaron and focused on me. "I saw the hand."

Chapter 22

Each slow, empty second confirmed the unthinkable. The grotesque scene wasn't a trick of the mind or a stress-induced hallucination. That ... thing ... had been witnessed by others. My lungs rebelled, refusing to fill as the enormity of our situation bore down, reshaping the world into something unrecognizable and terrifying.

"What the hell is going on?" Declan whispered.

It had been a human hand. The thing that'd come out of the ground and grabbed Pete's remaining leg and torn him from us. I knew what a damn hand looked like. A filthy, dirty starfish of dead, grey flesh, the nails encrusted with muck. I saw it again and again, the odd, rippling movement, each finger moving independently with no relation to the other as if something inside was pulsing, wearing the hand like a glove, frayed at the fingertips.

It was a small thing to have such power, such force. That hand had ripped Pete away from the three of us as if we were nothing as if our joint strength didn't exist.

I could feel fiery acid in my mouth, because it wasn't even the worst thing. I rubbed at my eyes, pressing till there were stars. I wished Aaron was right. I wished it was a 'nameless thing' that had taken Pete from us because it wasn't. Because I knew exactly what it was. I even knew its name.

"It was Dan," I said. I had to make myself say it, form the words consciously before forcing them out.

"What?" Blank faces from everyone.

"It was Dan's hand," I said it louder, with emphasis, as if it would help. I found I was shaking again. Trembling. "Okay? It was Dan Taylor's hand. The man we met down at the campground, the one who ... died."

Declan's lips opened and closed a couple of times. "That's impossible."

"I know what I saw." I had a horrible urge to laugh but squashed it down.

"No. He's dead. We killed him." Claire's eyes were on me, unblinking. Shit. I didn't know she was even listening.

"I'm sorry, but it was him." Or his hand, at least. The frayed bits at the fingertips hadn't been hand; they were something else, they were worms.

"Wait." Declan scrambled around to goggle at me. "You killed someone?"

Exhaustion crashed over me like a tidal wave, seeping into every fiber of my being. My bones were leaden, dragging me down with their impossible weight. The urge to surrender to oblivion tugged at my consciousness, promising a temporary escape. Nonexistence seemed like a mercy—a respite from the horrors that refused to fade.

"We had to do it. He was ... We couldn't let him suffer. They were in him; they were eating him. He..." God, how did you explain it to someone who wasn't there? I shook my head.

Declan was still gawping at me like I was Hannibal Lecter. "A person? You killed a person?"

I had the fleeting, now-irrelevant thought that I'd been right. If we ever got out of here, we would have a hell of a time explaining what we'd done to Dan, making people understand.

"We had to." It was all I could say.

"But what if—"

"There was no fucking 'what if,' okay? We had to do it!" I yelled at him. "You weren't there, you don't know."

There was a brief silence after this, and then, to my surprise, Claire raised a palm towards Declan as if to quiet him, then turned back to me. She was pale, her face oddly immobile.

"Calm down," she said. "It wasn't Dan, okay? How could it be? That's crazy."

"Yeah, that's crazy," Declan echoed her.

If I hadn't been so tired, I'd have leaped across and punched him, as Aaron had done earlier. Instead, I closed my eyes.

"Okay, whatever it was, looked like a hand. I get it, I saw it." Claire's words hung in the air, their purpose unclear. Was she trying to bolster her fragile grip on hope, or attempting to distract us all from the raw wound of Pete's absence? Her voice seemed to dance around the edges of our shared grief, desperately seeking any topic that didn't lead back to the horror we'd witnessed. "But what if it's what they ... if it's what the worms grow into—"

"It had his ring on, okay?" I sat up with a jerk. The need to silence her, to silence everyone, welled up like a tidal wave. "Dan's stupid pinky ring," I blurted out, the words catching on a sob that tore free. The absurdity of the statement hung in the air, a testament to the fragile thread of sanity we were all clinging to.

A band encircled the smallest finger, its crevices packed with grime. Despite the layers of muck, there was no mistaking Dan's garish ring. Beneath the filthy camouflage, hints of the eagle wings had still caught the light, a perverse beacon of recognition in this tragedy.

Claire fell silent again. After a while, I didn't even know if she was still there with us, mentally. I tried to think. Dan was dead; we knew it. Then I thought of his wife, and it took me a little while before I realized what had triggered the memory of Mel. Her body, heaving from the weight of worms inside, feasting.

It helped not to think about Pete and Wade.

More memories of Mel's corpse surfaced unbidden—those unnatural twitches and movements playing on repeat in the theater of my mind. Each jerky motion etched itself deeper, a macabre dance that defied death's stillness.

Dan's body had done the same. The night after we ... After he died, the movements in his dead body had almost driven me insane. I'd thought it was because he was being consumed from inside, but what if it was something else?

Or something more? What if eating wasn't *all* they did?

What the hell were these things?

"What if the worms can... use the bodies?" Everyone looked at me blankly, like I spoke a different language. They hadn't been privy to my internal thought processes.

I turned to Claire. "You remember how Mel's body moved?"

She frowned at me. "Dan's wife? Those twitches and spasms? Like ... like Dan?"

"And Malik," Aaron said. His eyes locked onto mine, wide with dawning comprehension. The color drained from his face, leaving it as pale as sun-bleached bone. A silent current of dread flowed between us, understanding passing without a word.

"What if the worms are able, somehow, to use the bodies. Like when they're in them. Coordinate somehow, to move?" Words tumbled out as my mind raced, grasping at logic to make sense of the insensible.

This verbal puzzle-solving had become a lifeline, a flimsy barrier against the crushing weight of Pete's death. But as the implications of my words sank in, realization hit like a knuckle sandwich. A cold sweat broke out across my skin, the world tilting sideways as the full magnitude of what I was suggesting became clear.

"That's insane." Declan's voice was a whisper, but from his face, he understood.

My head swayed in a disbelieving shake, a futile gesture against the impossible. The insanity of it all screamed in every fiber of my being. Of course it was madness—pure, unadulterated lunacy. But the cold, hard facts stared back, unflinching. Sometimes, what was real defied reason, and sanity became a luxury we couldn't afford.

"Tell me something about all this that isn't insane?"

"Wait, so you're telling me they're ... those things, worms, are using dead bodies?" Declan's face was contorted, the ends of his mouth pulled down. "Using human bodies like puppets? To what? To grab things?"

Thoughts scattered like splinters in a hurricane, each attempt to grasp them more futile than the last. My mind's eye kept betraying logic, flashing unwanted glimpses of Pete's face. These jarring snippets of memory threatened to derail any semblance of clear reasoning, turning the simple act of thinking into a grueling obstacle course.

"I don't think it's only human bodies," I said, turning to Claire. "Remember the bird? We all thought it was a bird ..." The words died as the world suddenly constricted. My chest tightened like a vise, each heartbeat a thunderous roar in my ears. The edges of my vision blurred as reality warped and twisted.

Fragments of memory surfaced unbidden—that fleeting glimpse of a claw during our misguided rock-throwing escapade, the hidden marks beneath Declan's trouser leg. In a bizarre tangent, thoughts wandered to the evolutionary marvel of opposable thumbs. It was my mind's desperate attempt to rationalize, perhaps. A grim realization settled: Declan's brush with the unknown had been a near miss, a twisted stroke of fortune in our increasingly treacherous world. On the faces of the others, my blank horror and incredulity was reflected back at me.

"I fucking told you." Aaron's face was chalky, and he was shaking. "I fucking told you. Malik ... Malik's body was trying to dig in the ground, and you didn't fucking believe me." He thumped his fist, hard against the rock. "You didn't fucking believe—" He sobbed.

Oh God. Aaron *had* said that. When he'd told us about their friend Malik dying, about Malik's body. He'd told us and I'd ignored him. The connection blazed into focus—those eerie twitches mirrored in Mel, Dan, and now this.

A chilling certainty settled in my gut as each piece of the horrific puzzle clicked into place. I'd thought I'd reached the limit of what I could handle, but a new level of terror opened up before me. My mind reeled, desperately searching for any alternative explanation, any shred of normalcy to cling to in this twisted version of life.

"I don't get it. If they could ... do that." Declan was white too, washed out and staring. "Why would they want to get in the ground, why not ..." He paused and made walking motions with a couple of fingers. "Like above ground?" He stopped and looked like he was about to vomit.

My head jerked in a helpless gesture, knowledge slipping through my mental fingers like sand. "Maybe they need the solid pressure to push against?" More gagging threatened.

"How many hikers do you think were in the park when it happened?" Aaron said suddenly. He turned to Claire and me, like we'd know.

A sharp inhale cut through the silence, my lungs suddenly remembering their job. The rush of air was a reflexive attempt to ground myself. "The whole park? Maybe thirty, forty? Who knows, probably would've been more, but the weather wasn't great."

"It's not just people though, is it?" Declan still looked shaky. "There's, like, animals and shit, too, right?" He rubbed his leg with slow repetitive movements.

I closed my eyes for respite. Declan was right, there were animals and shit too. Many, many times more of them than hikers, some of them big, some of them with claws. Could worms use claws? I opened my eyes. What the hell was I thinking? Had I actually gone bat-shit crazy?

"Do you think we're safe here?" Declan went on, unaware I was losing my mind. For all I knew we were all losing our minds.

"I mean, what if they get out of the ground, like, climb up—" He stopped abruptly.

We all considered this.

Aaron shook his head. "I think if they could, they would have already."

Claire gave a great gasp then and sobbed. We all shut up.

The light faded, shadows creeping across the stone where I laid, my mind a battleground of unwanted thoughts. Pete's face kept swimming into focus, followed by the phantom sensation of his body being wrenched away. Wade's absence loomed large in the gathering darkness.

Aaron's words about Malik's body echoed in my head, a cruel game of 'what if.' But even if we'd believed him, would it have made a difference? The leap to swimming subterranean corpses to ... whatever this was ... it was too vast, too absurd. My brain kept skittering away from the implications, unable to fully grasp the full nature of our situation.

The bizarreness of it all formed a barrier, a last line of defense against complete understanding. Maybe that was a mercy.

In the end, we made a fire with the wood Pete had managed to pass across before ... well before. At first, I'd been appalled at the idea, but Pete had died for those damn sticks.

Aaron indicated I'd lost my mind. "Are you taking the mick?" he said savagely, and I wondered briefly if he was about to come over and start thumping me like he'd done to Declan. He was right, it was stupid, I was ... *I don't know*. I sighed, and he went back to making a little heap of the wood. There wasn't a lot, not a lot to show for a life.

The fire lasted a while, longer than I expected. Aaron, Declan, and I heated bits and pieces. Claire lay on her sleeping bag with her face turned to the darkness.

I should have made her eat something. You'd be amazed how comforting hot ramen can be when you've had nothing warm for days. The noodle of choice when your companions were killed in appalling ways. I made coffee too—what the hell, the world had gone mad anyway.

And I had Wade's water bottles now.

Morning dawned clear after a cold, wretched night. I didn't feel like I'd slept at all when I woke, but I must have. I'd dreamt of water. Cold, clear spring water running over my hands, washing the blood away. Asleep, I'd thirsted for the water, yearned for it but couldn't drink it, as it was full of blood.

Everyone else was still sleeping, so I freed myself from the pile of clothing that now served as my blanket and got up as quietly as I could. I frowned at the others with rampant envy. Oh, to be asleep, unconscious, unaware.

I made my way back over to the edge of the gully and looked down at it. Then I watered it, relieved the place Pete died was out of sight on the other side of a boulder.

Going to the gully wasn't morbid curiosity; I wanted to know how far up it extended, what it looked like where it met the bottom of the rim. We'd have to climb up and around there when the others woke.

The sunrise over the basin was beautiful. From up here, I could see right out across the park. It was still stunning, the trees a thousand shades of green, the lake a little patch of bluish slate. This living hell was gorgeous.

A flicker of movement caught the corner of my eye, triggering an instinctive flinch. But instead of the terrors I'd come to expect, a small rabbit materialized, as if conjured from a more innocent world. The creature looked impossibly young, barely more than a kit. Its presence was a surreal reminder of life before ... all this.

I was transported back to a time when such a sight would've been mundane. Now, it seemed almost absurd in its cuteness, like a Disney character accidentally wandering onto the set of a gritty apocalyptic film.

The rabbit performed its signature hop-walk, a brief dance of caution before settling on a new patch of grass. As it began to nibble, I found myself captivated by this tiny pocket of normalcy in our absurd existence.

Besides birds, it was the first animal I'd seen alive since ... Well, I couldn't remember. Probably since we'd got to the park, because I couldn't remember if I'd actually seen anything before the meteor hit or had only heard scurrying and rustling. I remembered Wade telling me about all the wildlife we'd see on our hike and felt a razor slice in my chest.

My body froze, every muscle taut with the effort not to startle this unexpected visitor. Sure, it wasn't exactly a rare snow leopard sighting, but right now, a rabbit might as well have been the most exotic creature in the world. Its presence kindled a tiny flame of hope in my chest—life persisted, even here.

If anything could outpace the dangers lurking below, I supposed a rabbit stood a fighting chance. Nature's escape artist, built for speed and survival. My eyes traced over its features, committing them to memory: those dark, liquid eyes seeming to absorb the growing light, the soft grey-brown fur blending seamlessly with the terrain. A flash of white on its tail stood out, like a tiny banner of defiance against the encroaching gloom.

In this small, living creature, I found an anchor to a world I feared we'd left behind.

Perched on the unforgiving stone, I waged a silent war against my thoughts. Names and faces kept bubbling up from the depths of my mind, each one a fresh wound: Pete, Wade, Hassan. The Taylors. Christ. Each memory threatened to drag me under, into a whirlpool of grief and horror I wasn't sure I could surface from.

My brain became a minefield, every stray thought potentially explosive. I focused on the rough texture of the rock beneath me, the cool air on my skin—anything tangible, anything present. Anything but the growing list of those we'd lost.

The rabbit nibbled and hopped, hopped and nibbled.

Then I thought about Bill. Thinking about Bill was good because it made me angry—angry with a burning determination. Anger was good; anger wasn't cold terror, anger wasn't despair.

Bill's image burned in my mind; every detail etched with the precision of hatred. That Wookie-worthy beard dominated his face, but his eyes ... those I'd recognize anywhere, even if he took a razor to that facial forest. I catalogued everything: his height, build, the lilt in his accent. Each detail filed away, ammunition for later.

When we clawed our way out of this abyss, I'd paint such a vivid picture for the cops they'd think Bill was standing right in front of them. And if the boys in blue couldn't track down this murderous bastard? Well, I'd plaster his face on every lamppost from here to Timbuktu. Offer a reward that'd make lottery winners jealous. Hell, I'd dedicate my life to—

A spray of soil and the rabbit was gone.

Chapter 23

The dirt was still raining down as I cringed back, scrabbling away from the edge of the rock. I sat there on my ass and stared in stupefied repulsion.

The thing that took the rabbit was a bear. My scalp prickled. The thing had *been* a bear. I was not keen on bears at the best of times, and this wasn't the best of times. Or the best of bears.

It certainly didn't move like any damn bear I'd ever seen. Those vile pulses below the skin were just as appalling under fur. My mouth was cotton dry. A fucking bear, for fuck's sake.

The desire to be anywhere but here pressed down like a physical weight, threatening to crush what little resolve I had left. As I hauled myself to my feet, the world swayed, my legs as sturdy as overcooked spaghetti. The trek back to camp felt like a journey across a tightrope, each step a battle against gravity and my rebelling body.

A bizarre sensation crawled through my jaw, as if my fillings had suddenly developed a mind of their own and were staging a jailbreak. The feeling only added to the surreal horror of our situation, my body finding new and inventive ways to express its distress.

Everyone was awake when I got back. They all looked subdued and traumatized but conscious.

"Hey," I said. Claire looked at me; her eyes were red and bloodshot. My thoughts stalled until I realized, yeah, red eyes could happen from crying too, not just from being eaten inside by worms.

Plopping down, I dug into my pack like a desperate archaeologist searching for buried treasure. Only instead of gold, I was hoping for something edible that wouldn't make my taste buds revolt. Protein bars—everywhere. Had I packed for the apocalypse or just lost my mind at the grocery store? Oh, wait. Some of these were Wade's. Great. A wave of guilt crashed over me at the thought.

Beyond the protein paradise, all I could find were packets of ramen and the Taylors' granola bars—another punch to the gut. Sighing, I grabbed a protein bar at random. At least in their identical wrappers, I couldn't tell which were mine and which were Wade's. Small mercies, I supposed.

"Did you eat something?" I asked Claire. She looked ... bad.

She tilted her head to one side. "What if this is hell?" she said.

On the other side of the pile of dead ash, the two boys went still.

"What if this is hell, and we don't know we're dead?"

Aaron's face wrinkled in consideration. "Like in that old show? On an island, right? What was it called, again? *Gilligan's Island?*"

As I watched him, a theory began to form. This guy's behavior could only be explained by some serious childhood misadventures. I was talking multiple rounds of 'oops, the baby slipped' levels of mishap. His parents must have played catch with him and forgot the catch part. Repeatedly.

It was almost impressive, really. The sheer number of times he must have kissed the floor as an infant to end up like this ... well, it had to be some kind of record. Maybe that was why he was so thick-skulled now—years of unintentional impact training.

"Here." I lobbed another protein bar over to Claire. To my horror, she didn't move, and the thing hit her in the forehead. "Oh shit, sorry."

I rubbed my eyes and wondered how many times *I'd* been dropped on my head as a baby.

It had to be worse for Claire than the rest of us. We'd all lost people, friends, good friends in the last couple of days, but it had to be worse when it was your partner, surely?

I thought of Ben. It was not a direct comparison, granted, given that we were no longer together, and things hadn't ended well. And I still didn't have my favorite jacket back, but even so, the idea of him being torn apart in front of me hit like a kick to the head.

The boys and I finally got up and moved, making our way slowly and carefully up and around the peninsula of scrub. Claire followed silently. She went where we guided her, putting one foot in front of another. I tried to avoid catching sight of her face, as the bleak desolation was gut-wrenching.

After a long morning, we reached the foot of the cliffs and started back down the other side of the rift, along the stone. It was slow going, but we eventually made it up and around.

Killing Wade and using his body had saved Bill half a day—a life for a few hours. The life of my friend, with his lame-assed sense of humor and atrocious fashion sense, blotted out in an instant, in my place. His kindness and patience, his insistence *Die Hard* was a Christmas classic and that tomatoes were a fruit. If I got out of here, I would have to explain to his family and his girlfriend what had happened. How would I even start?

A strangled sob escaped me, and I slipped, my foot skidding down the side of a rock into a crevice. I pulled myself up, shuddering, and looked back at the others. I had to concentrate, keep my shit together.

We kept going. Then, the stone began to dip in a gentle slope. The trend was slight at first, but then it grew steeply, and sure enough, what I'd feared would happen happened: we came to another wide swathe of dirt across our path, nothing but grass and weeds. Well, shit.

I stood and waited as Declan, Claire, and Aaron arrived behind me. Random rocks and boulders were strewn through the area as if dirt from above had swept down amongst them like a tide over millennia.

"No way across?" Declan asked.

"I don't know," I said. "There's no way around it, though."

My finger traced a line upward, drawing attention to the imposing overhang looming above us. The rock face jutted out like nature's awning, defying gravity and common sense in equal measure. Below this stone sentinel, the landscape transformed into a no-man's land of scrubby vegetation, as if the cliff had sucked all life from its immediate surroundings.

The barren strip ran right up to the base of the rock, a stark dividing line between two worlds. My eyes darted from one protruding rock to the next, mentally connecting these stone islands across the expanse, each outcropping a potential lifeline in our vertical sea of peril.

On either side of the gully, there were definite stepping-stone possibilities. In the middle, though, where it dipped down, there was nothing but a few flat stones, barely sticking through the ground's surface. They were hardly bigger than a foot, with soggy, damp moss around them.

My chest was a ball of ice. There was no other way. It was stay here and die or try to jump, stone to stone and ... well, die.

I tried to block out the memories of yesterday, of Pete and what'd come out of the ground. The ice ball expanded into my stomach.

Next to me, Declan was doing the same thing I was, searching for a way across. "I think we can do it," he said. "Maybe."

Aaron said nothing. I glanced his way, and he stared out over the gap, as if he wasn't seeing what was there. Claire was quiet too. She'd crouched on the rock, leaned forward, balanced on one hand. Her head drooped like she didn't care enough to look. My head hurt, whether from dehydration or the general shit-ness of things, I didn't know.

"We're going to have to try it," Declan said, his Adam's apple bobbing. "I'll go first, if you like."

I frowned; he looked pitifully young. "Are you sure?"

"Yeah, I can't stand waiting about, you know."

I nodded. "Yeah, alright." I turned back to Aaron and Claire, and neither looked good. "Okay, how about you go, then Claire?" I tilted my head at Declan, hoping he understood it would be better if I followed her in case she got wobbly. She still had a frozen, lost look, as if she didn't know where she was going. "Then Aaron, yeah?"

In hindsight, I should have thought out the order better.

"Yeah, whatever." Declan's gaze was so intent on the swathe that I don't think he even heard me.

I took a swig of my precious water. The cool trickle of water across my tongue offered a tiny distraction from the relentless pounding in my skull. Each precious drop came with a twinge of guilt—Hassan's bottles were long gone, and now Wade's supply was dwindling. Claire and Declan nursed the last of Pete's water, the shared resource a grim reminder of our dwindling numbers and supplies.

Declan set out over the first few rocks. That bit wasn't too bad, as only a couple of places needed a real jump. He got to the middle and stood, assessing the way forward.

I followed to have a look, leaping easily to where he was.

When I reached him, he said, "What do you think? That way or across there?"

He pointed with a hand that trembled.

The soles of my feet itched. Neither option was a good choice. At the bottom of the damp gully, there was no straight path across. We could either go slightly up the hill, where the potential steppingstones were smaller and smaller but stuck up more, or go downwards and around. Downwards had more rocks, but they were flush with the ground. I was having little flutters at how close the earth was.

Aaron and Claire made their way to where we were hesitating and scuffled to a stop, balanced on a half-submerged boulder behind us. I checked over my shoulder on how they were doing—Aaron had a hand on Claire's arm, keeping her upright.

"What do you think?" I asked them.

Claire slowly focused on me then shook her head; I doubted she was up to much, but I was hoping to keep her present, alert.

Aaron looked at me, his face twisted in exasperation. "I don't *know*."

Declan pointed again down the slope. "I'm going to go that way; there's more steppingstones."

Before I had a chance to reply, to point out that the rocks that way were barely above the ground, he leaped.

Jump, leap, jump, scramble, and he was up the other side—just like that. I tried to track and memorize the route he'd taken. Everything was quiet, still.

My lungs expanded with a deliberate inhale as my eyes swept the terrain, searching for any sign of movement. The stillness was both a relief and a concern. Satisfied, I pivoted towards Claire, extending a hand in her direction.

"You next."

She stepped across to join me on my last decent rock. She blinked, nodded, and then jumped over to the first flat stone Declan had used.

A spray of mud flew up beside her rock. It was so close. Something sliced through the ground between Claire and the next, barely-there stone. She squealed, a high-pitched sound of panic.

Dear God.

I jumped instinctively, without consideration, and threw myself out over the gap. Uphill, away from Claire, to the curve of smaller rocks leading upwards and across. The noise and the impact I made might distract attention from her.

The first leap was fueled by a spike of adrenaline. My foot slammed onto the target—a treacherously small, rounded outcrop barely larger than my boot. For a heart-stopping instant, the world tilted as my sole skidded across the slick surface. Then Armageddon let loose. Dirt and pebbles exploded around me, a miniature landslide triggered by my precarious landing. Each flying particle felt like a countdown, ticking away the seconds before disaster struck.

A nightmarish appendage broke from below—some unholy fusion of hoof and abomination. Its movement defied nature, pulsating and rippling beneath matted, sodden fur. The monstrosity swiped across the rock before me, a grotesque obstacle in my path. But physics cared nothing for the laws of sanity; my body hurtled forward, irresistible impetus carrying me past the point of no return. As my foot came down, it hit something that moved, something that was knocked partially aside by my landing. There was a flash of whitish grey, and flesh gave horribly under the sole of my boot.

Unlike standing on a real finger, there was no resistance, no solidity from bones and cartilage, only a smoosh like rotten fruit. I skidded, and from the side of my eye, I registered, rather than saw, that Claire was still going. She reached the other side.

A spray of grit flew up and hit me in the face. I was blind. I blinked but couldn't clear my eyes. I had to keep going. I leaped for where the next rock should be, hit something solid, and breathed for the first time since I'd jumped. I could see out of one eye now, and below my boot was stone.

Reality blinked, and madness took the wheel. Something massive surged from below, rocking the stone beneath my feet. The precarious perch teetered, threatening to topple with me still aboard. The scattered shale that had offered meager protection now betrayed me, lifting and tipping my fragile sanctuary.

Desperation fueled an impossible leap. Traction was a distant memory as I hurled myself from the tilting rock. The next outcrop rushed to meet me, my knee slamming into its unforgiving surface before sliding off onto the dreaded bare surface.

In that split second, fear became a tangible force, propelling me upward. The feel of soil against skin ignited a primal terror, sending a molten surge of panic through my veins. My body reacted before my mind could process, launching upward in a move that defied gravity and reason. A heartbeat later, a hand of nightmare swiped through the ground where I had just been.

It flailed, the fingers grasping and moving independently. I caught a glimpse of it, the fingertips worn away, the vile squirm within, the glint of a wedding band.

It missed me. I couldn't believe it missed me. If we'd been on less pebble-filled ground, it would never have happened, but here among the rockiness, it must have hit something and been deflected. I reached the other side and scrambled my way up, clawing at bare rock with my hands, and beached myself like a manic, panting whale on the stone shore.

Exhausted muscles gave way, sending me sprawling onto my back, the pack a makeshift pillow against the unforgiving ground. The vast sky stretched above, indifferent to the pandemonium below. Each desperate gasp felt like trying to breathe through a straw, black spots dancing at the edges of my vision. The thunderous rhythm of my heart drowned out all other sounds, a frantic drumbeat counting out my survival.

All the while, a voice in the back of my mind screamed about the brief, terrifying contact between my knee and what harboured death. I pushed the thought away, focusing instead on the simple act of existing, of drawing one gasp of air after another.

Declan and Claire's frantic shouts slowly penetrated the fog of exhaustion, their waving arms finally registering in my peripheral vision. Reality reasserted itself, dragging me back from the brink of oblivion. With a groan that seemed to start in my toes, I hauled myself upright, muscles protesting every inch of the way. Eyes squinting against the harsh light, I forced myself to focus on the commotion, dreading whatever new crisis had emerged.

Oh shit, Aaron. I'd forgotten him, I couldn't believe I'd forgotten a whole person.

He was still on the other side, on the last safe rock. Although I wasn't sure how safe the rock was now, as sprays of grit were flung up across the channel. Clods of dirt and pebbles rained down, and Aaron twitched and quailed as they hit him.

It dawned on me what Declan and Claire were yelling at him. Surely, he couldn't be so stupid?

"No, wait!"

"Go back, go back!"

"Don't do it!"

I didn't think Aaron heard them. His face was shroud colored, and his lips were contorted, pulled back so his teeth showed. His eyes flashed up and down the gully.

I leaned forward to add my voice to the others. "*Don't—*" It tore helplessly from me as Aaron moved.

A fist of disbelief, of dread, hit me as Aaron threw himself forward, his face pure panic.

Chapter 24

Aaron leaped straight onto the ground towards us.

"Noooo! You stupid, *stupid*—" Declan's voice was a wail of despair.

Aaron didn't try for either of the routes we'd used; he simply pelted straight toward us. I didn't know if he thought the frantic activity to each side made the middle safer.

He was going to make it.

"Nooooo—" Declan lurched toward the edge of the rock.

Aaron managed a flurry of steps before something tripped him, slicing up and clipping his ankle. I flinched. He staggered then, still running but unbalanced. My thoughts congealed. He fell, hit the ground full length, flailed, then lifted himself on his elbows.

A second later, a great flume of dirt shot up, and a hand reached for his middle. Sharp panic shot through me. A snaking arm hooked him around his waist. A sickening crack rang out. He was pulled down with such violence his feet hit his pack. Mud and pebbles rained down around the collapsing hollow. He was gone, folded into the earth. I pressed my knuckles hard against my teeth.

"You stupid, *stupid* fuck." Declan crumpled down onto his haunches on the rock. His face was red and twisted, furious and hurt. "Stupid, stupid, stupid bloody—" He grabbed a pebble, stood, and threw it as hard as he could out over the gully. "You *stupid*—" He broke off into sobs, scrabbled up another rock, threw it as he sobbed. "Stupid, stupid fuck." He did it again and again till there was no more to be found.

I sat and stared at the dip where Aaron had disappeared. All was still again in the gully. I imagined the feasting going on beneath the surface and sick revulsion twisted in me.

Unbidden, the horrific questions bubbled up. The sensation of being dragged below, earth closing in, the living world receding. How long before the soil filled every airspace, before suffocation set in? My eyes slammed shut, a futile barrier against the invasive thoughts. Still, they persisted, setting my teeth on edge, threatening to chatter with morbid curiosity.

Three minutes. The number surfaced from what ... happened with Dan. Three minutes without air. The knowledge sat heavy, a grim fact I wished I could unlearn. Yet here it was again, suddenly, terribly relevant.

Please, God, let him not be conscious. With everything that had happened, I actually thought I'd become numb and developed some immunity to the razor thrust of terror and choking revulsion.

Yeah, I was wrong.

At last, Claire moved and made me realize I couldn't stay flopped where I was. Between us we hauled Declan up, made him climb up the side of the slope of rock, farther away from the gully. Then he collapsed, and I hadn't the heart to try and drag him any further. He sobbed; furious anger replaced by unadulterated grief.

I'd barely looked at Claire's strained, pale face. I'd barely parted my lips to speak, to ask stupidly if she had any idea what we should do when it happened.

Below us, something burst from the ground. At the gully's base, where rock met soil, remains burst forth, flinging debris skyward in a grotesque fountain.

It emerged further, each nauseating increment revealing more horror. The mass oozed upward, undulating as it breached the surface.

Instinct drove me back, then paralyzed me. My head was full of buzzing. I stared, transfixed by the impossible sight. The ... thing ... teetered on the edge of gravity's dominion. One heartbeat. Two. Its movements defied human biomechanics, barely vertical yet unmistakably animated by some internal force. My mind reeled, unable to process the sight while my insides roiled in protest.

Quivers rippled along the figure, a perverse puppetry keeping it upright. Finally, my lungs remembered their job, drawing in a ragged breath that tasted of fear and revulsion.

Declan retched, and then I caught movement as Claire stood. I flinched as she jumped back down, down across the rocks to the gully.

"Don't—" I said, reaching instinctively toward her. I didn't know why, as she was well out of reach and quite safe.

The urge to shield her from that abomination surged through me. It stood there, a monument to decay and violation of natural order. Where a face should have been, erosion had left only hollows—eye sockets and a gaping maw teeming with unspeakable movement. Patches of bleached bone peeked through remnants of scalp, a macabre mosaic of what once was human.

Despite all of it, I knew who it was or had been. The night Mel Taylor died, she'd worn a nightdress of sorts, like a T-shirt, but with a stupid ruffle of lace around the neckline. It had a keyhole with a loop and a

211

button in the shape of a daisy. When you spent hours sitting beside someone as they died in agony, some things made an impression.

The urge to heave coursed up my gullet as I stared at the sullied remnants of lace, at the button, dangling. The T-shirt was gone, as was most of the skin and flesh beneath it. Bare rib bones showed, but the repulsive noose remained.

Claire squatted down to get a closer look. I raised a trembling hand.

What the hell was happening? The body ... the remains of Mel's body, was protruding out of the ground from the knees up now. Nauseating bulges and ripples, ridges and contractions, held it here, upright. The arms were flabby tubes, twitching at its sides, the hands were bare spatulas, the fingers worn away. My head was full of horror, and I wanted to get as far away from that abomination as possible.

I caught a hint of a different movement then. The head pulsed beneath the torn, tattered scalp. Dirt and worms cascaded from the eye sockets, as if the press within couldn't be contained. The body ran through a great upward convulsion, and the skull distorted, bulged, and then returned to its normal shape.

Below me, Claire moved to regain her feet, a heartbeat too late.

There was another writhing, upward wave of contraction, and then the head exploded.

SPLUCKK— A disgusting wet pop, followed by a hail of worms.

They hit Claire like shrapnel. She screamed, a shrill, slicing sound, quickly cut off.

In the abrupt quiet, lumps of tattered skulls fell to the ground with tiny, dull thuds. Then a pattering rattle, like rice at a wedding—worms spraying out across the ground. The smell hit me like a smack in the face, putrid, rotting flesh, and a sharp chemical stench.

Below me, Claire scrambled away up the rock, scraping with her heels before she turned over and crawled back up the stone, clawing desperately. When she reached me, she was panting, making tiny noises of infinite distress. She slapped her arms. I caught a glimpse of her agonized face, mouth wide, eyes desperate.

Oh God, her face was covered in little red dots. Something moved in her hair, then disappeared. Oh God. The tail end of something disappeared into her cheek. I flinched from her. I couldn't help it.

She quietened and curled herself up, hunched on the rock, rubbing at her skin as she sobbed.

Paralysis gripped me, muscles locked in a rictus of disbelief. My body felt fused to the rock, a living statue frozen in fear. The world narrowed to a pinpoint, everything buckling around the impossibility before us. Each breath came as a ragged gasp, air catching in my throat like jagged shards.

Declan's movement shattered the stillness, jolting me from my trance. He picked his way over, face contorted into a mask of confusion and pain. Our eyes met, and his lips worked silently, grasping for words that didn't exist.

A lifetime later, we moved. I approached Claire, sliding my feet along the rock as if I might be tipped off the hard surface at any time.

"Claire—?" I caught myself before I asked if she was okay.

She wasn't fucking okay. She would never be okay. I wanted to smash something, pound something with my fists, kick the everlasting shit out of something.

My eyes betrayed me, scanning Claire involuntarily, searching for any sign of the impossible. Declan, proving himself the better man, crouched beside her. He offered her a water bottle, his actions a stark contrast to my paralysis.

I squeezed my eyes shut, wondering if Declan had missed what I'd seen.

"Thanks." Claire's steady voice cut through my thoughts, a surreal counterpoint to the situation.

A primal urge to scream clawed at my chest, barely contained behind clenched teeth. Claire's quick glance my way revealed skin cleared of those telltale marks, now just blotchy from tears. But her eyes ... God, how fast it was happening.

I'd always scoffed at the notion of 'reading' someone's eyes in books. But now, I understood. It wasn't the eyes themselves, but the face around them—skin contorting into a mask of disbelief and hopeless despair. The sight hit like a physical blow, forcing me to look away.

"Look," I managed, voice tight. "We'll get you out, get you to a doctor. We're almost there." The words rang hollow, desperation seeping through every syllable. "We're almost there," I repeated, as much to convince myself as her.

Claire took a deep breath that turned into a half-sob before she stopped it. She nodded and gave me a faint smile.

Christ, how did she do that?

We kept going. What else was there to do? Declan was blank now. I worried if I let him stop, I'd not get him upright again. It was mid-afternoon, and all I could think was to keep going, get out of there as fast as we could, and get Claire to help. She was, strangely, managing better than Declan.

About an hour later, we managed to stumble onto the high rim trail. I stood and gazed at it like a long-lost friend. It twisted and turned around the rim in front of us and gave me a little trembly spot in my innards. A tiny smidge of hope. We were so high up now, surely, we couldn't be far from the last climb? One last ascent then we would be out of the caldera, out where we could get help.

Claire caught up to me, then Declan. His eyes were red-rimmed and his face blotchy, but he was more present. We all stood and looked up at the trail.

"I need a break." Declan flopped onto a rock.

I didn't want to stop; we had to leave. Now, right now, before Claire—

"You guys should eat," Claire said, taking a seat herself. "Have some water."

How was she so calm? Coherent? In her place, I'd be a blithering wreck. She even seemed ... I didn't know. Not cheerful, that was absurd, but *managing* somehow?

"You should eat too," I said at last. Surely it would help keep her strength up?

"It's alright," she said. "I'm good."

'I'm good?' How the hell was she 'good?' I hugged myself a bit. It was cool up here, in the breeze. Was Claire in some kind of denial?

Gravity seemed to intensify as I lowered myself onto a nearby rock, the weight of our situation pressing down on my shoulders. My hand moved on autopilot, fishing out yet another protein bar from my pack. The sight of it killed any hunger, but survival trumped appetite. Even if Gordon Ramsay himself had materialized with a five-star meal, I doubted I could've mustered enthusiasm. Still, I forced down a bite, each chew a massive effort against a rebellion of taste buds and common sense.

If Claire was functional, did it matter if she wasn't processing what'd happened? Nope, damned good thing, actually. I wished I could block the knowledge somehow, wipe it from my brain.

Declan emptied his water bottle, one of Pete's, I noticed, and stuffed it back in his pack. "How long before we get there?"

I had no idea. "A few hours? By tonight, definitely. Maybe." I couldn't stop my gaze from sliding back to Claire's face. "Soon."

Now we'd found the trail, and it should be quicker going, much quicker, unless we ran into more tainted ground. The trail hadn't been made to keep on stone after all. It ran around the rim which, coincidentally, was mostly on rock, but probably not all of it.

The view was spectacular, and a fall of tumbled boulders below us led down to a carpet of miniature treetops.

"We should get going," I said, glancing at Claire again. I had to get her out of here as quickly as possible.

She was also looking out at the view, at the fall of the valley. I waited for her to turn around, but she didn't. She merely nodded without looking at me and reached for her pack. Declan groaned, straightened, and struggled into his straps.

It was late afternoon, and the line of shade was about three-quarters of the way across the basin. As we came around a bulge in the rim, the tall smoke plume from the meteor impact was stark against the sky, standing out like a giant middle finger to the world.

I was increasingly worried about Claire. Her lagging pace gnawed at my nerves. My mind, a treacherous thing, kept circling back to the atrocity potentially unfolding within her. Each glance at her face became a desperate search for signs, every expression a potential harbinger of the unspeakable.

Declan took point, leaving me free to shadow Claire. The trail, at least, offered some assurance that he wouldn't wander off a cliff in one of his fugue states.

Again, Claire halted, her gaze fixed on the sprawling park below. This recurring pause set my teeth on edge.

"Come on," I urged, gentle but insistent. The words 'Are you in pain?' hovered on my lips, unspoken. The thought of her feeling *them* already ... I couldn't bring myself to voice the question.

"Let's go," I said instead. "We'll be there soon, you'll see." The promise felt hollow, but it was all I had.

Helplessness clawed at me. All I could do was watch, encourage, and silently pray that each step brought us closer to salvation rather than damnation.

We trudged forever, step after step, boots scraping on stone, gaining height as we went. I had no idea when or if we'd reach the Dante's Crag climb, so I kept hoping it would be around the next corner. It wasn't.

Declan had disappeared around a bend when I looked back to check on Claire for the hundredth time. This time, she'd taken her pack off as well as stopped. God dammit, didn't she know we needed to hurry?

"Are you alright?" I called. Stupidly.

She smiled at me, a lopsided grin, one side of her lips quirked up. "Sorry, mate," she said, then she was gone.

Chapter 25

One moment Claire was there, the next, she disappeared from the edge of the trail out into thin air. All the air went out of my lungs in a hard uuuuugh. A second later, she landed below with a sad, distant thud.

My legs gave way, depositing me onto the unforgiving ground. A vast emptiness consumed me, as if every ounce of hope and strength had been drained away.

The cliff's edge beckoned, a dark whisper promising a final solution, but even that seemed beyond my reach. Exhaustion had seeped into my very bones, age and despair conspiring to root me in place.

Slumped there, a discarded marionette with cut strings, I wondered about Declan. Would he return? Uncertainty hung in the air, adding another weight to the crushing burden of our situation. Part of me couldn't summon the energy to care, while another part clung desperately to this last thread of human connection.

If I'd had the chance, would I have stopped her? If I could have raced back to her, bridging the distance in time? No.

And would I have been brave enough to do the same if I were in her shoes? If I saw worms eating away at my skin, knowing what lied inside me, squirming, feasting?

Probably still no, not by jumping off a cliff.

Declan wandered back down the trail. I heard him, but didn't bother looking up. I didn't want to have to tell him. I wanted to try and shut it out for a few more minutes, or perhaps forever.

"Where's Claire?" he asked.

My gaze finally lifted, meeting Declan's weary eyes. His face was a canvas of exhaustion, smeared with dirt and peppered with patchy stubble. The words were trapped in me, refusing to materialize. Instead of speaking, I managed a slight nod toward the trail's edge. Understanding flickered across Declan's features as he turned, approaching the precipice with cautious steps.

"Oh," he muttered. He came back to sit beside me. We sat in silence for what felt like a half hour, maybe an hour. The shadow cast by the sun traversed the basin, marking the passing of time.

At one point, Declan grabbed Claire's abandoned backpack and rummaged through it, searching for any remaining food or water. I closed my eyes. I didn't want to see. There was a heavy lump in my chest, pushing its way up, suffocating me.

Declan pulled out a worn leather pouch that housed her passport, documents, bank cards. "Should we take this?" he asked.

A nod, heavy with unspoken understanding, accompanied my outstretched hand. The passport—a small, weighty token of a life cut short—would find its place at the bottom of my pack. A grim cargo to be delivered to a family I'd never meet, a final confirmation of identity for someone I barely knew.

The cover flipped open, revealing a name: Claire Duffy. Her face, impossibly young and unblemished, gazed up from the photo. The contrast between that frozen instant of hope and our current reality struck like a physical blow. My eyes slammed shut, a futile barrier against the flood of emotions threatening to overwhelm.

Eventually, Declan stirred.

"Let's get away from here," he suggested, gesturing towards the cliff edge where Claire had jumped.

"Yeah," I agreed. "Let's get away from here."

We climbed the trail until dusk began to blur our surroundings, then stopped. I wasn't sure if it was a break or if we were stopping for the night. The urgency was diminishing. We needed to warn the world, to escape this place before these things got out, but I found it difficult to focus.

Instead, I tried to force myself to think about tomorrow. I wondered if we would reach the climb at Dante's Crag and whether we would be capable of making the ascent. The idea made my mouth go dry. Then, I tried to shake it off. *Don't think about heights.* Tomorrow had to be better; there was hope. There had to be hope. If only I didn't feel so tired, so numb.

God, I wanted a day when nobody died. Was it too much to ask? If no one died, it would be a good day. Particularly as there were only two of us left now. If someone died, it was fifty-fifty it'd be me, and even then, it was ignoring the fact that both of us could die.

Goddamn it, shut up, brain. I turned to where Declan was sitting, looking out across the basin. Was he looking at it a little too intently? Was he getting a little too close to the edge? I had a ringing in my ears, followed by an urge to move and sit between him and the drop-off. I told myself not to be stupid. Claire had only done ... what she had done because of what was inside her. Because she had known what was there, eating.

Declan wasn't going to jump. Yes, he'd lost all three of his friends, but he wasn't going to jump. I tried to think of something to say to him. He'd taken Aaron's death much harder than I'd expected, given how at odds they'd always seemed. But then, maybe he'd known him for a long time. After all, the deaths of the others had hit me hard, but nothing like as hard as Wade's. Wade and I had known each other most of our lives.

A fragment of advice surfaced from the murky depths of memory—the importance of acknowledging those lost, not erasing them from conversation. But the realization brought a fresh wave of guilt: how little I knew about these young lives so abruptly ended.

My mind fumbled through a fog of exhaustion and grief, grasping for something, anything, to say. After what felt like an eternity, words finally materialized, clumsy and inadequate: "Did you know Aaron for a long time?"

The question hung in the air, a feeble attempt at connection, at normalcy. Even as it left my lips, I felt the weight of its insufficiency.

Declan turned and looked at me blankly. "The stupid twat was my brother."

Shit. I must have missed that somewhere along the line.

He rubbed at his face like he wanted to erase his head. "Mum's going to kill me."

What? I just looked at him.

"She was so worried, you know? About us coming here? Not here, here—" He circled a hand to indicate the park. "America. Like, she was worried we'd get shot." He snorted at this. "How am I supposed to tell her Aaron was killed by—"

My mind wandered to a surreal scenario: my mom received news of my worm-induced demise. Her imagined response, complete with pursed lips and a raised eyebrow, was, "Was he at least wearing clean underwear?"

A snort-giggle escaped before I could stop it. The sound, born of trauma, exhaustion, and my brand of idiocy, startled even me. In a fleeting, paranoid flash, I wondered if it was the first sign of worms feasting on my brain.

Declan's head snapped around, his eyes wide. "What the fuck?"

Guilt crashed over me. He had been pouring out his heart about his brother, and here I was, laughing like a loon. There was no way to play this off as a random chuckle, so I spilled it all—the morbid imagination, my mom's fictional response, the whole absurd mental journey.

Bracing myself for a well-deserved uppercut, I was blindsided by Declan's reaction. After a beat of silence, he let out a snort that rivaled my own. Suddenly, we were howling with laughter, the sound echoing off the indifferent rocks around us.

Hysteria, it seemed, was contagious. To anyone else, our outburst would have seemed insane. But teetering on the edge of despair, it was a lifeline to sanity. Well, as sane as you could be when you intimately knew my mother.

Eventually, Declan's laughter subsided, and he shook his head while still occasionally hiccupping. "Man, you are messed up," he said.

We sat in silence for a little while longer, and I assumed we had stopped for the night. As I reached over to grab my backpack, something hairy and at knee-height suddenly charged towards us on the trail.

Chapter 26

A surge of adrenaline coursed through my body, awakening every nerve ending. The flinch was instinctive, primal—my muscles contracted before my brain could even process the threat. Fear, cold and sharp, raced along my skin like electricity, leaving a trail of goosebumps in its wake.

"What the—?" Declan's eyes bugged out of his head, and he scrambled backward.

The thing yapped.

I could not believe my ears or my eyes. It was the Taylor's dog.

The damn thing was alive. It reached me and danced frantically around, tongue lolling in manic excitement.

I rolled onto my knees, and the animal launched itself at me, squealing and yipping like a siren. He tried madly to lick my face, and I held him away, trying to stop him. I had no idea if he was infected with worms. I guessed not, or he wouldn't be able to run so fast. Or would he?

Under my hands, his frantic little body felt bony. He was absolutely filthy, covered in burrs, and stank to high heaven.

"It's alright," I called to Declan. "It's a dog." I couldn't remember its name.

Declan came cautiously to where I knelt.

"Man, it's dirty," he said.

The dog, noticing Declan's presence for the first time, barked at him.

"Hey, it's alright." He stooped to extend a hand to the animal.

I went back to undoing my pack, this time to dig out something for the dog to eat. We had the remains of Claire's food now too. I pushed the thought to the back of my mind and rummaged around to check what I had.

Meanwhile, Declan hunkered down and was making friends with the bouncing dog. Yeah, it was exactly as brainless as I remembered.

I closed my eyes on the sudden stabbing recollection of Josh Taylor heading off to save this stupid creature, dying lost alone in the wilderness. I'd almost forgotten the kid existed. How the hell was that possible?

"Barney!"

I lost my balance and fell backward onto my ass. The yell came from further up the trail. A great bubble of astonishment, a mad spurt of hope, bloomed in my chest. Seconds later, a small, muddy figure stomped down the trail.

"Holy shit," Declan said.

Yep, couldn't agree more.

It was Josh Taylor. The kid was indescribably filthy but alive. From head to toe, he was coated in the brown soil of the basin.

"How the hell did you get here?" Probably not the best way to greet a missing child, but seriously, I barely stopped myself from saying, "How the hell are you still *alive?*", *so, you know, better than it could have been.*

Josh put his hands on his hips and squinted at me. "Oh, it's you."

"Um, this is Josh Taylor," I said to Declan.

He nodded, probably not remembering the name.

"I got stuck," Josh said with a frown, answering my earlier question. "Up there. There's a bit where it's too far to get across. There's no rocks like back down that way." He pointed back down the trail behind us, and I understood he meant the gully where Aaron had died. Where

Claire—where Mel Taylor's corpse—I had a quiver of revulsion at the thought.

Mel was Josh's mother. My brain did a little tap dance around that. The kid had crossed those same rocks, alone. While beneath the ground was probably his mother's body. I tried not to think about it.

"Do you have any food?" Josh looked at my open pack with interest. "I'm starving."

"Sure." I rummaged for something to appeal to a kid and found a granola bar.

I sucked in air through my teeth when I remembered it was from Dan Taylor's pack. I hadn't been able to bring myself to eat it; I had stuck to the monotony of my endless protein bars. I had bought what I planned was a week's worth of the things, but it turned out it was enough for a lifetime. There had been a couple of Taylor's bars left in Wade's pack too; I presumed he had felt the same.

"Here." I passed the granola bar across, hoping my thoughts about its origin wouldn't occur to Josh.

He either didn't notice or care. He plonked himself down on the rock beside us and tore the thing open, which attracted Barney's immediate and intense interest.

The little dog sat neatly and looked up at the boy with hope. I dug out another bar to give to the animal. By the time I had opened it, Josh's was gone, so I passed it to the boy and fished out another for the dog.

I made the mistake of chucking it onto the ground, where Barney promptly tried to choke himself to death by inhaling it whole.

Gack-hurruff-gak.

Idiot animal. I retrieved it and broke the bar into bits, feeding it to him a little at a time. He still inhaled it, but at least didn't choke.

"How did you get here?" I asked Josh. "Up on the trail, I mean?" The last time I had seen him had been down in the basin, well before we had any idea what was really happening.

He had finished the second granola bar and was peering to see what else was in my pack. I dug out a packet of Claire's beef jerky and handed it to him. Maybe it would slow him down.

Nope. In fact, the chewiness resulted in enthusiastic, open-mouthed mastication.

Given I had seen some pretty horrible sights in the last few days, you would think this wouldn't bother me. Not so, I discovered. I averted my eyes. Granted, it wasn't up there with watching a corpse's head explode, but still ... ick.

Yeah, I had been told many times I used sick humor as a defensive mechanism. Also, that I was not as funny as I thought I was.

Declan's face contorted into a mask of bewildered disgust as he watched Josh's vigorous chomping.

The absurdity of it nearly triggered an inappropriate laugh, which I barely managed to suppress. Josh, apparently catching Declan's less-than-impressed expression, gulped down his mouthful with an audible swallow.

His eyes darted between us, a mix of confusion and wariness evident as he blurted out, "Who are you?"

"Um, I'm Declan. It's nice to meet you."

"Why do you sound funny?"

Ah, kids.

"Because I'm British. Where I come from, you sound funny."

Josh screwed his face up at this, then dismissed it as incomprehensible. "I don't sound funny." He returned his attention to the jerky.

The kid managed half a pack then promptly fell asleep, flaked out on the bare rock almost mid-chew, head on his filthy pack, and slept.

His mouth gaped open, a symphony of snores filling the air. A fleeting, uncharitable thought wondered if his gob ever got a rest. But on its heels came a darker concern—would those snores transform into screams of internal agony?

Anxiety clawed me, only slightly soothed by the memory of his clear, un-reddened eyes. The image of bloodshot gazes—Mel's, Dan's, Claire's—flashed unbidden through my mind, a grim parade of commemoration.

My hand found its way to my forehead, as if the pressure could somehow push away the intrusive thoughts and mounting tension.

"I guess we're spending the night here then?" Declan said.

He had dug out some food from his pack and was feeding it to the appreciative dog.

"I guess so," I said.

A few hours later, Josh woke up. "I'm hungry."

Declan was asleep, snoring softly, so I rummaged some more of Claire's food for the kid. The dog didn't so much as stir; he was in a food coma after everything Declan had fed him. The stars were out, a million wormholes eaten in the sky.

Josh scarfed down a packet of jerky and a couple of little bags of savory biscuit things. The chewing noises were noticeable in the still night, but at least it was dark, so I didn't have to see the process in detail.

Also, it seemed he had plenty of water, which was strange, but I was happy I didn't have to share my precious supply.

"Did you know my dad's dead?"

The words hit like a bolt of lightning, freezing me in place. Thoughts spiraled at dizzying speed. How could Josh possibly know about his father's fate?

My head swiveled towards the boy, his silhouette barely visible in the darkness. Starlight caught his face, illuminating a ghostly pallor that seemed to emphasize the impossible knowledge he possessed. Words formed and dissolved on my tongue, each attempt at a response dying before it could reach my lips.

"And did you know that dead people come out of the ground?"

Oh, God. Well, my question had been answered, horribly. I nodded.

Josh looked at me intently. "Is my mom dead too?"

Memory surged unbidden—Josh's anxious face tilted up, his question about his mother hanging in the air. The weight of that lie still sat heavy, the false reassurance I'd offered now a bitter taste on my tongue.

In the present, Josh's gaze bored into me, unseen but palpable in the darkness. The urge to shield him warred with the raw need for honesty. This time, truth had to win out. The kid had already lost too much to be betrayed by another lie.

"I'm sorry, buddy, she is," I said.

The kid was silent. A subtle shift in his expression caught the dim light—a brief protrusion of his lower lip before his mouth tightened into a thin line. The darkness obscured the finer details, leaving uncertainty about the moisture in his eyes. But Josh's face, what little could be discerned, had become an unreadable mask, emotions locked away behind a blank façade.

"I'm sorry," I said again.

He nodded, a quick emphatic jerk. I expected him to cry then, but he looked out into the darkness, the stars a milky swathe above us.

"I saw my dad," he said. "He was dead." His voice went a little wobbly. "You could tell. But I didn't see Mom."

Oh God. What did you say to that? His experience hung in the air, a cloud of unimaginable horror. The confusion, the fear, the raw shock of seeing his father's body in such a state—it was beyond comprehension. Unbidden, an image of Wade flashed through my mind, his form twisted and defiled in the same grotesque manner. The thought alone sent a knife of anguish twisting in my gut, a bitter taste rising on my tongue.

The gap between what Josh had gone through and my imagined scenario yawned wide, yet even this glimpse into his trauma left me reeling. How did a child process such a nightmarish sight? The weight of his ordeal pressed down, a suffocating blanket of empathy and helplessness.

I had absolutely no idea what to say to the boy. There were simply no words of comfort.

"My dad was a doody-head."

My eyebrows shot up. That came out of left field and was also a surprisingly accurate diagnosis for one so young. The kid's assessment wasn't far off the mark. Dan Taylor's track record certainly leaned towards the doody-head end of the spectrum. A flash of guilt followed the thought—speaking ill of the dead felt wrong, but honesty demanded acknowledgment. Dan's actions had left much to be desired, even if his fate had been undeservedly cruel.

Josh's voice got real small then. "I didn't think he'd leave me there. I thought if I went off, he'd have to wait till I found Barney." I caught a flash from his eyes as he glared at me accusingly. "But when I went back, you'd all gone."

"What do you mean, went back? We thought you were on the other side of the landslide. We looked, searched. How did you get back?"

"Um, yeah, I couldn't get down the trail, where it'd all fallen down. I heard you all yelling, so I hid."

"You hid?" I was gobsmacked. What the hell?

"If you found me, you'd have made me go back."

"You little shit," I said.

Josh grinned. His teeth flashed white, the swine.

I was flat-out furious and astonished. All the time we spent looking, it had never occurred to me that the kid might hide from us.

"But how did you get around the landslide?" There had been no possible way through. I had trouble getting my head around this. "How the hell did you get back to the campsite? How did you find the dog?"

"I dunno." Josh pooched out his lower lip. "I got lost for a bit. Then I found where we stopped when I left, and everyone was gone. So, I thought maybe if I went down the hill instead of on the trail, I'd get around the bit where it was all—" He broke off to flap a hand about, presumably to indicate the landslide.

I couldn't believe he'd survived. He'd gone off a marked trail into the wilderness. It would be incredibly dangerous for a young child, even without murderous trees and an infestation of man-eating worms, let alone what came out of the ground later. It boggled the mind, or at least it certainly boggled mine.

"But I got lost, I couldn't find the campground."

My head shifted in unconscious negation, the motion a sign of incredulity. Catching myself mid-gesture, I willed the movement to cease, muscles tensing against the involuntary response.

"So how did you find the dog?"

"I dunno. He found me."

I frowned at the animal sprawled at Josh's feet. He was fast asleep on his back, snoring in little snuffles, with one foot poking dramatically skywards.

Now, that truly boggled my mind.

"I was yelling for Dad, and I didn't know what else to do. Then Barney found me."

Huh. Well. I guessed it proved miracles could happen.

"We should probably get some sleep, bud. Hopefully, we'll be out of here tomorrow."

"And we'll take Barney?"

"Um, sure," I said. In truth, I had no idea how we were meant to get a dog up a cliff.

In the morning, I woke gasping from a dream about Claire, as if there weren't enough night terrors in my waking hours. I sat and tried to shake it loose from my head.

In the dream, Claire approached the rotten remains of the body again as it swayed, poised below us. This time, though, it'd been Pete's body, and it lifted its arms in horrible invitation. Worms dripped from the ragged tips of his fingers and from his eye sockets, tangling in his beard. Claire leapt into his arms, and instead of the body's head exploding, the pair vanished into the ground.

If the dream was my subconscious trying to reunite the couple in death and somehow make things better, it didn't work. What would Claire have said? "Didn't bloody work, did it?"

No, it didn't bloody work. It didn't bloody, bloody, bloody work. Gritty eyelids scraped against dry eyeballs as I rubbed them, a futile attempt to clear the fog of exhaustion. My tongue rasped against the roof of my mouth, a desert landscape of thirst and neglect. Each swallow was a struggle, reminding me of how long it had been since water had passed my lips.

I understood now, though, why Claire had gone back down the rock into the range of the thing. She'd wanted to know if it was Pete's body.

The ragged corpse had been so filthy, so tattered and torn, so worn away, I'd only known it for Mel Taylor by the snare of fabric around its neck.

A while later, the others stirred. Declan sat up in his sleeping bag, blinked a bit, then scratched himself.

"Wow, I need a wash," he said, sniffing an armpit before struggling out of his bag.

Yeah, fat chance of that happening. I doubted there was any chance before we got out of here, as there wasn't much water up around the rim.

Declan stuck his bare feet into his shoes and shuffled off down the trail. His movements must have woken Josh because the kid stirred and flopped back and forth a couple of times.

"Morning," I said.

"Grumphf."

"Hungry?" I tried.

This got his attention, and he sat up. I dug around and threw him a breakfast bar-looking thing of Claire's. I got no thanks. I guessed I wasn't the best in the morning either. He tore the bar open, and the dog on the end of his sleeping bag didn't so much as twitch.

As Josh chewed, I racked my brain for something to say that wouldn't involve his family or what had happened to them. Jeez, it wasn't easy.

"Why are you so dirty?" I asked.

Josh blinked at me owlishly. "Yeah, I fell in the mud a bit. Before I got up onto the rock."

My eyes flared. "A bit?" I tried not to think about worms in the mud.

"Well, a couple of times." He scrunched his face up in concentration. "Like five or six."

I snorted. I couldn't help it. For some reason, I found the idea of the kid falling over again and again funny, like some kind of silent-movie banana-skin skit.

Josh looked at me with furious indignation. "It's always slippery near the water."

His hands went to his hips. There was mud caked into his head in big globs, like hair product. "It wasn't only one creek, you know, they're all slippery, like whenever I needed water."

Every muscle in my face strained against the inappropriate urge to grin. The absurdity of it clashed violently with the gravity of our situation. Here was this kid, standing before me—a living, breathing miracle in the midst of our calamity—and all I could do was fight back laughter. The incongruity of it all threatened to bubble over into hysterical mirth, a testament to our frayed nerves and battered psyches.

Declan wandered back up, grunted at us, settled himself looking out over the basin, and fished in his pack for breakfast.

I ate my cardboard protein bar as Josh tried to wake the dog. Barney had flopped over in the night and appeared to be sound asleep sprawled on his side. The snoring had stopped, and the furry body lay silent and still.

"Wake up, Barney." Josh poked at him. Nothing happened.

A little frisson of ice ran up my chest. Josh pushed the animal with both hands. Still no response.

Oh no, how long was it since the dog had been on bare dirt? Had he—?

Josh shoved him again. "Wake uuuuuuup, Barney."

Chapter 27

T he dog gave a great grumphing groan and opened his eyes.

Air rushed into my lungs, a shaky inhalation that rattled my entire frame. A laugh caught my breath midway, before gusting out. This simple act of respiration felt monumental, as if each molecule of oxygen carried the weight of our precarious situation.

"Cripes," I said. "I thought he was ... sick when he wouldn't wake up."

Josh wrinkled his forehead at me. "No. Barney's always like that in the morning."

Okay then. Phew.

In the end, the dog staggered to his feet and blinked blearily, did one of those big, 'front legs out, butt in the air, tongue curled stretchy' yawns. He took a few stiff steps, sniffing.

"Do you have any more food?" Josh asked. "I'm hungry."

The kid must have hollow legs. Barney wandered over to Declan and sniffed at his back.

"Let me see what I've got," I said to Josh.

A sudden movement caught my eye, drawing my attention just in time to witness a scene of canine irreverence. The dog, with impeccable timing and zero regard for human dignity, raised his hind leg. In one fluid motion, he christened Declan's back with a stream of liquid audacity.

"Aaaagh, you little bollocks!" Declan scrambled away, twisting his arm to pull at the back of his T-shirt.

"*Barnneeeeeey*," Josh wailed. "Not again."

A laugh escaped before I could stifle it, earning a withering glare from Declan. His scowl then shifted to the unrepentant canine, eyes narrowing dangerously. For a heart-stopping instant, visions of the dog sailing over the trail's edge flashed through my mind. But Declan merely wrestled out of his sodden shirt, revealing an intricate tattoo sprawling across his left pectoral. The design resolved into intertwined letters, a personal story etched in ink on skin.

"You've got a tattoo," Josh informed him.

"Cool, huh?" Declan said.

Josh looked at him with incredulous disgust. "No," he said and shook his head. "Only *old* people have tattoos."

I snorted again.

"You little gobshite," Declan said. He'd wiped himself off as best he could with the pissed-on shirt, then pulled out another and struggled into it. It was exactly as filthy as the one he'd taken off, but at least not soaked in warm dog urine.

Exhaustion hung heavy in the air, mingling with the collective irritability born of stress and sleepless nights. Yet beneath the surface, an undercurrent of cautious optimism burgeoned. Dante's Crag loomed tantalizingly close—a beacon of potential salvation. The prospect of escape, of finally breaching the boundaries of this nightmare, felt almost tangible.

'Today could be the day,' whispered a small voice in the back of my mind. 'We *should* make it out.' The word 'should' carried the weight of our hopes and fears, a fragile bridge between our current hell and the promise of safety.

When I got back from my trip down the trail and back, the boys were on better terms.

"He only did it 'cause he likes you," Josh was telling Declan.

"He's a bit of an idiot, isn't he?" Declan said with a grin.

I settled myself down and pulled out another protein bar. For once, I actually felt hungry.

Josh frowned at Declan. "He's a good dog," he said defiantly. "No matter what my dad—" He broke off, a bit damp around the eyes.

"Yeah, he's a good dog," I said. "Come here, boy." I waved a bit of protein bar at him, and he shot across to me. Yep, idiot.

"Some people like him," I told Declan, feeding Barney the treat. "Not me, of course. I think he's a little prick, but some people like him."

Josh laughed. Mission accomplished.

Declan wandered back to where he'd slept and rolled up the sleeping bag he'd inherited from Pete.

Josh stared at me for a little while, like he was going to say something, but then bundled up his sleeping bag, badly, not much rolling involved. He stuffed it randomly into his pack. Luckily, there didn't seem to be much else in there.

"Was it my fault?" he asked me.

I goggled at him a bit. His fault? What—that he'd crammed his sleeping bag in like a pile of balled-up laundry? Hell yes, entirely.

"What happened to my dad?" He huffed, taking a deep breath. "If I hadn't gone to find Barney ..."

Ah, jeez. I didn't have a joke big enough for that. Also, I thought I'd gotten over the urge to slap Dan Taylor up the back of the head. It turned out I hadn't.

"No," I said. "Absolutely not."

Josh looked at me dubiously. I guessed kids got used to not being told the whole truth.

"Okay. Do you remember the day we met you?" I asked him. His brow wrinkled, then I got one of those emphatic nods.

"Do you remember when we went to the spot you guys were using as a bathroom?"

Another nod.

"And your dad was digging about in the hole and got some worms out? Then he put them on his hand?" I extended my cupped hand to demonstrate.

Recollection dawned on Josh's face.

"That's when it happened. That's when he got bitten, and that's why he died."

I checked whether Josh had taken this in. He was a stoic little bastard.

"That's why he died?" Josh asked.

"Yeah, I'm sorry bud."

"And my mom?"

I nodded and held my breath in hope he wouldn't remember Dan saying his mom was in the hospital and me lying to back him up, but the kid didn't say anything.

My gaze drifted down to Josh, catching sight of his protruding lower lip—a subtle sign of his inner turmoil. The kid's composure was nothing short of remarkable, a stark contrast to the chaos surrounding us. A fleeting thought crossed my mind: how would my younger self have handled this adversity? Probably with a lot more tears and hysteria. Hell, even now, the urge to break down and howl at the unfairness of it all simmered just beneath the surface.

"Well," I said, and glanced over to Declan. "We should probably get going, huh?" I turned back to Josh. "Are you ready?"

He made a sound like 'sh-yah.' "I'm all packed," he said, his eyes sliding to where Declan and I still had gear out.

The dog was sniffing about, poking at some empty food wrappers, then his ears pricked up. I frowned at the animal. I didn't hear anything. He stood, stiff-legged, intent. Staring up the trail. He sniffed, his foxy little nose tasting the air. Then he took off up the path, doing his yap-yap thing.

God damn it.

"Barney!" Josh flung himself after the dog, abandoning his pack where it sat.

God damn it!

A silent exchange passed between Declan and me—my eye roll met with his head shake. Alrighty then. Message received, loud and clear.

With practiced motions, we tucked away the remaining odds and ends, our movements a well-worn choreography of survival. Packs settled onto shoulders with familiar weight, a reminder of how far we'd come and how far we still had to go. Josh's bag found its way into my grasp, an extra burden willingly shouldered.

And just like that, we were moving again. Another leg of our journey had begun, each step carrying us closer to ... well, something—hopefully, salvation.

At first, I was grouchy about having to carry the kid's stuff and pissed at him for taking off like that and taking off in a place where everything was trying to kill us. For about five minutes, I kept expecting to catch up with him, give him an earful, and hand him his pack, but there was no sign of him.

An uneasy sensation coiled in my gut, a silent alarm bell ringing. Logic whispered its doubts: Wouldn't Josh, having caught up with the dog, doubled back to ensure we were following? A glance at Declan's face mirrored my concerns, his furrowed brow a testament to our shared unease.

Our ascent continued, punctuated by periodic calls of Josh's name. Each shout hung in the air, unanswered, before fading into the indifferent landscape. The eerie silence that followed each call stirred a sickening sense of déjà vu, memories of other unanswered cries haunting our steps.

Where the hell was the kid? We might never know if he'd gone over the edge of the trail. Below us, way down below the steep drop, the treetops made a green carpet. If he'd slipped and fallen, the boy was gone, completely gone.

"Jooooooooooooosh!"

A half-hour later, my voice was getting hoarse, and we still hadn't found him. The sick feeling had solidified into dread. I'd managed to lose Josh Taylor for the second time.

The trail had gone up and over a hump, and we were heading down again. Down towards bare ground. To the side of us, the hill flattened out into a shallow slope instead of a steep drop.

The trail's stone was still wet with dew, and I'd slipped a couple of times on the surface. I had my head down, picking my way, when Barney shot back up the trail towards us.

He was by himself. Oh crap, where the hell was Josh?

The dog hit me at speed, front legs rebounding off my thighs. Then he did the mad, hoppy thing, bouncing off his back legs so his front paws hit me exactly where they shouldn't.

"Get down," I told him. "Where's Josh?" Like the dog could tell me.

Declan caught up to me and the pair of us looked down at the dog gyrating around us.

"Do you think he's gone over the edge?" Declan said.

"No sign. If he went over, it must've been back there, at that drop-off." My hand gestured towards our recent path.

Barney, either misinterpreting my point or driven by some canine logic, suddenly bolted back the way we'd come.

"Barney!" My shout echoed off the cliff face, mocking me with its "ey-ey-ey."

The dog didn't so much as twitch an ear. Great. Josh Taylor's dog added to the list of things I'd managed to lose.

Declan's face scrunched in thought as he stared after the vanished mutt. "Does the dog coming back mean Josh never made it this far?"

"Could just mean the dog's an idiot," I offered.

Declan's eyebrow arched. "Newsflash."

"We should press on," I said, my mind racing. "If Josh went over back there, well ... there's nothing we can do. But if he's in trouble further ahead, that could explain the dog's return."

My hand waved vaguely, thoughts still forming. "Maybe that's why ..."

"Why what—?" said Declan. "Why the dog's fucked off again?"

We stood and looked up the trail, then back down. There was no sign of either Josh or Barney.

"Do you want me to take that for a while?" Declan extended his hand for Josh's pack, and we started again.

We were approaching another bulge in the side of the rim and heading downhill. The ground ran up towards the trail's rock. I had a horrible feeling that up ahead, we'd find bare vegetation and danger.

If Josh had gone off the trail onto open ground ... the fist in my abdomen clenched tighter. Just one day, I'd wanted one day where no one died.

We went on. The trail ran down and down, further towards the encroaching dirt. I got farther and farther ahead of Declan, my sense of urgency back. Straggly trees and bushes infringed the trail, that was how close to the terrain the track had dropped.

I was eyeing this vegetation keenly as I came around a bend, so I was slow to register the figures.

Two of them stood on a rock beside a narrow gully of bare ground, one tall, one short, and one Josh Taylor.

"Hello again," Bill said.

Chapter 28

My heart leaped like a salmon. I instinctively twisted a hand behind me to Declan. I had no idea if he could see me, so I could only hope he'd understand to stay back out of sight.

"What are you doing?" I asked idiotically.

It was obvious what Bill was doing or intending. He held Josh in front of him, a cruel grip on his neck. Bill's fingers dug into the kid's skin. The barrel of his gun was pressed hard against Josh's head.

All my happy thoughts of vengeance, of sinking my fist into Bill's stupid hairy face, vaporized, leaving nothing but terror.

A subtle shift in the air betrayed Declan's movement behind me. In my mind's eye, I saw him creeping forward, curiosity overriding caution. In confirmation, Bill's gaze was fixed on the ridge at my back, tracking something unseen.

Paralysis gripped me, each heartbeat stretching into eternity. The certainty of Josh's fate settled like lead in my belly. No matter what move I made, the kid's death warrant was already signed. The weight of this knowledge pressed down, stealing the very air from my lungs.

My thoughts darted about like headless chickens. Should I try to rush Bill? I was too far; he'd shoot me before I reached him, but it might give Josh a chance. Was I actually brave enough to do it? I felt like I was about to wet myself. Would it be better to try to distract Bill, hoping something might happen? I couldn't think, couldn't think.

The boy's face was blank and pale, his eyes dilated.

I was strung up with frantic disbelief and confusion. I couldn't believe this was happening. After Josh had managed to survive for days alone in this hellhole, now he was going to be snuffed out in an instant, and I didn't know what to do to stop his death.

The kid's breath came in short, sharp pants as he stood as still as possible in Bill's grip, his eyes blank and staring.

My focus flipped back to Bill, and something struck me. Why had he not shot the boy and jumped already? Why had he waited here? Did even Bill have some compunction about killing a child? Or had Josh told him we'd be along, and he was waiting for a more mature stepping stone? A larger one? If that was the case—

A sudden cacophony of barks shattered the tension. Whirling around, I caught a glimpse of fur and fury as Barney streaked past, a canine missile locked onto Bill.

In that split second, the little dog's intentions were anyone's guess. Was this a fearsome attack or just an overeager greeting? But Bill, faced with the oncoming ball of energy, didn't wait to find out. He jerked back, the gun swinging wildly to target the approaching pooch.

Time slowed, the scene unfolding in terrible clarity. Bill's finger tightened on the trigger; Barney was oblivious to the danger as he bounded forward. The absurdity of it all—this tiny dog potentially changing the course of our future—struck me even as horror blossomed.

"Noooo." Josh whipped about and socked Bill directly in the balls. Smack.

It was impressive. Despite weighing around sixty pounds, he put all his weight, strength, and fear into that blow. He was perfectly positioned as well.

"Ahhh." Bill instinctively doubled over. His grasp on the back of Josh's neck loosened. Then, he drew his gun hand back to strike the kid's head.

My chest was going to burst. This was my opportunity, my chance to intervene, to stop Bill and save Josh. To make up for failing to save Wade. I desperately lunged toward the two of them.

And stumbled over the dog. I crashed onto the ground and landed forcefully on my hands, nowhere near Bill and Josh. Damn. Barney joyfully pounced on me with excited yelps.

"Get off, you little shit." I swiped frantically at the animal, trying to see what Bill was doing. My awesome display of athletic grace had amused the hairy asshole and distracted him. He sniggered as he looked at me, flailing around.

It gave Josh the barest chance, but it was enough. He slipped out of the man's loosened grip, ducking his head to dislodge Bill's hand, then shoved hard with both hands. Using the strength of his leg muscles, he caught Bill on the hip. My limbs tingled in hope.

It was enough to cause the man to wobble. He raised a foot to re-arrange his body, to plant his feet back down more sturdily. He never did—Josh pushed again. A spark of tremulous optimism swept through me as he shoved a third time, more of a collapsing-forward headbutt than a thrust. This time, he hit Bill on the side of the knee. The man's arms windmilled, his mouth a silent gaping circle.

Halfway to standing, I watched Bill's desperate dance with gravity. His arms twirled uselessly before he toppled backwards off the rock.

A tremor rippled through the ground, felt more than heard. The surface between the gully's bordering stones seemed to inhale, a pre-monition of horror. As Bill's body met the soil, an eruption of dirt obscured him from view. Then, a nightmarish sight: a forest of undu-lating, ripple-fingered appendages burst forth. For one eternal second, they reached and grasped, their pulsing movements defying nature. With a final spray of earth, Bill vanished, gobbled whole by the insatiable ground.

No thud. No scream. Just the terrible silence of the impossible made real.

A tempest of emotions surged through me—revulsion and triumph battling for dominance. Legs trembling, I lurched forward, peering into the hollow that had become Bill's grave.

"Take that, mother*fucker*." The words burst forth, raw and primal. My fist shot skyward in a gesture of fierce victory. A wildfire of vindictive joy blazed within, consuming rational thought. Each pulse of savage satisfaction seemed to scream: *That's what you get, asshole. That's the price for Wade's life.*

"Yeah, take that mudda fucka," Josh piped up behind me. He'd regained his feet, too, and copied my air punch with his small fist.

Whoops. I started to tell him those were bad words; he shouldn't imitate me. But fuck it, Josh Taylor had earned the right to say whatever he wanted.

"Oh my god." Declan scrambled over to us. He looked down at the hollow in the ground where Bill had disappeared, then back at Josh with admiration. "Well done, man."

Barney frisked around us. It struck me then that Josh knew what would happen when he had pushed Bill off the rock and onto the ground. This young child had deliberately caused the death of an adult.

Looking down at Josh, my vision blurred with unshed tears. An overwhelming surge of ... pride, of all things, threatened to burst my chest wide open. The absurdity of it wasn't lost on me—what kind of world had we stumbled into where this was cause for celebration?

But there he stood, this indestructible force of nature disguised as a kid. Josh Taylor, survivor extraordinaire, had weathered the storm of horrors solo and emerged unscathed. Like a cockroach after the apocalypse, he'd endured what should have been unsurvivable.

A smile tugged at my lips, unbidden and genuine. Fondness, an emotion I'd thought long buried, bloomed warm in my chest as I gazed at this impossible child.

"Did you bring anything to eat?" he said. "I'm hungry."

Yep, cockroach.

The three of us sat back from the edge of the rock, away from the chemical waft in the gully. We were stuck again; there was no way across, but right now, it didn't matter; we had a celebratory vibe. It was party time in hell.

We dug out food and drink. There wasn't much water left. Josh had a splash, I had a couple of drops, and Declan was out completely. I shared mine with Declan and stuffed the empty bottle in my pack, hoping we'd find water soon.

Declan fed the bottomless pit that was Josh, and I broke up another protein bar for Barney. He sniffed at it suspiciously before chowing down; maybe he had a brain in there somewhere.

We were perilously close to dehydration.

As I sat and chewed, I recalled all the shots we'd heard across the basin. Before we'd even met Bill, before ... Wade. Before we'd known what those shots were. All those single shots, and I wanted the jerk to die all over again.

A part of me yearned for closure, imagining one of those grasping appendages as Wade's final act of justice. The thought nestled in my mind, a comforting fiction I chose to believe.

Earlier musings about what constituted a 'good day' in this hellscape suddenly seemed laughably naive. No deaths equaling success? Dead wrong. Today, Bill had died, and the world felt lighter for it. A grim satisfaction settled in my bones. Against all odds, this blood-soaked day had become something to celebrate.

Josh was petting Barney. "See," he told us. "I told you he was a good dog. Did you see him get that mudda fucka? He could be an attack dog. He bit that mudda fucka."

Hmm, maybe there needed to be a conversation after all. I didn't think the dog actually bit Bill either, more bounced off his nuts, maybe. I looked at Barney, the attack puffball. He sat and panted, gaping in a gormless grin beneath his beady little eyes. Um, okay. I glanced at Declan, and we exchanged smiles.

"So, how are we going to get across this?" Declan nodded at the gully.

Josh looked at him. "The man said there was no way across."

"We should check for ourselves," I said. I'd be damned if I'd take Bill's word for anything.

So, that was what we did. We didn't bother taking our packs uphill. Even from where we started, it was pretty clear there was no way around the top. We went to check anyway, but the dead peninsula of ground ended up against a sheer cliff.

So, we tried downwards, to where the gully sprouted scrub, then trees, as far as we could go before there was nothing but sloping terrain beneath the spreading tree canopy.

The only possibility was a fallen tree trunk sprawled, almost entirely across the gap. At first, it looked like the answer to a prayer, and Josh was madly keen to cross it.

"I can do it, easy-peasy."

"Hmm, maybe. Hold on, bud." On closer inspection, I wasn't so sure.

The area was in deep shade and the reclining tree trunk was covered in a layer of slimy green moss. Although the wood looked sturdy it could be rotten, might not hold weight.

More concerning was the evidence that someone had recently tried and failed to cross. On our side, where the crown of the tree had heeled over, long bare branches rested on rock, and there were the remains of fresh footprints. Someone had stood on the mossy trunk and slipped off.

Boot marks were through the green carpet, and residue of it was on the rock beside the tree. Someone had tried to get across but decided it was too slippery.

Cautiously, my boot found its way onto the moss-covered log, testing its stability. The verdant layer yielded slightly under pressure, a silent testimony to years of decay beneath.

At ground level, Barney's wet nose worked overtime, investigating every green trace with canine thoroughness. As my foot connected more firmly with the log, a dull thud resonating through the wood, the dog's ears perked up. In one fluid motion, he bounded onto the log beside me, his attention instantly drawn to older indentations marring the mossy surface.

Those footprints, I realized with a chill, were likely Bill's, the final visible marks he'd left in this world. Barney's inquisitive snuffling took on a more ominous tone as he traced the path of our nemesis, unknowingly following a dead man's trail.

"Get off," I told the dog.

Barney's eyes met mine, his body frozen in place. A memory flashed unbidden—Mel Taylor's frustrated shouts at the unresponsive animal echoing across time. The recollection stung, sharp and unwelcome. A heavy exhale escaped my lips, an attempt to expel both the stale air and the painful reminder of our losses.

Meanwhile, in my blip of distraction, the dog calmly trotted down the tree trunk, nearly reaching the other side. Then he slipped and scrambled.

"Barneeeey." Josh jumped onto the log to follow.

"No." I extended my arm to stop him, but missed, lost my balance, slid on the rock, and ended up on my knees.

The dog also tumbled down. He rolled off the log onto the root ball of the tree, on the opposite side of the gap, partially embedded in the ground. I tried to regain my footing, to reach out, but Josh was already crossing, already halfway balanced on the slippery trunk.

Time froze as I watched, muscles taut with tension. The urge to shout, to demand his immediate return, clawed at me. But fear sealed my lips—what if my voice broke his focus, sending him plummeting? Silence became both shield and torment.

A cold sweat prickled across my skin, nerves jangling like live wires. Every slight movement, every shift in balance, sent a jolt of adrenaline coursing through my veins. The fragility of the moment weighed heavily, each second stretching into an eternity of anxious anticipation.

Josh edged downwards along the tilted trunk, step by step, across the gully. The dog was scrambling to right himself among the mossy tree roots. I tried not to think what he might be rolling in. Josh's pack was hanging unevenly, with only one arm through a strap. My shoulders tightened.

The kid was going to make it.

Then he wobbled, tried to catch his balance, and fell.

Chapter 29

Josh dropped a leg to either side of the tree. The kid landed right on his balls. I winced as he hit, but he managed to fling his arms around the log and cling on.

"*Owwwww.*"

My heart thudded in my throat. Across the gully, Barney clawed his way up the gnarled tilted roots and bounced onto the rocks. He perched there, gaping in a happy grin.

I swear the damn dog was going to be the death of me, of all of us. In the instant, my eyes flicked to Barney, Josh's pack shifted to one side. It dragged at him as it fell and pulled him around the mossy tree trunk till he was hanging upside down. He screamed in three short, shrill bursts.

The emerald ground beneath him heaved. I drew in a sharp swig of dread. A spurt of wet sludge pitched upwards. Something swiped, knifed through the green, and missed the loose dangling strap of Josh's pack by a hair.

"Drop it, drop your pack!" Declan shouted.

It had all happened so fast I was still sprawled among the dead tree branches where I'd slipped. Declan crawled out onto the tree trunk as I struggled to right myself on the slick rock. He still had his pack on, and his weight changed the balance of the tree. It shivered through what was left of the dried branches under me.

Josh let go of the trunk with one hand and let his pack fall. In a massive slurry of dirt and moss, it was gone. The ground beneath Josh writhed in unnatural motion, a nightmarish display of emerging appendages. Glimpses of fingers and palms breached the surface, a grotesque garden sprouting from the soil. The sight sent a shudder through my body, every sinew screaming in protest at the impossible scene unfolding before me.

Declan had straddled the tree trunk and used his hands to inch towards the kid. A splatter of dirt hit him in the face, and he spat and blinked.

Josh was upside down, clinging to the log. He couldn't see what was happening below him, but I assumed he could feel the clods being thrown up, hitting him.

Summoning every ounce of strength, I heaved myself upright, throwing my full weight onto the tree's end. My muscles strained as I pressed it against the unyielding rock, becoming a human anchor. Each of Declan's movements reverberated through the wood, the vibrations telling a story of his cautious advance towards Josh's precarious position.

"Hold on, I'm coming." Declan made his way forward, his hands slipping and skidding through the slick green moss.

From below, grit, slime, and pebbles were flung up repeatedly, as what was beneath the ground fished upwards. Hands, talons, and paws searched and clawed. I had no idea what some of the animals were or had been. Now, they were obscene marionettes.

My viscera revolted. All I could do was pray that what happened to Claire wouldn't happen again. There was no way any of us could get out of the way in time if another body protruded from the ground, if another head burst and sprayed us with worms.

Barney barked abruptly from the other side. It startled me so much that I almost wet myself.

"Shut up!" I roared at him, although he wouldn't listen.

"Hold on, we're almost there." Declan had reached where Josh was suspended. "Give me your hand."

The trunk dipped perceptibly, groaning under the combined burden of Declan and Josh. My eyes darted between the ground under the bowing wood and their precarious forms, each second an eternity of suspense. The urge to look away warred with the necessity to remain vigilant, leaving me frozen in a state of helpless observation.

Josh was frozen, unable to release his hand. Declan reached forward, underneath the log. He grabbed a handful of shirt and waistband, then hauled and rotated the kid until he was clinging to the top of the trunk.

Josh was making odd, sobbing noises but managed to start inch-worming forward, down the tree to the roots. He never once released his grip.

Declan moved to sit back up but didn't make it. The bulk of his pack pulled him to the side, and he slid around the slippery trunk exactly as Josh had done.

"Shit, shit. Help!" He tilted his head to the side and glanced at me, his eyes frantic. He scrabbled, trying to pull himself back up. On the slick surface, it was impossible. The weight on his back pulled him down, and all he could do was cling, as Josh had done.

With frantic fingers, I clawed at buckles and straps, urgency overriding finesse. My pack fell away, a dead burden discarded without a second thought. Freedom of movement gained, instincts took over. In one fluid motion, the log became my bridge to Declan.

Legs coiled around rough bark, hands grasping for purchase, as inch by precarious inch, I edged forward. Each movement was a careful balance of speed and caution, the need to hurry warring with the knowledge that one wrong move could spell disaster.

The slimy green moss was incredibly slippery. Under my grasping hands, it slid from the wet log like a layer of oil. The scent of decaying flesh, mixed with the distinct, sharp odor of worms, hit me in the face.

On the other side, Josh had reached the bottom. He collided with the raised roots with a jolt. The trunk shook. Ants crawled on my scalp.

The log split, broke, and fell. The base of the tree bent, cracking directly above the roots. I desperately clung on as the trunk descended a foot to the ground. It landed with a thud and then bounced.

All I could do was hold on tightly and hope that the entire tree trunk didn't splinter into nothingness. Below me, Declan was still hanging on, upside down. With the steeper angle, his head was only a couple of feet from the bottom of the gully, and his pack, hanging from him, was almost touching it.

The ground beneath him churned in grotesque motion, a nightmarish sea of writhing forms. The soil was alive, pulsating with an unnatural hunger that defied comprehension. The sharp, rank scent intensified. It burnt into my nostrils. Dirt was flung up in swathes. The world was filled with the sound of spattered mud and desperate whimpers.

Suddenly, momentum took control. The world tilted as gravity pulled me down the trunk, straight towards Declan. Desperation fueled futile attempts to halt the slide, fingers scrabbling for purchase on the slick bark. Declan's frantic struggle with his pack strap became a terrifying countdown.

The damp surface offered no mercy, as slippery as black ice. Inexorable motion carried me forward, a human projectile on a collision course. Impact. The sickening thud of body against body. Declan's feet, torn from their tenuous grip, scraped across my arm and wrist. A trail of moss and mud marked their passage, a grim reminder of our shared peril.

His pack hit the churning sludge a second before his legs. For a brief, heart stopping beat, my mind went blank. Declan's arms were still wrapped around the trunk. I flung myself flat on the log to reach down, to try and grab him, to pull him back up.

His face below me was a mask, eyes round. Beneath his head, the ground exploded, sending a harsh spray of mud across my face.

Declan screamed, his voice stretched high. Then I saw it.

All the churning in my guts froze.

Chapter 30

It was a snake, but not a live snake. It shot up, then dove down. It wrapped around Declan's neck, and then pulled him into the ground. No live snake moved like that, animated by vile pulsations under the skin. My mouth was dry as dust.

The creature's strength was overwhelming. As it attempted to drag him down, its monstrous form proved unstoppable. The horrific scene unfolded with brutal efficiency, leaving me frozen in shock and revulsion.

Declan's head landed with a thud and a brutal gush of blood. I gagged and locked eyes with him for a split second, then his head was gone. Pulled beneath the desecrated surface by another grotesque brown coil.

His neck spewed red before his body was also pulled below. Hands, claws, and hooves burst through and around him, piercing his backpack and entering his body, and dragged him down in a shower of dirt.

I clung to the tree trunk, choking on a sob.

"Come on!" Josh screamed at me.

He had reached safety. The kid was standing on the rock on the other side.

A primal urge to scream at him, to blame the dog for this debacle, clawed behind my eyes. But terror had stolen my voice, leaving me gasping for air too thick to breathe.

Below, an eerie calm descended upon the gully. The frenzied activity had ceased, replaced by occasional movements in the disturbed soil. Sickening odors wafted up, a nauseating mix of decay and something unnatural, hinting at the morose feast taking place out of sight.

Spontaneously, my mind conjured images too horrific to dwell on—of writhing forms and violated bodies. The thought of what might be happening to Declan sent a violent shudder through me, my body rebelling against the very idea.

"Get up *here*." Josh danced up and down on the rock. Tears streamed down his face.

Steeling myself, I forced my body into action. Cautiously, I slid towards the broken end of the trunk where it disappeared into the soil. Every fiber of my being screamed with tension as I neared the bottom. Focusing intently on my hands, I inched forward, hyper-aware of each movement.

Josh screamed then, a high-pitched shrill, piercing the air. Beside me, a body had emerged from the ground.

It wasn't a swipe, or the slash of a limb, but the start of an awful balancing act. Dread sank its knuckles into my gut.

The ground beneath heaved, sending more terror through me. Scrambling to my feet on the slippery wood, I launched myself across the gap. My fingers scrabbled desperately at the remnants of the root ball, tearing through dirt and debris in a frantic climb out of the gully.

The body had writhed its way out a couple of feet now. It wasn't human. It was an animal of some kind, had been an animal, maybe a mountain goat, maybe a deer. Its head was floppy, and its front legs were broken flags. The astringent smell was subtly different.

A great pulse ran through the body, and the head partially raised. My mouth filled with liquid revulsion. I tore my eyes from it and struggled up the rock, concentrating on hauling ass out of there.

Josh was gone. I hoped he'd gotten out of there, up across the stone where it was safe. My breath tore at my chest as I heaved myself up and finally made it out of the crevasse up onto a plateau of rock on the other side.

A shiver of thankfulness ran through me. In front of me ran flat sheeting stone, seamed with patchwork channels, not tumbled boulders, not something to climb up or through. If I could get up, I could run.

But the rock face greeted me with a treacherous covering of moss. Each attempt at finding purchase was a battle against gravity and fear. Josh's voice cut through the air, words lost in the rush of adrenaline. A quick glance back at the gully sparked a desperate hope that he'd found safety on higher ground.

With a final, exceptional effort, I hauled myself over the edge, collapsing onto a mesa of solid rock on the far side. The world spun as relief and exhaustion warred for dominance.

"Keep going!" I bawled at Josh. He was still looking back at me.

I stumbled to my feet.

Every movement felt like wading through molasses, each second stretching into eternity. Muscles burned with the effort of propulsion, pushing beyond their limits. Behind me, a sickening, wet pop sent tendrils of dread racing up my spine.

SPPLUUUCKK!

Desperation fueled a final lunge forward, grasping for those precious extra feet of distance. The sound echoed again, louder this time, reverberating through the gully with terrifying clarity.

Impact with the ground sent shockwaves of pain through my body as I rolled, finally coming to a stop. Heart pounding, I twisted to look back, to see if my efforts had been enough.

In that instant, the line between life and death hung in precarious balance.

The rattle of debris rained down barely a body length from me. Worms, skull fragments, dead flesh. The canopy of trees in the gully may have collected some and the steep rocky sides of the gap might have deflected a bit. But not enough, not enough to stop it.

As I retreated, another wave of stench assaulted my senses. The familiar, putrid odor of decay now carried a new, acrid chemical note.

Though reasonably confident I'd escaped unscathed, doubt niggled at the edges of my mind.

The frantic sprint had left me drained, muscles screaming for respite. Every fiber of my being craved collapse, a brief reprieve from the horrors we'd witnessed. Declan's final, anguished expression threatened to overwhelm me, but I forced the image aside. Safety demanded distance from that accursed gully.

Higher up the rocky slope, Josh and the dog waited. Each step towards them was a battle against exhaustion and gravity. As I finally reached the kid, a new wrongness permeated the air.

Josh's face was a mask of wild-eyed terror, jaw working frantically as he struggled to form words. Only clicking teeth and strangled sounds emerged. Abandoning the attempt at speech, he jabbed a trembling finger behind me.

"Look," Josh finally croaked.

I turned, eyes scanning the landscape. At first, nothing seemed amiss—just bare rock, tree-tops lining the gully, and a dull grey sky. Then, everything shifted.

Literally. The stone itself appeared to move, a crawling, squirming mass of layered motion. A seething carpet of death advanced towards us, individual components indistinguishable but unmistakably swift. And they were coming for us.

Josh stood frozen, eyes vacant, body quivering. I grabbed his arm, yanking him from his trance.

"*Run*," came the whispered command.

We bolted. Amidst the overwhelming terror, a fleeting sense of gratitude registered—the flat rock beneath our feet gave us a fighting chance. Obstacles or uneven terrain would have sealed our fate.

Josh suddenly pulled away, screaming at Barney. The dog stood ahead, rigid and bristling, barking furiously at the encroaching tide.

Atta boy, scare 'em off, flashed absurdly through my mind, a spark of dark humor in our desperate flight.

The relentless rhythm of survival drove us forward, each footfall against the stone sending shockwaves through weary bodies. Behind us, inexorable death continued its ruthless pursuit.

All I could think was, "What the fuck?" We were supposed to be safe on the stone. It was what we knew, for certain, in all this insanity: we were safe on the stone, on solid rock.

I plowed on. My legs felt like they had turned to stone themselves. I hauled them onwards, threw each one forward after the other. My chest burned.

We weren't safe on the stone.

Whenever I looked back, the creatures were there. Following us. The ripple of movement, skittering, squirming across the rock. I pictured them sniffing at our footsteps, tasting us.

It gave me an odd sensation, like my teeth were loose in my head. I looked and ran. Looked and staggered.

The high rim trail offered little respite as I clambered onto it. Each torturous step brought a gain in elevation, the climb relentless in its demands. Muscles screamed in protest, but the urgency of survival pushed the body forward. The path ahead promised no ease, only the grim necessity of continued ascent.

Finally, my body waved the white flag. From all-out sprint to stumbling walk to face-planting on the ground. How far? A mile, maybe?

Who was I kidding—probably half that. The real question: how long could those nightmare-fuel rejects keep up the chase?

I dragged myself onto a convenient rock hump and risked a look back. Nothing moving. Small mercies. Josh and Fido had vanished—another point for the 'not totally screwed' column. If that rippling hell-carpet caught up, maybe they'd wear themselves out on yours truly and leave the kid alone. Silver linings, right?

Sitting there, trying not to keel over, a lovely realization hit me like a brick to the face. I'd been a grade-A moron. Thought I had the worms all figured out, did I? Newsflash, genius: you couldn't know jack about something that shouldn't exist. Congratulations, you won the Idiot of the Year award.

Eyes peeled, scanning for any twitch below. Those things moved like greased lightning on steroids. The mere thought sent a shiver down my spine.

Death. Not just a possibility now, but a certainty. Weirdly, that crushing realization almost took the edge off the whole 'I accidentally killed Declan' guilt-fest. Almost.

If I closed my eyes, the tree trunk beckoned, a treacherous bridge to suffering. One slip, one lapse of care, and suddenly the world tilted. A collision, a desperate scramble, and then ... nothing. Funny how one stupid decision could change everything.

Bright side? Ha. What a joke. This rock might as well be a headstone. Death circled like a vulture, promising agony with every beat of its wings. No food, no water, just the clothes on my back and an endless expanse of wilderness. Dante's Crag might as well be on the moon.

Josh and his mutt were long gone, probably smart enough to avoid this mess. Thoughts pinballed around my skull, each one more useless than the last. But Declan ... no. *Don't go there. Don't see that face, that horrific scaled noose.*

Claire's face swam into view instead. Brave Claire. Would her courage rub off when the skittering tide came creeping up the trail? Finding a high place wouldn't be the problem. It was the jumping that turned my legs to jelly.

Heights. God, what a laugh. "Not good with heights," that was what people heard. A comfortable lie, easy to believe on solid ground. But up here, with nothing but air and certain death below? Phobia didn't begin to cover it.

Was it karma, that throwing myself off a cliff was probably now my best choice? Was this my punishment for killing Declan? And Dan? I now had a worse phobia than heights, of course, as above all things, I now feared being eaten alive.

If I hadn't previously had a phobia of being eaten alive, it was only because I'd never known it was an option, a horrendous, heart-stopping, throat-closing option. One that made jumping from a great height seem appealing, but maybe it was only because I was nowhere near a cliff?

"Heeeeeeeey." Josh reappeared above me, hopping from level to level back down the track. He wobbled to a halt, panting.

"Come on—I've found a rope. It's hanging down the rock."

Chapter 31

A flicker of movement caught my eye, but Josh's words sank in slowly, like a stone through murky water. A rope? The kid had actually come back? The world tilted on its axis, hope bursting through the cracks of despair.

"Hurry up," Josh said. "I need a boost up to get the rope, I can't reach it."

I hauled myself painfully to my feet and staggered onwards. Time blurred. Suddenly, we were there—the looming face of Dante's Crag. And there it was—a lifeline dangling from the heavens. I gazed motionless, afraid the slightest movement might make it vanish like a mirage.

"It's a rope, right?" Josh yelled up at me.

Words failed. A nod was all I could manage as I scrambled up for a closer look. The boulder beneath my feet felt like the only solid thing in the world. Below, Josh and Barney were specks against the unforgiving landscape.

And there it was. Red as a lifeline should be, with little white and yellow dots winking like stars of hope. It snaked up the cliff face, anchored at intervals by metal loops. Each one sang a tiny song of salvation.

My fingers twitched, aching to grasp that braided promise. But a whisper of dread still lingered. How long had it been here? Would it hold? And even if it did ... could I conquer the paralysis that gripped me whenever solid ground fell away?

It was at once the most heartbreakingly wonderful and terrifying thing. Someone had left their rope; someone had managed to get out and, knowing others could be trapped, had left their rope. A surge of thankfulness swept over me; the sheer compassion lined my eyes with moisture.

With what was chasing us, after all the horror, after Bill, after watching Bill murder Wade just to step on him, to save his own miserable life, after witnessing such depths of humanity, this felt like hope. This felt like kindness, like a small glimmer of redemption for humanity. We weren't all assholes.

And, more importantly, Josh and I were going to get out. We had made it. After everything we had gone through, here was escape at last. It was almost too much to comprehend, the idea of normalcy, of help, safety, counseling, coffee, toilet paper, getting the hell away from what was chasing us, and alerting the authorities before those damn things scaled the rim.

The rope also scared the living hell out of me.

The lifeline swayed gently, taunting me. No choice. This was it—salvation or ... well, best not to dwell on the alternative. My chest swelled with determination, even as my innards performed nauseating backflips.

Fingers quaking, I reached out. The rough braid bit into my palm, solid and real. A tug. It held. But for how long? And what waited at the top?

Shadows lengthened, stretching grasping fingers across the rock face. Daylight was bleeding away, and with it, our chances.

Hassan's face flashed unbidden, a king-hit of memory. The sickening crack as he'd hit the rocks below. The absolute finality of it.

Not this time, a voice growled in my head. *Not us.*

"*Heeeeeeeeeeeeey!*" Josh yelled up at me with impatience. "I need help with Barney."

He'd managed to pick the dog up, barely, and was arched awkwardly backward, trying to hoist him up the rock. The furball was looking supremely annoyed at being manhandled and was struggling to get back down. As I looked at the pair of them, I remembered dogs couldn't climb ropes.

Josh's eyes shone with hope as he cradled Barney, oblivious to the crushing truth. How did you tell a kid to leave his best friend behind?

The sun dipped lower, casting more darkness that reached for us with hungry tentacles. A cold knot of dread tightened in the pit of my stomach. Bad enough to face this climb, but now ...

Barney whined, squirming around to lick Josh's face. Loyalty in the face of horror. It was almost enough to break what was left of a heart.

"We have to go." The words tasted like ash. "Now."

A breeze like death's cold breath ran across the face of the cliff. Climb or die. Some choice.

My gaze traveled back to Josh and Barney, an island of innocence in this purgatory. A sigh escaped, heavy with the weight of what came next.

"Hand over the furball." The words came out gruffer than intended. Might as well let the kid have his moment. Bring the dog up to the bottom of the rope for one last goodbye before ...

Barney kicked, a bundle of anxious energy. Muscles strained around my spine as I hauled the dog up. Then—*ping*—a sharp protest from an abused back. Pain flared, hot and insistent.

"Damn it," the curse slipped out through my gritted teeth.

Wade would have been proud of me, though, as I managed not to say it too loud.

Meanwhile, my brain kept turning over. Someone had gotten out, which meant either help or fiery death was coming. The authorities would take one look at what lurked in this godforsaken place and reach for the big red button. Visions of mushroom clouds bloomed behind my eyes. A fitting end for this nightmare.

I looked at the cliff. I had no idea how long the rope had been there; it could be days, could be ten minutes for all I knew.

Was it possible to wait here for help? The closer we came to climbing, the more irrational my thinking became. We had no food, no water, and nothing to keep us warm overnight. If we stayed and waited, what state would we be in tomorrow? Not good, I'd bet, not great shape for climbing if it came to it.

Going without food was doable, water was non-negotiable. But hell, I wanted to wait. More than anything, the desire to avoid climbing that cliff burned strong. My hand absently rubbed at the sore spot on my back.

"You know, someone's gotten out," I said to Josh. "We could wait for them to send help." It was rubbish, but my fear of heights had temporarily hijacked my brain and overridden both my fear of flaming death and my fear of being eaten alive. *Go figure.*

The kid looked at me like I was crazy. Which I probably was.

"No way. We have to get out." He had one hand on the rope and wiggled it back and forth. "I can climb this. Easy peasy."

My skin itched all over as the rope swayed. "Um, are you sure?"

"Ye-*ess.*" An eye roll.

Was that sarcasm?

"We have to go, now." Josh looked at me, lip quivering.

The truth hit like a gut punch. Rescue? Ha. More likely a scorched-earth policy once word got out. The rope was a mocking reminder that someone had already escaped this hell. Right now, they could be spilling secrets that would seal our fate.

Josh's eyes were narrowed now, dubious. "Anyway, it's worse than before—" Barney jumped up to paw at him, interrupting. My anxiety spiked, waiting to hear what Josh considered worse than being eaten alive.

"—we don't have anything to eat."

Ah, okay then. We all had our priorities, I guessed.

"Come *ooon*." He tugged at the rope impatiently. "Let's go already." He was almost hopping up and down.

I braced my knees. "Alright." I considered. "I think you'll have to go first," I said. "So, I can still hold the rope for you."

And also, if I chickened out and couldn't do it, the kid would be safe. I looked down. Barney had sat himself eagerly at Josh's feet. He goggled up like he expected to be fed. Josh looked at him. His lower lip drooped, and I registered exactly when it dawned on him: dogs couldn't climb ropes.

"Josh," the name came out as a croak. "Barney ... he can't ..."

The words hung in the air, sharp as broken glass. Suspicion dawned on the kid's face, twisting it into a mask of disbelief and pain.

"We're taking Barney, right?" His voice cracked, desperate for reassurance.

Yeah, sure kid. In my head I framed the words to break it to him the animal wasn't coming, that we had to leave him here, probably to be caught by the tide of scuttling death. I tried to speak, but nothing came out.

Oh no. I couldn't do it, I couldn't tell him Barney wasn't coming. So, I lied.

"I'll bring him."

I waited for Josh to realize that there was no way I could carry a dog up a cliff, but he nodded. "Okay. Cool."

Jeez.

Well, it was probably for the best. If I'd told him flat out we couldn't bring Barney, he'd be a mess, not the best frame of mind for climbing a cliff.

Josh bent over to say goodbye to the pooch. "Now you be a good boy," he said, with completely unfounded optimism.

The rock face loomed overhead, its sheer height sending a wave of dizziness through me. Forcing myself to focus, I tried to assess it objectively. Not too steep, decent footholds scattered about. With the rope, the kid stood a fair chance.

Grasping the line, I pulled it taut. The rough braid bit into my palm, solid and real.

"When you reach the top," I called to Josh, "yell down. Can't see where this thing ends from here."

Awkward, but also good. If I did manage to climb the damn thing, Josh wouldn't know I didn't have Barney till I reached the top.

My eyes traced the rope's path upwards, losing it against the darkening sky. A fullness unexpectedly filled my bladder. This was it. No more stalling, no more excuses. We had to climb, ready or not.

The kid set off, and my chest tightened. But damn if Josh didn't make it look effortless. His small hands gripped the rope confidently, toes finding purchase on the sloping rock face. Up he went, scaling the cliff with the ease of a seasoned climber.

A mix of relief and envy washed over me. For Josh, this was just another adventure. No paralyzing fear, no second-guessing every move. Just pure, instinctive motion.

"Piece of cake," I muttered, watching his steady ascent. The words tasted bitter. Now it was my turn, and suddenly that rock face looked a whole lot steeper.

Before I knew it, he was out of sight. I could tell he was still climbing from the vibrations through the rope, so I tried to hold it as tightly and still as possible. Maybe he seemed quick to me because I had to go next. A bare minute later, Josh called from above.

"Hey! I'm up. It's easy."

Hmm, yeah, easy for some.

The dog's eyes met mine, dark pools of ... something. Desperation? Understanding? Barney sat there, unnaturally still, as if he knew what was coming. A lump formed in my throat.

"Oh jeez," the words slipped out, barely a whisper.

This wasn't just leaving a pet behind. This was abandonment in the face of unspeakable danger. Barney's tail gave a half-hearted thump against the ground, a pitiful attempt at optimism.

We stared at each other, human and dog, while the weight of the impossible choice pressed down. The rope swung gently, a constant reminder of the urgency. But how did you explain the unexplainable to those loyal eyes?

"No," I told him.

His fluffy little ears went back on his head. Oh, for crying out loud.

"I've got no way to take you, buddy. If I had my pack, I could've stuffed you in it. But I don't."

Crouching down, I found myself explaining the situation to Barney. Ridiculous, sure, but anything to postpone that climb. My hand sank into his fur, surprised at how small he actually was beneath all that fluff.

Suddenly, he was up, tongue swiping across my cheek. "Oh dammit," I muttered, caught off guard by the gesture.

My hands instinctively went to his chest, holding him at bay. But, something clicked. He was light, mostly fur and spirit. An absurd thought crossed my mind—could he fit in my shirt?

We locked eyes again, and I could almost hear the unspoken question. Was I really considering this? The rope creaked softly above, a reminder of the perilous climb ahead. But leaving him behind ...

My fingers tightened slightly in his fur. Maybe, just maybe, there was another way.

Dammit again. Why did it have to occur to me? It wasn't fair. I put my head down on Barney's hairy one and sighed. He twisted and stuck his tongue up my nose. Ugh.

I wasn't much for tucking in T-shirts usually. I wasn't saying it was because there was a little extra padding around the middle these days, that might be disguised by a hanging-out shirt. It was purely a fashion choice.

Anyway, I tucked my shirt in, looked at the dog, then looked at my front. I undid my belt and redid it a notch smaller. A sharp stab awoke the sore spot in my back, but I decided to ignore it.

"What's going on? What are you doing?" Josh shouted down from above, his voice tinny in the mild breeze.

For heaven's sake. I let the annoyance sweep through me as it helped settle my nerves.

"I'm sorting out the dog!" I bellowed back up. "I'll tell you when we start; now shut up."

Determination took over. Scooping up Barney, I attempted to stuff him into my shirt collar. Two seconds of frantic wriggling later, awareness set in. Impossible.

Depositing the furball back on the ground, I caught his look. Great, now the dog thought I was the village idiot.

Plan B. Teeth clenched on my shirt hem, I squatted down. Barney bounced around like this was the best game ever invented. After a ridiculous struggle, I managed to pin the furry menace against my chest.

"Hold still, you maniac," I muttered through a mouthful of cotton. The whole situation was absurd. Here we were, at the base of a deadly climb, and I was wrestling a dog into my clothing.

But damned if I was leaving him behind. We were in this mess together, might as well face that climb as a team. Even if that team included one very wriggly, possibly insane canine passenger.

Arms clamped tight, I spat out the shirt hem and yanked it down over Barney's squirming body. Staggering upright, I stuffed the fabric into my trousers, fumbling one-handed with my belt. Pretty sure the shirt was now tucked into places it had no business being, but desperate times and all that.

There I stood, sporting a panting, furry beer belly. Letting my arms drop, the canine bundle sagged alarmingly. Barney twisted, but miraculously stayed put.

This was a terrible idea. No doubt about it. Yet a tiny, clearly deranged part of me felt relief. At least I wouldn't be facing that climb alone. Even if my climbing partner was currently stuffed down my shirt, panting hot dog breath onto my chest.

"We're both idiots, aren't we?" I muttered to my furry passenger. Barney's tail moved against my skin in response. Yeah, great team we made.

The rope hung before us, a challenge and a lifeline. With a silent prayer, I reached out. No more delays. Time to see if this insane plan would get us up the cliff or kill us both in the attempt.

Chapter 32

Duck-walking to the rope, I cradled the Barney-bulge like some bizarre, furry pregnancy. Each awkward step was a test, gauging how secure my canine cargo remained.

Surprisingly, the impromptu harness held. Barney shifted slightly but stayed nestled against my chest. His warmth seeped into me, a constant reminder of the added stakes in this climb.

"It's you and me, bud," I told the dog. "What the hell, if I don't make it, maybe you'll break my fall." I reached out and grabbed the rope, testing to make sure it was still secured. I was filled with butterflies. They weren't just fluttering in there; they were having some kind of manic rave.

Barney stuck his nose out of the neck of my T-shirt. I sincerely hoped he wouldn't try to get his whole head out of there, as he'd probably choke me if he did. The feel of his fur against my naked skin was strangely unpleasant.

"Alright, we're coming up!" I shouted to Josh.

"Okay."

Okay.

I took my first step off the ground, pressed my toes into a ridge of rock and hauled myself up. The dog shifted in his cocoon.

"It's alright, bud," I said. "You're all right." I tried to tell myself I was talking to the dog.

The climb started surprisingly well. Hand over hand, foot after foot, I inched upward. The upper part, where cliff gave way to slope, was tantalizingly close. Just a bit further and maybe, just maybe, the vertigo would ease.

But looking for footholds meant looking down. And looking down meant ...

It hit like a freight train. Reality slammed into me, every neuron screaming about the drop below. Muscles locked. Skin crawled. I became one with the rock face, a petrified statue clinging for dear life.

Eyes screwed shut, but it didn't matter. The awareness of empty space yawned beneath me, a gaping maw ready to consume me whole. My tongue, dry as sandpaper, stuck to the roof of my mouth.

Hands, now painful claws, refused to budge from the rope. Face pressed against cold stone, as if I could meld into it and disappear. The enormity of the situation crushed down, an invisible weight pinning me in place.

This was it. The end. Frozen here forever, or until gravity won its inevitable victory. Tiny sips of air whistled through my constricted throat. Time lost all meaning—seconds, minutes, hours blurred into an eternity of paralyzing fear.

And all the while, Barney's warmth against my chest. A reminder of the stakes, of the impossible choice that led to this terror on the cliff face.

"What are you guys dooooooing?"

A second after he heard Josh's voice, Barney struggled. Pinpricks of alarm shot through my wrists; he had been still, but now he wriggled.

That woke me up fast. I couldn't feel my hands. The dog kicked and turned. My shirt partly untucked.

"Stop it, Barney, no." It was like the animal couldn't hear me, wouldn't, his movements became frantic, and he was going to fall. The bundled fabric moved under my belt.

The world narrowed to a pinpoint of sensation. Sweat beaded on my forehead, trickling down to sting my eyes. Each shallow breath rasped in my ears, impossibly loud against the deafening silence of the cliff face.

Muscles trembled from the strain of immobility, a deep ache setting into joints locked in desperate grip. The rough texture of the rope bit into my palms, a constant reminder of the tenuous lifeline.

Against my chest, Barney's rapid, rhythmic panting provided an unexpected counterpoint to my erratic gasps. His fur tickled my skin, an obnoxious sensation given our precarious position.

The air felt different up here—thinner, colder. It nipped at exposed skin, a sharp contrast to the heat radiating from my overtaxed body. Somewhere far below, a pebble skittered down the cliff face, the sound unnaturally crisp in the still air.

Time stretched, elastic and unreal. Were we seconds or hours into this frozen picture? The distinction blurred, lost in a haze of adrenaline and primal fear.

Then Barney crapped on me.

Inside my shirt. Spurted a miniature ejection, horribly warm against my skin. Dear heaven, it stank. I believed the correct term would be 'lost control of his bowels.'

Pllllrrrrrp. Oh, dear God there was more of it; how could there be more?

It was the wretched protein bars I'd given him in the morning. That was why he'd been wriggling, desperate to get out. Sheesh. I could feel warm liquid spray down my belly and seep under my waistband, through to where I'd tucked my T-shirt in so emphatically. I groaned. The dog stuck his nose out the neck of my T-shirt and licked me on the neck. Ugh.

"Come on, what are you doing?" Josh called down. His voice had gotten all high-pitched.

"Your stupid dog's just shit on me!" I bellowed upwards.

There was a choke of laughter from above. Damn kid.

Being crapped on had woken me up, though, broken through my static paralysis. Don't get me wrong, I was still shitting myself, maybe not literally like the damn dog, but at least shitting myself and able to move.

I managed a step up, felt for a new toe hold, and hauled myself and my reeking burden upwards again.

I was able to focus on something besides the soul-crushing terror of my position. Admittedly, I was focused on foul-smelling dog diarrhea, but if it got me moving, who cared—I got a big waft from my shirt—oh, good Lord, I cared.

It stank so badly. At least Barney had stopped wriggling, which I assumed was from shame.

The thought of my shirt untucking nagged at the edges of consciousness. A problem, sure, but one that paled in comparison to our other worries. Still, the urge to fix it gnawed.

The likely state of affairs inside that makeshift dog-sling was ... less than pleasant. A grimace twisted my features as I imagined tepid, wet dog mess waiting to greet any exploratory hand.

Nope. Not happening. Bad enough to be stuck on this godforsaken cliff without adding that horror to the mix. Besides, a wet, potentially shit coated hand on the rope? Recipe for disaster. One problem at a time. First, conquer this paralysis. Then, fix the shirt, deal with whatever mess awaited. Priorities, even if they involved dog shit at dizzying heights.

It was beyond revolting. My mind, desperate for distraction, latched onto the unpleasant condition of my midsection. Focus on that, I commanded silently. The warm, wetness creeping into places it had no business being.

Something gave way far above me with a scrape and then came loose. The rope whiplashed down directly on me. A metal peg caught me with a slash across the head. A slither and clink echoed as it hit the ground below me, far, *far* below me.

Pain blotted out everything. It felt like my skull had been split open by a sledgehammer. I clutched my head, expecting to feel raw brains and spurting blood. There was nothing, nothing but pain. I pressed hard to the place and rubbed, trying to ease the stabbing throb. Eventually, the blossoming agony dispersed enough that panic could nudge its way in. I fought down the urge to hyperventilate.

I clung to the cliff, a human fly without its safety thread. My head throbbed, an icepick of pain lodged behind my right eye. Vision blurred, making the world a smeared watercolor of potential doom. *And let's not forget my new fashion accessory—a shirt full of dog crap.*

We were in deep trouble this time. I'd faced death before in the past few days, but this? This was a whole new level of "oh shit." You'd think I'd be used to it by now, but no. Each time hit like a haymaker straight to the nose.

My stomach roiled, a grim echo of Barney's earlier indiscretion. I wondered, with a detached sort of curiosity, if I was about to join him in the "soiled pants club." Wouldn't that be the cherry on top of this disaster sundae?

Then, because the universe clearly needed a laugh, my foot slipped.

We hung there, Barney and I, suspended between solid ground and empty air. I had a fleeting, ridiculous thought: At least I wouldn't have to explain to Josh why his dog was a pancake at the bottom of a cliff.

Time stretched like taffy. I could almost hear the mocking laughter of gravity as it prepared to claim its prize.

Then, over my panic, over my fear, a great wall of anger hit me.

For *fuck's* sake. Could I not have one morsel of time to panic and mourn my imminent death? I was majorly pissed. Completely, irrationally furious.

The anger propelled me upward, each movement a middle finger to fate itself. I hauled us higher, one precarious hold at a time. Barney's weight shifted with each move, a furry pendulum in my shirt.

We came out of shade and into the late afternoon sun. Sweat stung my eyes, mingling with dust from the cliff face. The rock bit into my fingers, but I welcomed the pain. It was real, tangible, something to focus on besides the yawning emptiness below us.

My muscles screamed in protest, but I told them to shut up and deal with it. We weren't done yet. Not by a long shot.

The sun beat down mercilessly, turning the cliff into an oversized frying pan. Heat radiated from the rock, making each handhold a test of endurance. But bring it on. I'd take blistered palms over a swan dive any day.

Inch by grueling inch, we ascended. The slope gradually became less severe, hope flickering like a mirage. Were we actually going to pull this off?

A pebble skittered past, dislodged by my foot. I refused to track its fall, to think about what it represented. Instead, I channeled every ounce of stubborn fury into the next reach, the next pull.

Screw physics. Screw probability. We were getting to the top of this godforsaken rock pile if it was the last thing we did.

Sweat beaded on my forehead, running into my eyes and blurring the world into a haze of brown and blue.

My skin was raw, scraped by rough stone and baked by relentless heat. Each handhold was a test of will, fingers screaming for relief but refusing to let go.

Barney wriggled as I moved, a constant reminder of our precarious situation. His fur, already damp with watery shit, stuck to my sweaty skin. Revolting.

The air thinned as we ascended, each breath a little harder to catch. But I pushed on, driven by a fury that burned hotter than the sun-baked rock.

My joints creaked in protest, unused to this vertical dance. But I silenced their complaints with sheer stubbornness. We had no choice but to keep going.

The cliff's face gradually softened its angle, offering a glimmer of hope. If the rope had failed lower down ... No. That thought had no place here. Only up. Always up.

Almost before I knew it, I'd reached the lip, where the cliff definitely decided to become a slope. I pulled myself up and over it, then lay on my side against the rock. I'd made it.

It would still be as deadly to fall from there, but it felt safer, it felt more like horizontal ground. My bones melted. I couldn't believe what I'd done. I flushed with the idea of it. I'd done it. I'd climbed a fucking cliff.

The dog squirmed around, and I got a heady waft of excrement. In my fright, then anger, I'd actually blocked out the smell, but now I could taste it in the back of my nose.

"What are you doing?"

I twisted my head up, and Josh was peering at me, maybe only ten feet further up. The empty pegs that had held the rope continued up to where he was, even though the rope probably hadn't been needed on this bit. At the sound of the kid's voice, Barney yipped in his shitty pouch and struggled again.

"*Barney*. Are you okay?" Josh bobbed up and down.

Is *he* okay?

The dog went frantic, digging and struggling to get out. Without gravity keeping him in the beer belly position, he managed to get his head out of the neck of my T-shirt. I choked slightly as I got a mouthful of fluffy hair.

"Damnit, stay still." I spat out fur.

It was no good, though, as the little swine had seen Josh above us. All I could do was keep a hold on the slope as he squirmed his whole body out through the neck hole of my shirt. I guessed it had been stretched out by his weight. Then with a flip, he was out, his great plume of a tail, liberally covered in diarrhea, swiped over my face.

I didn't even care if he fell off the cliff then, although he didn't; he bounded up and over the edge. A noisy reunion went on above me.

"Barney. Eww, Barney, you smell. Good boy, don't get it on me."

Ohhh. Dear God in heaven, it was in my mouth, my *mouth*. I put my forehead against the rock and spat, then spat again.

Somehow, I managed to drag my sorry ass up the last few feet of rock, up and over the top onto genuine flat ground again. I lay back and let a swamp of relief flow through me, I was up, I was safe, I'd made it.

I let the knowledge sink in that I'd actually, finally gotten out. I was out. Whatever was in the park below was trapped there, away from me, contained within the enormous stone basin.

"Barney's covered in poo," Josh helpfully informed me.

I opened my eyes and found the kid staring down at me.

"Yeah, so am I," was all I said.

Josh's nose wrinkled. "Eww. That's nasty."

"No shit." I closed my eyes again.

The world slowly came back into focus as I stopped shaking. Five minutes of blissful stillness, but reality couldn't be ignored for long. The state of my clothes, my skin, the shitty fabric still tucked against me—it all cried out for attention.

Josh's impatience was palpable, his bouncing a visual reminder of our unfinished journey. Just the rim left to conquer, then down to the parking lot. To people. To help.

No phone. No keys. No plan beyond "find someone." But none of that mattered now. We'd done the impossible—scaled that cliff with nothing but stubbornness and a shirt full of dog.

Hope, fragile but persistent, bloomed in my chest. We'd made it out. Against all odds, we'd clawed our way back to the world of the living. Whatever came next, we'd face it. Because after that climb? Everything else seemed manageable.

"Can we go already? It's getting dark." Josh was keen to get going. "And I'm hungry."

Of course, he was. "Tell you what, bud, you scout up the trail a little way while I try and clean off some of your dog's crap okay?"

"Me and Barney can do it. You hurry up."

Barney had already disappeared up the path. Josh took off after him.

"Don't go too far!" I bellowed after them.

I had nothing to wash with. The best I could do was strip off my bottom half, remove my underpants, and swab as much shit off me as I could with them. These were underwear I'd worn a couple of days too, so not pleasant, even without the added dog feces. Then I threw them away and put my trousers back on.

Inside, they were wet but less so than my boxers and T-shirt. The front of my shirt, particularly the bottom, was liberally soaked in diarrhea, but with it untucked, it felt marginally less revolting than before. At least it wasn't against my skin.

It was the best I could do. Man, I stank. I headed up the trail, jiggling my jewels into a comfortable position against the wet fabric. Repulsive.

I caught up with Josh, where he sat waiting on a boulder.

"I'm really thirsty," he said.

The dog was tongue-out panting too. The little bastard was probably dehydrated after losing half his body weight in shit.

"Not long now," I said. Dear God, I wanted to get out of there. Finally, finally, I was going home. "Come on, let's go."

The trail was mainly stone, with a few scrubby plants clinging to the cracks. The sky was a clear, darkening blue against the silhouetted rock of the rim. We scrambled up the last few feet, reached the top, and stopped.

We were a good few hundred feet above the valley's dip. Down to the right would be the parking lot. I looked at the timbered area below us, the treetops split by the access road, and further to where the slope leveled into a great sweep of plain.

My eyes swept across the horizon, taking in the sprawling vista of hills. But something was wrong. Terribly, horrifyingly wrong.

Smoke plumes. Not one, not a dozen, but hundreds. Thousands. Each one a beacon of destruction, a harbinger of the nightmare we thought we'd escaped.

My lungs seized, refusing to draw breath. The realization hit like a physical blow, stealing the air from my chest.

In my mind's eye, I saw it all unfold. Each plume marking a meteor strike. Each strike seeding the earth with those ... things. The worms. Growing. Breeding. Spreading without the stone walls of the basin to contain them.

I imagined their relentless hunger. Starting small, then working their way up the food chain. Dead bodies rising, puppeted by an alien will. Feeding. Consuming. Unstoppable.

The truth crashed down, brutal and unforgiving. There was no safe haven waiting for us. No home to return to. The horror we'd fought so hard to escape had simply gone global.

Josh's excited chatter faded to white noise. The memory of Barney's warmth against my chest felt like a cruel joke. We'd climbed that cliff, defied death itself, for what? To witness the end of everything?

I wanted to scream, to rage against the unfairness of it all. But my voice, like my hope, had died.

There was nowhere left to run.

None of us were going home.

Acknowledgements

As always, enormous thanks to my wonderful husband Chris Duffy, without him none of my books would have been finished.

So much gratitude to Anna Tynan and Katie Parker-Riccio, brilliant writers who had the patience to alpha read for me and teach me so much about writing. Big thanks to amazing horror writer Wil Forbis, for beta reading and giving me valuable feedback, and much gratitude to bestie Lucy Norman for all her support.

Also, so much appreciation for Alexandria Brown and Tina Beier at Rising Action Publishing for taking a chance on 'Wormies' and for all their hard work on whipping it into shape.

This book, set in the US, was written in the UK (in the North Yorkshire village of Cononley*), by an Australian writer, for a Canadian publisher, which gives us all a free pass for any terminology, language or spelling anomalies. That's just how it is, I don't make the rules.

And finally, a big thank you and apology to my Cononley neighbour, Caren Wilson for using the names of her grandsons and dog (names only – any resemblance to people is purely coincidental, apart from Barney, that little bollocks is entirely himself).

*Shout out to the Cononley WI book club and the Skipton Library writers' group.

About the Author

Louise Jensen Duffy, writing as Ernest Jensen, is an Australian author living in Scotland who writes horror and historical fiction.

Louise won the 2023 Cheshire Novel Prize, with a previous title being longlisted for the 2022 Cheshire Novel Prize. She was longlisted for the 2023 BPA First Novel Award and was also shortlisted for the 2022 Comedy Women in Print Award, winning the CWIP Runner-up Unpublished Book to Screen Award.

To date Louise has written five novels and, while technically they're her first foray into fiction, she spent the last twenty-odd years writing for government, which has given her a solid foundation in creative writing.

Nameless Things is her first horror novel.

Looking for more chills and thrills? Check out Rising Action's other horror stories on the next page!

And don't forget to follow us on our socials for cover reveals, giveaways, and announcements:

X: @RAPubCollective

Instagram: @risingactionpublishingco

TikTok: @risingactionpublishingco

Website: http://www.risingactionpublishing.com

On a tiny, isolated island off the southern Alaskan coast, three girls have vanished without a trace, and Audra's close friend—the island's therapist—has been found murdered. A recent storm has severed all communication with the outside world, leaving Audra, the town's lead detective, trapped and at the head of a very personal case.

Her lead suspect, Valorie, the daughter of a notorious cult leader and the town's outcast, was discovered blood-covered and dazed at the crime scene. Valorie's memory is a gaping void, a dark well hiding traumatic secrets, including the truth about the teenage kidnappings that haunt the island.

As Audra digs deeper into the town's twisted history, it becomes clear other murders on the island, dating back decades, might be connected. The clock is ticking for the missing girls, and every clue leads Audra to question even those she's known her whole life.

Valorie must confront the horrors of her past while Audra's investigation becomes a descent into madness. On this cursed island, the line between neighbor and nightmare blurs, revealing that true horror often wears a familiar face.

Unfurling on Aug 26, 2025

Anita Walsh, still reeling from her husband's sudden death, finds herself haunted not only by grief, but his "Negative Image," a new phenomenon where the deceased prey on those they loved in life, turning intimate memories into nightmares. This spectral figure uses their shared past as a weapon, systematically dismantling her friendships, career, and self-worth. Desperate for escape, Anita plunges into a quest to sever the ghostly bonds that tie her to her tormentor.

As society grapples with the rising terror of NIs, a charismatic extremist proposes a radical solution to isolate the haunted from the unafflicted, gaining dangerous followers. Anita, alongside another victim of this spectral affliction, must navigate their personal hauntings and societal threats to prevent the breakdown of their community.

With its gripping narrative and eerie exploration of love and betrayal, Negative Images marks Rebecca Schier-Akamelu as a powerful new voice in horror. This novel delves deep into the psychological horrors of grief and the supernatural, making it a must-read for fans of horror and ghost stories alike.

The haunting begins July 22, 2025

THE HAUNTING AT MORSLEY MANOR

Where the dead don't rest, and the living may never leave...

GEORGE MORRIS DE'ATH

World-famous paranormal investigator Eric Thompson's career took a nose-dive after a particularly gruesome case which left most of his camera crew dead. His partner and best friend also abandoned Eric, leaving him floundering.

He is soon approached by a mysterious woman who has purchased the supposedly haunted, but previously off-limits to paranormal sleuths, Morsley Manor. To drum up publicity about the house, she hires Eric to perform and host a paranormal investigation on the premises.

As he ventures over to England to uncover the darkness bleeding through the veins of Morsley, horrors begin to spring from every corner and Eric soon begins to realise that not all is as it seems...

Evil is unleashed on September 23, 2025

Newlywed Sam has always wanted to be a part of a normal happy family. When her mother-in-law falls ill, Sam dutifully moves her family to Edenic Camillia Island to care for her. The island residents, namely the older women, welcome Sam and her daughter Emma with open arms, endless cocktails, and plenty of superstition.

It seems perfect until it's not. The house next to her mother-in-law's is creepy—not only that, it's where Ben's first wife died.

Sam's teen daughter Emma isn't interested in spending the summer in Camilia. It gets even worse when Emma starts to see things—knowing that there are ghosts trying to warn her of something, but what?

Despite Emma's pleas, Sam doesn't want to rock the boat with her new family. Emma won't pretend nothing is happening, especially as the messages become more grim and frequent. What secrets are buried on Camilia Island? And why are all the residents keen on keeping them quiet?

Something is wrong in Bunker, Illinois.

Nora Grace Moon thought her toughest challenge this semester would be managing her OCD, but when her deceased roommate turns up as a reanimated corpse, her world starts to collapse.

When her uncle sends her a cryptic message, Nora realizes it must be a call for help. She reaches out to fellow gamer Wesley for advice, a US Marshal with real-life skills for tactical survival, not just in-game. They venture out into a world that is growing more and more deadly by the moment—not only are the undead spreading, but other humans are taking advantage of the societal breakdown. And unknown to Nora and Wesley, they have been targeted by an ancient archeological society who will stop at nothing until they have what Nora has: an artifact that will unleash a new world order of the undead

IRL is a paranormal thriller about leaving the online world and dealing with things "In Real Life."